MW01286452

ANGEL FROM THE EAST

BLOOMS OF THE BITTERBRUSH
BOOK ONE

BARBARA A. CURTIS

Copyright © 2024 by Barbara A. Curtis

All rights reserved. No portion of this book may be reproduced or transmitted in any form or by any means - photocopied, shared electronically, scanned, stored in a retrieval system, or other - without the express permission of the publisher. Exceptions will be made for brief quotations used in critical reviews or articles promoting this work.

The characters and events in this fictional work are the product of the author's imagination. Any resemblance to actual people, living or dead, is coincidental.

Unless otherwise indicated, all Scripture quotations are taken from the Holy Bible, Kings James Version.

Cover design by Evelyne Labelle at Carpe Librum Book Design. www.carpelibrumbookdesign.com

ISBN:

Thanks be to God—and to all those who helped with this story.
O magnify the LORD with me, and let us exalt his name together.
Psalm 34:3 KJV

And suddenly there was with the angel a multitude of the heavenly host praising God, and saying, Glory to God in the highest, and on earth peace, good will toward men.
Luke 2:13–14 KJV

CHAPTER 1

Caldwell, Idaho, 1897

Impulsive and foolish...impulsive and foolish...
The rhythm of the locomotive lumbering away from the Caldwell platform picked up its tempo, grinding the words into Eliza Roberts's soul. Already, merely standing next to the depot, she regretted disembarking in Idaho.

The train's smoke seeped into her lungs, reiterating the truth with each breath she took. She didn't belong here any more than she had in New York City. Once again, Mother, Father, and Aunt Belinda had been right. She was too impulsive —just as Grandfather had been, traipsing off to this forsaken wilderness. *"In search of what?"* Aunt Belinda had asked more than once. *"His foolish dreams?"*

Two cowboys slithered onto the platform. The shorter one winked and tipped his hat. "G'day, miss. May I offer you some assistance?"

Eliza gave him her perfected schoolmarm glare. "No. Thank you."

Laughing and slapping his hand against his leg, he turned

back to his companion, and they meandered down the street toward a nearby saloon.

Eliza clutched her carpetbag close to ward off the December wind that stung right through the fibers of her coat and wound beneath her scarf. Dust flew everywhere, piling up ankle deep, coating townsfolk's shoes and stockings and her own blue traveling dress. The particles billowed onto the train platform, slipping past her lips, into her mouth. A gritty film covered her teeth, clawing its way down her throat like the taste of disappointment her family liberally flavored her life with.

"Darling, you're already twenty-one—and a spinster like your aunt."

"Eliza, you're reckless, just like your grandfather, God rest his soul."

"Eliza Roberts, believing in God is all well and good—but it's a private thing. Don't embarrass us by talking about such things in public."

Eliza sighed, then coughed as yet more dust entered her nose. Her mouth. Down her throat. Once she accomplished her mission—a few weeks at the most—she'd resume her journey on to California. She was a teacher, after all, not a rancher. Then this town could go on smelling of horses and unwashed cowboys without her...or her dreams.

Recollections of Grandmother were hazy, but Eliza did remember her parting words when she'd left New York for the West years ago. *"Be a light for Jesus."* And that, Eliza intended to do—to the little ones out in Los Angeles.

Within minutes, the platform was empty of passengers except for Eliza. Where were the buggy and driver promised to escort her to the Double E? Even though Caldwell purported itself to be civilized, she had no idea what dangers lay between the depot and her inherited ranch.

She stepped into the small station and spotted a telephone.

"May I make a call?" she asked the man standing over it—presumably the stationmaster.

"Where to?"

"New York City."

"New York City. I see." He stared at her a moment. "That'll be quite expensive, you know."

"Yes, sir." She pulled money from her carpetbag and settled up with the man—hopefully not more than the true cost. But he seemed kind. Then he put the call through.

Three rings and then Eliza heard someone take a breath. Mother?

"Hello," came Aunt Belinda's clipped voice. Not surprising since her spinster aunt spent a lot of her time at the brownstone, anyway.

"Aunt Belinda, this is Eliza." She sat on the chair the man pushed her way, keeping an eye on the window in case her escort arrived while she was inside.

"Goodness, child. Where are you?"

"I just arrived in Caldwell."

"Idaho?"

"Yes, Grandmother and Grandfather's town."

"Hmph. Why ever did you stop there? This will delay your arrival in California." Aunt Belinda's sniff carried quite pointedly over the phone line.

"I wanted to see where Grandmother and Grandfather lived since I'm so close."

"You are not close. Now be on your way before you miss your respectable teaching job in Los Angeles."

Her job wasn't even secured yet. Whether Aunt Belinda didn't know that or just chose to ignore that technicality, Eliza didn't stop to give room for more questions. "May I speak with Mother or Father?"

"They are not present. We did not expect a call from you

from the middle of nowhere, so they did not stay home to await word from you."

Oh. "Could you let them know I arrived safely?"

"I will. And I will let them know you will be continuing on your way shortly."

"I don't know—"

"Thank you for calling. Good day." And with that, the line went dead.

Eliza stared at the phone a moment.

"Miss—is everything all right?" the stationmaster asked.

"Y-yes. Thank you. I'll wait outside for my ride. Thank you for the use of your phone." She hurried out to the platform. By now her ride should be here.

But he wasn't.

Almost twenty minutes passed, and a trio of unkempt cowboys approached, their sly grins promising things she would not approve of. Had men here nothing better to do than bother every woman they laid eyes on, no matter how plain or proper? Eliza captured the blond hairs whipping about her face and stuck them back in place under her bun and hat.

"Where are you?" She grumbled to the unseen—and very late—driver. What kind of an escort would be so slacking?

She tugged her coat tighter, squeezing out the chill of fear. Even in this wild land, she was sure it would be improper to meet a man's gaze—but if she must, she certainly would.

Eliza searched the faces of townspeople hurrying past, but still, no one seemed to be expecting a gangly lady arriving from New York City. She looked up and down the dirt road and frowned. Grandfather Roberts had written of birthing calves and chasing regal stallions, riding the open range and praying beneath a multitude of stars, of flaming sunsets and hot chuck-wagon meals.

Not of alkali and sagebrush that extended as far as she could see. Not swaggering cowboys with raucous laughter and low-slung holsters. Not more saloons than a town this size should even claim.

How could this be the place Grandfather had written of so grandly?

"Oh, Grandfather." No one was around to hear her talking to herself, her voice the only sound amidst the jutting peaks of his beloved Owyhees in the distance that trumpeted the loneliness of this land. "If I'd come while you were still alive, I would have seen the ranch through your eyes." He would have explained what had prompted him to pack up Grandmother and head West years ago—leaving behind his family, even his only grandchild, in New York—for this wilderness. There had to be more to Caldwell than dust and desolation. A reason her grandparents had stayed here. Being a light.

And that was what she would be here, too, for her brief stay. Someone praising God just like the angels at Jesus's birth. She smiled. That would be her mantra as well. *Glory to God in the highest, and on earth peace.*

The nicker of a horse caught her attention, and she turned as the driver of a small wagon tied the reins to a post. At last someone was here for her! She stepped closer to the edge of the platform, hiding behind a beam to observe her driver.

Tall, close-cut hair, broad shoulders... But instead of leaping onto the elevated boardwalk, he turned back to his horse. They were like a matching pair with the same shade of brown hair. He cradled the mare's head in his hands, scruffling her forelock as a father might tousle a child's hair.

The horse nuzzled the man's shirt pocket, and the man made a noise, not quite a laugh. "All right, Ruby. You win." He bent, and the horse pulled a carrot from his pocket with a soft whinny.

"I'll be right back." He patted her on the shoulder. "I guess you deserve your treat now—as you'll have quite a load to carry when I return."

Eliza pulled her stomach in. Quite a load, indeed!

The horse's ears flicked toward the man as he turned. With a slight—but still noticeable—limp, he climbed the steps to the boardwalk and headed toward the station.

Eliza stepped into the open, intercepting the brown-haired man, wondering at his clean-shaven face in a land where she'd expected all men to be mustached and bearded.

"Excuse me, sir." She hated being brash, speaking first to a man, but obviously, he was to fetch her, as she was the only passenger left.

He stopped. Nodded. "Good afternoon, ma'am."

Eliza felt like his mare, perking her ears up at his even-paced voice. Had he recognized the fear in her eyes? For he was treating her as gently as a skittish horse.

When he tipped his cowboy hat upward, his dark brown gaze revealed a kind man. Finally, she felt safe.

"I'm awaiting an escort to my grandfather's ranch. Are you perhaps the foreman of the Double E?"

Shadows darkened those brown eyes. "No." The sudden gruffness in his tone matched the scowl now on his face.

Eliza lowered her gaze in what she hoped was an apologetic, demure manner. "Please forgive me."

The man's jaw tensed. He shifted his weight, favoring his left leg. When he spoke again, he was less brusque, though still unsmiling. "Do you need any he—"

Before he finished, a tall, rugged cowboy vaulted onto the platform and doffed his hat toward Eliza. His shaggy black hair gleamed in the sun, his pale blue eyes sparkling. "Excuse me, ma'am, but I believe you must be waiting for me. Benton Calloway." He extended a hand. "Foreman"—he darted a pointed look at the other man—"of the Double E Ranch."

The first man took a step back but didn't move beyond that, as if intending to listen to the exchange.

Eliza shook Mr. Calloway's hand, feeling his rough,

workman calluses. Here was the man who had worked along-side Grandfather, the man left in charge of his beloved ranch.

"I'm Eliza Roberts. Thank you for coming to meet me."

"I apologize for not being here on time to meet your train, ma'am. Cows don't always follow the train schedules." He chuckled, then slid his hat over his heart. "I do want to express my sympathies to you in the passing of your grandfather."

Eliza choked back tears, wishing again she'd gotten a chance to really know Grandfather—more than just through his handful of recent letters. "Thank you, Mr. Calloway."

"May I load your bag into the wagon?"

"Yes, thank you." Gratefully, she relinquished her carpetbag to the charming, raven-haired cowboy. "My trunk is over there."

"Your...trunk? Yes. Of course." He smiled. "Are you ready to head out to the Double E, Miss Roberts?"

"Oh, yes." Excitement assuaged her earlier fears. At last she would see the land her grandfather had loved.

Benton Calloway gripped Eliza's elbow, urging her forward. "Good day," he said with a look of dismissal as he brushed past the other man.

Eliza climbed into Mr. Calloway's wagon. She glanced back at the man still standing on the platform, his scowl twisting his features into a rigid mask, all trace of his earlier gentleness gone. Plastered on his face was restrained rage.

She prayed her path would never cross his again. He was exactly the kind of man her father had warned her about.

~

*C*aleb Morgan stalked away, as much as his bum leg allowed, not bothering to acknowledge Benton Calloway's departure.

That despicable scoundrel...

He tried to stop his thoughts from heading further down

that useless path, but once again, he failed. *He's nothing but an underhanded coyote...*

Almighty God...

His words never got much beyond that, especially not after seeing that man again face-to-face. Whenever he thought he was getting on with his life, there was always a reminder of what Benton Calloway had done to him, what he'd taken away. And on cold days like this, the pain in his leg with each step he took never let him forget.

Dear God in heaven... He tried again, but still no words came, except for one final plea. *Forgive me for despising that man.*

Caleb was tempted to turn and look over his shoulder to be sure the gangly young lady was safe. But he didn't. Her confident stance and the penetrating, knowing gaze in those clear deep-blue eyes told him she would be just fine without his help.

Mr. Roberts's granddaughter, indeed. He should have known by one look at her that she was kin to Miz Elizabeth. Long like a white pine with bitterbrush blooming on top, Mr. Roberts used to say of his missus. That fit Eliza Roberts exactly —tall and stately like a pine tree, her hair almost as yellow as spring blossoms on Miz Elizabeth's bitterbrush edging the backyard. And adventurous, coming all the way from New York by herself. That showed grit such as Miz Elizabeth had, though he couldn't imagine anyone having the same heart that Mr. Roberts's wife had possessed. She'd been the true heart of the Double E, no doubt about it.

But this newcomer had Mr. Roberts's look of determination too. And the way her gaze had rested first on him, then on Calloway, sizing them each up before speaking a word to either...

Yes, this granddaughter most likely could handle Benton Calloway on her own. And hopefully, she was wise enough to see beyond his charm of doffing his high-end Stetson—which he made sure folks knew was beaver fur—down to that wretched soul hidden underneath his vest.

"Howdy, Caleb." The stationmaster stood in the doorway, patting the top of the box he held in one arm.

"Leviticus."

"Looks like your saddlery supplies came in at last. Business must be doing purty good, eh?"

Caleb nodded. How much of the scene had the man overheard? No one ever said anything to his face about why he had left the Double E or started over in town and established a saddle-making shop in an old barn. Especially when he'd been like a son to Mr. and Mrs. Roberts. Yet whispers flew like lariats around Caldwell. People speculating why he lived in town while Calloway now managed the Double E.

Caleb accepted the crate with two arms, the weight straining his still-tender ribcage. "Much obliged." He turned to leave, wishing the man would walk back inside. Caleb needed no one to witness the effort it'd take to not stumble down the steps from the elevated boardwalk into the dusty street just to load his wagon. His custom saddle-making shop was only three blocks away. Three blocks, and he needed a wagon to carry one box.

"Caleb. Hold up." Leviticus's boots sounded on the planks behind him.

Caleb stopped and turned back to face the older man. "Yes?"

Leviticus eyed him head to toe. "Do you need any—"

"No." Caleb spun around—another mistake, as the crate banged against his ribs. He took the steps faster than prudent and stumbled on his landing, stirring up yet another unwanted cloud of dust.

"Hey, watch it." A town drunk staggered around him and onto the steps. "Who'ya think ya are? Dirtying up our nice town?"

"Sorry," Caleb mumbled. Even the drunks usually steered clear of him—though quite possibly they were friends of Benton Calloway.

"What does it matter, anyway, what people think?" he whispered to Ruby. She nickered low, a sound that had become her offer of companionship. "God knows the truth."

And He also knew the heart of that rattlesnake who had just whisked off Mr. Roberts's granddaughter. She had actually come. A few months too late, but she was here. And probably would be gone within a few days. Someone as proper and cultured as she was wouldn't stay in this barely tamed land. He could only pray she'd be safe from harm during her visit.

A few months ago, he would have been the one escorting her out to the Double E. Now she was at the hands of Benton Calloway—and though Caleb had been taught to be a gentleman, watching out for ladies, there was nothing he could do for Miss Roberts.

He gave Ruby a pat on her withers. "May the good Lord watch over her."

And it certainly was up to God Almighty Himself—as Caleb was no longer employed at the Double E, much less still the foreman.

CHAPTER 2

"The Double E is just over that rise, ma'am," Mr. Calloway said.

Eliza's heart beat quicker, but she simply nodded at the foreman.

For the last several miles, there had been little conversation between them. He was polite, even friendly, yet she was the one who remained quiet. She didn't want to offend him about the land where he lived, but it was not what she had expected.

Even miles away from town, the land was lined with sagebrush and alkali. And dust. From the first steps the team of horses had taken away from the depot, they were hoof deep in dust as they pulled the wagon down the street. Eliza could only imagine what kind of hardships her grandmother must have endured in this rough land. And how lonely she must have been, with her two children and a granddaughter left behind in the East, only to die almost nine months ago out here without ever seeing them again.

But now that she was about to catch her first glimpse of the ranch, she leaned forward, scanning the horizon. Perhaps Mr. Calloway and Grandfather had sat on the broad porch at night under twinkling stars, discussing the day's business, planning for the morrow. Surely, what she lacked in knowledge about ranching—which was everything—would be carried out in good hands with this foreman. She'd stay long enough to feel as though she knew the life her grandparents, Elizabeth Rose and Elliott Roberts, had shared here. And if she could find the love of this wild land her grandfather had written about in the handful of letters she had, maybe she'd understand why he had abandoned his family for this place. Then she would sell the ranch and continue on to California to take a position as a schoolteacher.

Eliza grabbed at her skirt, trying to tame it against the wind that barely seemed to stop for a breath. "You love this place, don't you?"

Benton Calloway looked her full in the face, relaxing his hands on the reins slightly. "You have no idea what this place means to me."

"Mr. Calloway, could you tell me what my grandmother was like? I only have a few faint memories of her."

A fun woman with a quick smile... *"Eliza, would you like to see this pen disappear?"*

He lowered his head a moment. When he looked back at Eliza, his voice was soft. "She was a good woman. A God-fearing lady. An excellent cook... The ranch isn't the same without her." He was silent for a beat. "If I may be so bold in saying, Miss Roberts, you favor her in looks."

Her cheeks were surely pink, and not just from the cold. "Why, thank you. I consider that an honor. How about my grandfather? You must have known him well. Could you tell me about him?" Eliza sat forward, eager to learn about the man he'd been.

The foreman's hands tightened on the reins, and the horses shook their heads in protest. "Your grandfather..." Benton cocked his head. "Did you know him at all?"

"He traveled west when I wasn't even eight, so mostly all I remember of him was that he had a beard and smelled like peppermint."

And that the day he left for this land, he had held her on his lap. *"One day, you will come to visit us on the big ranch I'm going to buy, yes? You'll tame a wild horse and be a cowgirl, my little angel."* For years, she had clung to that promise before realizing it was never going to happen.

A rut in the road jarred her to reality. Well, maybe the promise was coming true—only, too late to matter.

Eliza held back a sigh. "Once he moved, he was estranged from his family. He was an adventurer, I believe, though my father rarely spoke of him. A few months ago, I went to live with my aunt, and it was only then he started writing letters to me."

Benton Calloway nodded. "Then you won't be surprised when I tell you. I do hate to speak ill of the dead." He paused. "But the truth is, he was an exacting, hard man."

Eliza's heart dropped. Then what her parents had said was true. But in his letters, Grandfather Roberts had been poetic, passionate, a man in love with his ranch, this land, his wife, and his God. Yet Mr. Calloway had known him in person, had worked for him. With him. And the fact remained that Grandfather had alienated his own family, cutting off contact with them. So this certainly should not surprise her, though it still saddened her immensely.

They traveled in silence for a few steps of the horses before the foreman spoke again.

"Up ahead." He pointed. "There it is."

Eliza stared at the splintered board dangling from a post by a rusty nail. *The Double E.*

"Could you stop for a moment?"

Mr. Calloway shrugged but pulled the horses to a halt.

The artistic lettering—perhaps designed by Grandmother?—

declared this the entrance to her ranch. Though the paint was faded and chipped in places, the sign offered a welcome of sorts. She inhaled, expecting a sense of elation at stepping into Grandfather's world, onto his land. But all she got was a mouthful of dust.

Eliza covered her mouth with her scarf and smothered back a coughing fit.

Mr. Calloway shook his head as if he'd expected as much. "Well, this is it."

He slapped the reins against the horses, and the wagon continued along the dirt road, past fences and more sagebrush. And then Eliza saw it—her inheritance. There was the barn, a few outbuildings, and the two-story house. But the white paint was peeling. And where were the cowboys lassoing calves or sitting on the rails that Grandfather had written about? The hens scurrying around, rummaging for food? The horses neighing in the distant fields? Where were the freshly washed clothes flapping in the brisk breeze?

Eliza shivered. There was no welcome. No feeling of peaceful solitude. The Double E looked abandoned. The only movement was the windmill behind the house being forced by the wind to rotate its blades.

As they approached the yard, a herding dog trotted out to meet them. Eliza sighed a breath of relief. Kep. If Grandfather's faithful companion was here, surely, all would be well.

"Move out of the way, Kep," the foreman called. When he pulled the horses to a stop, he jumped from the wagon and walked around to the other side to help Eliza down.

At last Eliza saw some sign of ranch life as a few scrawny chickens wandered into view from around the side of the house. Kep planted himself between them and the garden fence, barking until they changed course.

The dog walked closer to her, sniffing the air and appearing to study Eliza.

"Hello, Kep." She patted him on the head, and he wagged his tail. "I'm glad to meet you."

"Mr. Calloway..." Eliza looked around. "Where are the cows? The horses? All the men?"

"Well..." He wiped his forehead with his sleeve. "We're down to just four horses—these two and my horse and George's horse. He's the only other cowhand left. And what cows we still have are out in the north pasture."

If it hadn't been for the worn sign at the entrance, Eliza never would have guessed this was the same ranch of which Grandfather had written. But as she stepped toward the house, she spotted the one thing that was exactly as Grandfather had described—the wide front porch. She climbed the few steps and stopped on the wide planks, taking in a deep breath of cold Idaho air. She was standing where Grandfather had stood each morning. And there were two straight-backed rockers. Which one had he sat in at the end of the day, marveling at the sunsets, writing letters to her?

"I wish I had been here while Grandfather was alive." Eliza smiled faintly at Benton Calloway where he still stood near the horses. Then perhaps she would have been able to see the glories of the Double E through Grandfather's eyes. If only he were here to explain them to her—to welcome her with a hug. She wiped away a tear, lest Mr. Calloway see it and think her silly.

"Yes, ma'am." He yanked on the halter of one of the horses before tethering the team. "I'll bring your bag."

"No, Benton." A short, plumpish woman had come out of the house and stood on the porch. "I'll bring it in. You can carry in the trunk." Tucking some gray hairs back into her bun, she turned to Eliza. "I'm Nellie, the cook."

"Miss Nellie." Eliza hurried over to greet her. "I'm Eliza. I'm so glad to meet you."

"I'm glad you're here, Miss Eliza. Come in. I'll show you upstairs to your room."

Nellie led Eliza to a room with a bed covered with a patchwork quilt in harvest yellows, sunset reds, and river blues set inside a border of plain browns and gray. Pale yellow curtains hung at the window, and a braided rug with deep browns and bold blues looked comforting for cold feet on a wintry morning.

"This is lovely," Eliza said.

"Your grandmother made it and always kept it ready in case someday—" Nellie abruptly stopped and grabbed the pillows on the bed, fluffing them up. "You take your time and get settled and changed out of your traveling clothes. I set out a pitcher of fresh water and a towel for you. Then come down to the kitchen and I'll fix you up with some apple pie." With that, she hurried out the door.

"Thank you, Miss Nellie," Eliza called after her.

She washed up first, then unpacked her dresses and few other belongings, laying them carefully into the deep drawers of the pine chest. Next, she changed from her blue traveling dress—sturdy and plain like herself. But it was comfortable and gave a semblance of elegance when she felt like a dust-blown nomad. She put on the straight-front corset her mother had insisted on packing. Perhaps if she carried herself well, she would look stylish rather than silly in this latest fashion that was meant to curve ladies into an S shape. For her first evening here, perhaps looking graceful was important.

Though her stomach gave a little reminder that she should hurry downstairs for the promised pie, Eliza sat in the straight-backed chair beside the bed. Had Grandmother placed it here just for this purpose, to be able to look out the window to the open land stretching as far as one could see? What a wonderful place to sit, to read and think, and most of all, to pray.

Eliza pondered Miss Nellie's words spoken before she'd

hurried off. Had whomever Grandmother set this room aside for ever come? Had it been for Mother and Father? Aunt Belinda? She sat up straighter in the chair. Maybe for her? Had Grandmother and Grandfather really meant for her to come one day?

After another little growl from her stomach, Eliza stood and headed downstairs. Maybe over pie she'd find the answers to all her questions from the one who probably knew this place the best—Miss Nellie.

Nellie was placing a plate with steaming apple pie onto the table as Eliza entered the kitchen. "Sit down, Miss Eliza, and eat. You must be exhausted and hungry."

"Thank you. I'm so glad to finally be here." Eliza took a seat and quietly ate her pie as she contemplated how to voice the concern that had been growing each moment she was here. "Grandfather's ranch is...certainly different from the way he described it."

"Things have changed since your grandfather took ill and passed on to glory." Nellie sighed and wrung her hands. "But one thing hasn't changed—the men that are left still need to eat." She bustled about the kitchen. "So I am still here with them."

"What kind of changes do you mean?" Eliza asked. The letters in her carpetbag had depicted the ranch as glorious. So where were the cattle? The hired men? The horses?

Nellie turned her head quickly toward the door. When she looked back, she didn't quite meet Eliza's eyes. But Eliza recognized the flash of something that had crossed Miss Nellie's face.

Fear.

Instinctively, Eliza stood and gently pulled Nellie into an embrace. "Thank you for your part in taking care of Grandfather. I'm sure it meant much to him."

Nellie nodded and after a moment pulled away. "Welcome to the Double E, Eliza. You're long overdue. Now, shoo. Go and take your rest after your long journey. Supper will be ready in an hour."

"Yes, ma'am," Eliza said, smiling, pretty certain that Miss Nellie was the one who really ran the ranch, or at least the main house. But as she turned to find her room, her last glimpse of the cook was that of her wringing her apron between her hands.

Eliza climbed the stairs and once in her room, she sat in the chair by the window again. If she closed her eyes, she could imagine what life might have been like here with Grandfather. She would have joined him on the front porch, rocking, watching the sun set together, listening to him tell stories about roundups and cattle drives. Almost everything she knew about him, though, was in the small packet of letters she had carefully wrapped and placed in her carpetbag. In them, he had spoken little of mundane facts of his life here. Instead, the pages were filled with his dreams and of the grandeur of God the Creator.

Eliza blinked her eyes open as an idea came to her. She had intended simply to get information about her grandparents and then sell the ranch. But now that she was actually here, what if she stayed a while before selling it? Maybe Grandfather had hoped she'd do more than just pack up his belongings and dispose of them. Would he possibly have wanted her to keep the ranch in the family, to keep it going? To pursue his dreams? Not that she knew the first thing about running a ranch, but couldn't she learn? If only Grandfather were still alive, he could give her some advice. He could tell her why he had left New York and brought Grandmother here.

As Eliza looked out the window at the land comprising the ranch, a peace pressed upon her heart. Perhaps she *did* have the ability to keep those dreams alive.

She reached for her bundle of letters, pulling out the envelope on top. Grandfather's final letter, attached to his Last Will and Testament, had been sent to her in New York from the Idaho lawyer.

My Dear Eliza,

When you receive this, my farewell to you, it will mean that I have left this earth. Though grief will be in your heart, rejoice also that I will be with the good Lord above. As you know now from my will, I have given you the joy of my last years, the Double E. Its prosperities should keep you comfortable for years to come. It has been my refuge, my place of seeking and walking with the Lord. May you find His peace here also, whether riding beneath the stars or sitting on the porch steps.

I hope that in heaven we are given the privilege of watching down upon the earth, as I long to see you finding joy each step of the way, my little angel.

May God bless you, dear one.

Love, Grandfather

Eliza, if you ever find yourself needing help in this land, seek Caleb Morgan. He is a good man and will assist you. I trust him with all I have.

Eliza stared at the letter. Who was this Caleb Morgan that Grandfather had trusted? And if he was such a special friend, why hadn't Grandfather mentioned him in his previous letters? Perhaps he lived too far away to be a daily part of his life or was too frail. All she had to do was to find Grandfather's elderly friend. Then she'd also find her answer as to what to do with the ranch.

Too excited to rest, Eliza ventured outside again, wanting to get a closer look at the ranch before Miss Nellie called her to supper. She'd start with the barn.

The two horses that had pulled the wagon nickered at Eliza as she approached their stalls. One at a time, she rubbed their noses. Then, noticing the small tack area with the harnesses, she peered closer, but how strange there were no saddles stored there.

"Do you need help, ma'am?"

Eliza jumped as Benton Calloway appeared from behind her.

"I was just looking around, trying to see the ranch as Grandfather loved it. It seems a bit...run down," she said hesitantly.

"I've been taking care of it the best I can after the passing on of your grandfather, ma'am." Benton bowed his head slightly, and his voice held a tone of hurt.

Eliza hastened to assure him. "Oh, I'm sure you have been."

Benton looked up again and into Eliza's eyes. "You might as well know—money has been scarce. I had to sell some of the cattle to have cash to pay the hired hands. Even so, I had to let most of the men go. That's how things became run down. Now that you're here," he said with an unexpected eagerness, "the ranch can be sold off."

Eliza frowned. "I'm not sure if I want to do that right away. The Double E is the only legacy of my grandparents that I have. I think I'd like to stay and try to get the ranch back the way it was before I sell it." She searched his face, looking for some sign that he understood her need to do this without thinking her completely illogical.

But Benton only stared at her in silence, his head cocked and eyes widened.

"Putting this ranch back on its feet is a mighty big job, ma'am," he drawled. "If you decided to sell, you should make enough money to live in style back East, as I'm sure you're accustomed."

"No." Her decision was right, even though Benton Calloway did not understand. "Grandfather loved this ranch. I'm going to do my best to make it into a place he'd be proud of." She smiled, hoping her announcement came out sounding confident. "I can be very determined."

"Yes. I see that. No one would think otherwise of you if you did return East, though."

"Now, Mr. Calloway." Eliza gave him a gentle smile. "I know you're just watching out for me and for my grandfather's interests. But I believe that we can turn the ranch back to the way Grandfather wrote about it. You have the experience. I have the determination. Together we can do this."

Benton nodded and turned toward the door. "Yes, ma'am."

"Mr. Calloway?" Eliza called after him. "Before you go, could you tell me where the riding saddles are?"

Benton stopped and turned around. "We don't have any fancy lady's side saddles for you, ma'am. That and the stock saddles—except mine and George's—were all sold after Mr. Roberts passed on. They brought a good deal of money, them being Morgans."

Had he practically spat the name out? "Morgans?"

"Mr. Roberts had them custom made by Caleb Morgan."

Caleb Morgan! Should she venture to ask Mr. Calloway? But at the glower on his face, perhaps now wasn't the time.

"They're worth something, with him being known across the state now."

"Where would I find this Mr. Morgan?"

Benton stared at the straw-layered floor a moment and swallowed, as if choking on something. He then turned a pointed gaze on her. "Ma'am, let me warn you. You're best off not having any dealings with that man."

With that, he turned and headed out the barn door.

CHAPTER 3

*E*liza slept soundly after her long journey. But when she awoke, she sat up, listening to the strangeness. How odd country life sounded. No trolleys clanging down the tracks, no horses clopping their shoes against the cobblestone, no children shouting from the streets as they played. It was almost...silent here. Except for Nellie's banging around in the kitchen and a rooster crowing and Kep's faint bark.

She climbed out from underneath the warm blankets and wrapped the pretty quilt around her as she peeked out the front window. Down below, George, the dark-haired ranch hand whom she'd met at suppertime, swung a bucket, splashing water along the way, as he trekked toward the barn. Chickens roamed the yard, stopping to peck here and there as if they couldn't wait for Nellie to toss them their breakfast. Perhaps Benton Calloway was already out in the pasture repairing fences.

With a big yawn, Eliza stopped gawking and hurried about getting herself ready. Apparently, ranch life started much earlier than she was used to.

Within minutes, she was dressed and downstairs. "Good morning, Miss Nellie."

Nellie turned her head but continued to stir eggs on the stove. "Good morning to you, Miss Eliza. But around here, I'm just Nellie. I'm glad you're up. Breakfast is just about ready. Would you ring the bell for me?"

"I'd be glad to." From the moment she had heard the lovely gong sound last night, she had felt a connection to her grandparents, glimpsing the ranch life they had loved.

When she returned from the porch, she stared out the back kitchen window.

"What are you looking at, child?" Nellie asked.

"Just how odd it looks with that one big clump of sagebrush on the edge of the yard. Your gardens are so neatly tended to, and then that just sticks out. Maybe I could cut it down for you."

"Oh, no, dear. Your grandmother never allowed that one to be cleared. It's part of the ranch. 'Don't you touch it,' she'd always remind the men. But come May, you'll see it's not sagebrush. It's bitterbrush."

"Bitterbrush?"

"When you smell the flowers, you'll know for sure it's not sagebrush." Nellie inhaled deeply. "Pretty yellow-petalled blossoms. But as pretty as the flowers are, it still looks like sagebrush the rest of the year. An eyesore, if you ask me. I don't know why Miz Elizabeth wanted to keep that thing. But she did. And both she and your grandfather were adamant that it must never be cut down. Now, come eat while it's hot." And with that, she scooped eggs and bacon and biscuits onto plates and set them on the table as George and Benton came in to eat.

Eliza spent the morning with Nellie, learning her way around the kitchen. This was the only place she could function confidently on the ranch. Nellie even allowed her to help a little, but the cook's bustling about and banging of pots and pans whenever Eliza asked a question about the ranch's condition or the people made it clear she should work silently. The most she was able to glean was that it was still a full-time job for Nellie to clean the main house and keep the two remaining ranch hands fed.

Once done with dishes and meal preparations and after being shooed out by Nellie, Eliza retired to her room. Curled up in the alcove, she settled in to read her Bible.

Judge not, that ye be not judged was the passage fresh on her heart.

Lord, let me live that verse. This is such a strange land here. Let me not judge these people against the ways I know from the East. Let me be a light to bring Your love to the West.

And when not praying and reading, Eliza had plenty of time to figure out a solution to the ranch's problems. Though Mr. Calloway was always reticent to state his opinion, she knew he firmly believed she should sell. There was no use in trying to redeem the ranch, he'd explained. The money was gone. He saw no other option than to sell it. But now Eliza thought of another answer. Caleb Morgan. Finding him, she knew for sure, was her grandfather's wish.

Now with a plan of action, Eliza hurried downstairs and found Nellie out back feeding the chickens.

"Nellie," she called, keeping back from the clucking hens as they left scratching in the dirt and flocked around Nellie and the food she tossed their way. "I'd like to ride into town tomorrow. Are there any supplies I could pick up for you?"

The cook set her pail on the ground and her hands on her hips.

"I don't have time to hitch up the wagon and take you. Benton should have brought supplies yesterday when he was in town. And we don't have a sidesaddle for you. Miz Elizabeth's was sold."

"No, I didn't mean for you to take me. And I don't need a sidesaddle."

"Well, we ain't got any saddle for you. Just Benton's and George's, and they need them."

"Of course. But I can ride bareback."

"Bareback? You being a city girl?"

Eliza grinned. "Of course. I may not know anything about a ranch, but I do know a few things about horses."

"Well, I might need heavy things—flour and sugar."

"That's fine. And if you have a saddlebag, I can carry whatever you need."

Nellie dropped her hands from her hips. Picked up the pail and shooed the chickens back to scratching in the dirt. "Very well. I'll make you a list. If you're bringing back flour and sugar, the least I can do is make a pie with it. Come along."

Eliza worked alongside Nellie the rest of the day, and by the time she tumbled into bed, she felt she had a solid friend in the cook.

The next morning, Eliza climbed onto her grandmother's mare, Rosey. Dressed in a long, full dress, she had no problem swinging her leg over to ride astride, something that was against all her proper upbringing, but out here, it proved the simplest way to ride. And who was there to see her and be offended in this land, anyway?

Old Kep escorted her as far as the entrance sign. At the gate, he sat on his haunches, flicking one ear forward, as if making sure the area past his guard was safe for her to enter.

"Thank you, Kep," Eliza called to him. "I'll bring you a treat from town when I return." Then she and Rosey were on their own. She tried her best to see the drab colors and tumbling weeds through Grandfather's eyes but finally gave up, resigning herself to the bleak-looking land.

After a few miles, Eliza spotted two riders approaching.

Swiftly, she swung her leg back over the mare's neck to ride in a proper lady-like fashion.

"Good day, Miss," one gentleman called while the other tipped his hat.

"Good day." Eliza nodded at them. "Excuse me—could you tell me how much farther it is to Caldwell?"

"Just around that bend, ma'am, and you'll be there."

"Thank you!" Eliza urged Rosey forward, and within minutes, she was once again in the bustling little town.

A lady with three little blond girls who were passing a market basket back and forth between them walked down the street. The girls' laughter overshadowed their patched and loose-hanging dresses and their mother's gaunt face.

"Hello," Eliza called to them. "I'm new to town and was wondering if you could direct me to the mercantile."

"That's the mercantile right there," the oldest girl—maybe around nine—said, pointing to a well-kept building.

"Thank you." Eliza smiled at her.

"We just came from there," the middle girl volunteered shyly. "Mr. Jacobs gave us some candy."

"We each got one today!" The littlest girl, with long braids, held up a piece of stick candy to show her.

"That was so kind of him. I'm sure I'll like Mr. Jacobs myself." She looked at the lady. "I'm Eliza Roberts. My grandfather was Elliott Roberts. Perhaps you knew him?"

"Yes, I did. He and Mrs. Roberts were wonderful people. My condolences to you."

"Thank you."

"I'm Maggie Billings, and these are my girls, Lila, Rosita, and Virginia." She pointed from oldest to youngest.

"I'm always last," the littlest girl piped up.

"I'm very glad to make your acquaintance." Eliza reached down to shake hands with each of them.

"Come, girls, we best be going now. Welcome to Caldwell."

"Thank you—and God bless you," she added as the lady turned away with a sad look in her eyes. Was she widowed and struggling to raise her girls alone? Or even going home to a drunken husband? Eliza watched for a bit as the girls once again swung the basket and chattered amongst themselves. Maybe she could find a way to help the family during her short visit here.

Eliza rode up to the mercantile, tied Rosey to the hitching post, and climbed the boardwalk to the door.

"Good day, ma'am." The skinny, silver-haired shopkeeper eyed Eliza as she entered the premises. "You're new in these parts."

"Yes. I'm Eliza Roberts, Elliott Roberts's granddaughter from the Double E." She held out her hand.

"Daniel Jacobs." He shook Eliza's hand. "My condolences on your grandfather. He was a good man."

"Thank you."

"Will you be staying? Or you just passing through?"

"I hope to be staying for...a time."

Mr. Jacobs nodded, pulling on one of his suspenders. "Did Nellie send you with a supply list?"

Eliza smiled. "She did." She pulled the paper from her pocket and handed it to Mr. Jacobs.

She watched quietly as he set about gathering the items. As sugar and flour and coffee piled up on the counter, Eliza wondered if he might give her the information she needed. All she had been able to find out from Nellie about Caleb Morgan was that he lived in Caldwell and made superb saddles.

"Will there by anything else, miss?" the proprietor asked.

"Actually, yes," Eliza said with a demure smile. "I need a saddle. I've heard of your legendary saddlemaker, Mr. Caleb Morgan."

"Ah, yes." Mr. Jacobs brightened. "Caleb. He's made quite a

name for himself. I guarantee you won't be sorry if you buy a Morgan. Two blocks up, one block over, and you're there."

Eliza nodded while inwardly, her heart danced with the easily acquired news.

"Shall I hold your purchases while you pay him a visit?"

"Oh, yes, thank you. It was nice meeting you, and may you have God's peace upon you." She smiled at his raised brows, then scooped her skirts with one hand and hurried out of the store, not stopping until she reached a small wooden barn-like building with *C. Morgan Saddlery* on a sign over the doorpost.

How she wished she could tell Grandfather she was here. *I've found Caleb Morgan, as you requested. Soon the Double E will be back on its feet.*

Eliza stepped across the threshold of the building and took a few steps inside.

"Is someone there?" a man's voice called out from somewhere in back.

"Yes," Eliza answered. "I'm looking for Mr. Caleb Morgan."

"I'll be right out."

"Thank you." Eliza surveyed the large open area. She didn't know much about saddles other than the feminine sidesaddle she occasionally had used—but these heavy, cumbersome-looking saddles had a sturdiness about them. Though bare of any designs engraved in the leather, they looked to be of high quality. And the leather flaps and the horn and stirrup casings must all be necessities for cowboys' rough riding. Even she could tell, as she rubbed a hand across the leather on one, that this man, Caleb Morgan, must love his work. She was looking forward to working with the man whom Grandfather thought of so highly.

Footsteps sounded across the plank floor, and Eliza turned. The man approaching her was not white-haired or even elderly.

"You're Mr. Morgan?" How could this man she'd

approached at the train station the day of her arrival be the man Grandfather had trusted? A man with rage-filled eyes?

"I am." He smiled momentarily, and Eliza caught a glimpse of the initial kindness and gentleness she had seen when he was patting his horse that day. The way he had first spoken to her. The anger didn't make sense. But she had seen it.

"I'm Eliza Roberts—from the Double E—Mr. Elliott Roberts's granddaughter."

Mr. Morgan nodded. "I'm pleased to make your acquaintance. I'd like to offer my sympathies at Mr. Roberts's passing."

"Thank you."

"Is there something I may do for you?"

"Yes." Now that she was here, she should go through with her intentions, to embrace what Grandfather had written. "My grandfather trusted you."

His eyes widened. In surprise?

"That's why I've come to you." She paused and looked into his dark brown eyes that somehow—at the moment, at least—spoke of goodness. Grandfather surely must have known what he was doing in choosing this man, though he was so much younger than she had expected. "The Double E is in trouble." A shadow darkened his eyes, but she pressed on. "I want to work with the foreman, Mr. Calloway, to restore the ranch. Will you help us?"

Mr. Morgan stared at her a long moment, then took a deep breath. "No."

"But my—"

"No." The saddlemaker crossed his arms.

One look at his face confirmed that no pleading would change his mind or persuade him to listen further. The deep scowl from that first encounter was back, embedded on his face.

She pulled herself up as straight and tall as she could. She would not back down nor be intimidated by this ill-mannered, coarse oaf.

Eliza turned the words over in her mind with which to answer, deliberately choosing each one—words that would let him know exactly what she thought of him and his manners. How she had come solely at her grandfather's request, how Elliott Roberts had trusted him alone so completely with all he owned, and how he had now dishonored Grandfather's wishes without even the courtesy of waiting to hear more.

Eliza put her hands on her hips, narrowed her eyes, and opened her mouth, ready to deliver her diatribe.

Mr. Morgan kept his arms crossed and widened his stance.

"*Mister* Morgan..." Though he was hardly deserving of the gentlemanly title.

Judge not, that ye be not judged. The words from her Bible, still lying open on her bedside table at the Double E, lodged in her heart. Slowly, they choked off the callous words she was about to deliver as precisely as physical blows.

The oaf raised one brow, as if ready, waiting for her to strike and wondering what was taking so long.

"I..." Eliza took a deep breath, fighting down the harsh words she still wanted to spew at him. This was hardly the message of love and peace she wanted to bring to Grandfather's town.

Then the fleeting image of her mother's finger wagging at her as a child dissolved the last of her anger. "*Temper, temper, Elizabeth Rose Roberts. One day, it will surely get you into trouble.*"

Mother was right. And that day had come.

Eliza swallowed. "I'm sorry to hear you won't be able to help us," she said softly. She stepped closer to a saddle that appeared to be finished and ran her hand lightly over the fine leather. "I see you do good work. I need a saddle for the ride home."

If Caleb Morgan's mouth hadn't yet fully dropped open at

the sudden change in her manner, it did when she tacked on, "Is this one for sale?"

～

A stock saddle? Caleb didn't know which shocked him most—her quick turnaround from a spitfire to a calm, proper lady, or her request for this stock saddle. That alone moved her out of the proper-lady category.

He closed his mouth and reassessed her. Well, he could certainly imagine she had the fortitude to disregard any fashion protocol and ride however she wished. She would probably not even be above donning a pair of man's dungarees —which she most likely would end up doing if she rode astride rather than on a lady's sidesaddle. But the way she suddenly turned from a raging madwoman to soft and gentle...*that* he couldn't understand.

He shook his head to clear it, though the gesture didn't help at all.

"Well...yes, I can sell you a saddle." He tried for an attempt at a civilized smile. "That's what I do."

She managed a small smile in return. "Please forgive me for my...bad temper."

Forgiveness? What kind of lady would so willingly ask for that? None he knew.

"Of course." Caleb could only guess what it cost her to ask.

Eliza stuck out a hand which he clasped, surprised at its strength and warmth considering she appeared a well-bred lady.

"Thank you," she said with such a sweet smile that her rather plain features seemed to glow with an inner light. She made him think of a picture of an angel he'd seen at church long ago. Or maybe she just so reminded him of Miz Elizabeth.

Gentle, calm, kind. Yet firm, able to keep the ranch hands at the Double E in line—and attending church—when she was alive.

Her magnetism drew him as he focused upon her eyes, so clear and blue. Beyond her frustration and anger with him, he could see peace in her soul reflected through those eyes.

Abruptly, he dropped his gaze to the floor and pulled his hand free from hers. If he wasn't careful, he'd end up imagining she was sincere and guileless, a woman whom a man could trust. And that he never intended to do again.

Eliza's eyes widened at his sudden action, and she took a step back. "I'm sure you have your reasons for not helping us."

Oh, there was a myriad of those. His hatred for Benton Calloway. His bum leg, ribs that still hindered movement if he wasn't careful. His commitment to his saddle business. But only one reason mattered.

That Elliott Roberts had ordered him to never step foot on the Double E again. And that was something he wasn't about to share. But he could certainly extend an olive branch and return her graciousness.

"Thank you, Miss Roberts, for asking. But I'm sorry that I'm not able to help you. However, I can assist you with a saddle."

"This one?" She again touched the one she'd been looking at. The bulkiest one in the shop.

Surely, she knew the inappropriateness of that one. "I do have a ladies' sidesaddle which you might like."

"I like this one."

"Miss, it's...not for sale."

She quirked an eyebrow at him.

"It's not finished."

She kept that brow up, challenging his statement.

"The detail work isn't done." Or his signature etching. "But I do have one in the back you might like just as well. I just finished it, actually." A stock saddle if she was insistent but one less cumbersome and also less expensive. Though, from the style and flounce of her dress, perhaps money wasn't a problem for her, just for the Double E.

"Thank you. I'd like to see it."

He turned to retrieve it only to discover her right on his heels. "I'll bring it out."

"I can walk to it, thank you. Though I do hope it's similar to that one. I like its sturdiness."

She kept up her chatter as they entered the back area of his shop.

"It's dusty and dirty back here, miss. I can—"

She waved a hand in dismissal of his objection. "There can't be any more dust in here than I walk through out on the street, is there?"

He almost chuckled. "No, I can't say that I can match that."

"Good. Then show me what you have back here."

He walked over to the one he had in mind. Sturdy, solid. And finished. One he would have no qualms selling her—as far as comfort and safety went, that was. Still, what was this New York City-bred woman doing in the dust and wanting a work saddle?

"I must tell you, though, Miss Roberts, this saddle is for riding hard and roping cattle. Ranch work."

"Hmm. Do you think it's well made enough, then, to withstand a ride to town and back?"

He dared not linger too long on the twinkle in her eyes. "Well, of course. It's a well-made saddle. Period."

"Then, sold!" She thrust out her hand again. And gentleman that he'd been raised to be, of course, he should take it. He gave it a firm shake as he would for any customer. And stole a peek into those eyes again, as he would not do with any old customer. And now her lips were smiling as well. "Let's settle up, and then I'll get Rosey saddled."

Rosey. Other than his own horse, Ruby, Rosey was the ranch favorite. Miz Elizabeth's mare. The Double R's, Miz Elizabeth had called the pair. And no doubt, even Ruby missed living out on the Double E. But he had to accept things and get on with—

"Mr. Morgan."

He jerked his hand back. Hen-plucked feathers—had he been holding Miss Roberts's hand this whole time? "Yes, let's settle up. Where is Rosey?" He didn't see her out at the hitching post.

"She's back at the mercantile."

Three long blocks away. But, he reminded himself, he was a gentleman. "I'll go get her. You may wait here."

"Oh no. I'll get her. I need to pick up my purchases from Mr. Jacobs, anyway. And I do want to bid him good day before heading back to the ranch. I'll return with her in just a little bit."

And with that, she whooshed out of his shop. Like a tumbleweed chased by a gust of wind. One that once upon a time he would have chased after as well.

He stared at his hand that had held hers—twice today—the connection still teasing his fingers. But what could come of it? She was only visiting the ranch. And even if she stayed longer, he wasn't welcome there, anyway.

He curled his fingers into a fist. The answer was *nothing*.

Absolutely nothing.

CHAPTER 4

*S*unday morning, Eliza dressed in her best for Grandfather's church. There she would sit on the same pew he had, soak in the worship through hymns and Scriptures, and praise the same God he had. And what a joy it would be meeting folks who had known and loved both him and Grandmother.

And afterward, there was to be a church dinner on the lawn, if the cold didn't chase it inside. She and Nellie had spent the last two days baking pies and chicken and biscuits to take. Secretly, Eliza hoped Mrs. Billings and her three sweet girls would join her and Nellie and feast with them. Maybe starting out the week with full stomachs would be a blessing to the family.

She entered the kitchen at the same time as Benton Calloway. His black hair, while still rather unkempt, was slicked back, giving at least a semblance of his having cleaned up.

"Good morning, Miss Eliza, Nellie." With a charming smile, he nodded at each of them, squirming his shoulders beneath the thin brown cloth of his suit coat.

George followed close behind Benton. "Howdy." George gave a shy smile and sat down at the table.

Eliza greeted them and helped Nellie fill the plates.

"Good morning, men." Nellie set the plates of steaming eggs and bacon before them. "Eat up and then we'll be leaving for church."

George took a deep inhale of the food on the plate in front of him. "Yes, ma'am. The wagon is all hitched up, ready to go."

Eliza loved the rule Grandmother and Grandfather had made and that the men were still abiding by even in their absence—that every employee of the ranch attend church on the Lord's day.

"Very good." Nellie took her own seat. "If you'd be so kind as to help Eliza and me load the food basket, we'll be on our way as soon as the dishes are washed."

"Will do." George steepled his hands. "Shall I ask the blessing for our food?"

"Certainly. Thank you."

George prayed, and at the amen, Benton shoveled food into his mouth without a word.

Eliza tried to picture the former times around this table that Nellie had told her about. How Miz Elizabeth, as the men called Grandmother, would fix delicious Sunday meals for them and she and Grandfather took care of the chores so the ranch hands and Nellie could have a day of worship and rest. No wonder she had been loved by their employees.

After breakfast, Eliza, Nellie, and George climbed into the wagon with Benton at the reins. This time, Eliza enjoyed the wagon ride as the alkali and sagebrush were familiar sights. Now she felt safe, accepted on the ranch, no longer fearful as she had on that first wagon ride.

Before long, the wagon arrived at a little white church in Caldwell. Outside, wagons and carriages and a Studebaker buggy congregated, the horses left to graze as the owners went inside to worship.

Nellie led Eliza down to the front pew, seating her in what she identified as Grandfather's favorite spot. A flock of ladies clustered around Eliza, greeting her with hugs as they welcomed the granddaughter of their friend Elizabeth Roberts. Benton and George wandered around talking with the menfolk.

As the congregation stood to sing the first hymn, Benton Calloway's deep voice boomed out from somewhere in the middle of the congregation. Eliza turned around, pleased to hear one of the Double E's employees singing to the Lord. But as she turned, her gaze wandered across the almost-full little church to the very last pew. There, slumped down in the corner of the bench, was Caleb Morgan, arms crossed and stone-faced. She didn't know why he was here, but it was apparent that it wasn't to worship.

In her quick look, she also spotted Mrs. Billings and her three little towheaded girls. Mrs. Billings stood with her head bowed, eyes closed, but the littlest girl waved at Eliza, then giggled. As soon as the service was over, she'd make a beeline to invite them to sit with her and Nellie at the potluck. If there was some way she could help this family during her short stay at the Double E, she surely would.

∾

*C*aleb glared at everyone around him. He might as well not have come for all the good the sermon would do him. But he came each week, anyway. Out of respect for what Mr. Roberts had required of his employees. Not that he was one of them anymore. Out of habit from his parents' training. And out of longing, holding on to a thin thread of hope that maybe one day he could pray and wholeheartedly worship again.

Caleb shut his eyes, remembering when he used to sit up

front on the first pew right beside Mr. and Mrs. Roberts, as though he'd been part of their family. Mrs. Roberts would pat his arm and call him their almost-grandson. He'd eaten at their family table, joined them for family Bible reading. Prayed and sung with them...

Benton Calloway's booming voice seemed to fill the entire church, grating on Caleb's ears. Caleb blinked open his eyes and scowled. That was why he was sorry he'd come. Because Benton Calloway was here. And in the few moments he'd had his eyes closed, Callie, the girl he had intended to marry, had slipped in and seated herself next to Calloway. Caleb forced his gaze away from the two of them nestled up cozily in the crowded pew. But instead of looking at the gray-haired widowed preacher, his eyes riveted again on the front pew, on the back of Miss Roberts's neat bun. He clenched his fists. The life he'd known less than a year ago was over. Miss Eliza Roberts, the real grandchild, had taken his spot—on the pew and at the ranch.

He tried real hard to concentrate on the sermon and was doing a decent job.

"But let me read what Jesus said." Reverend Thompson slid his spectacles on. "'Ye have heard that it hath been said, thou shalt love thy neighbour, and hate thine enemy.'"

Caleb sat up a bit. Had Jesus said that? Must be, since the reverend was reading straight out of the Bible. But somehow, that didn't sit right—that Jesus didn't see anything wrong with Caleb hating his enemy.

"Now, some people would stop there. And that would be a grave mistake. For that is what was being taught in Jesus's day, not what He was teaching. Read on with me to see what Jesus is really teaching here. 'But I say unto you, Love your enemies, bless them that curse you, do good to them that hate you, and pray for them which despitefully use you, and persecute you.' Some mighty strong words, I'd say."

Love Benton Calloway? Bless him and do good to him? Pray for him?

All impossible.

"But impossible, you say?" The pastor looked over the congregation, and Caleb squirmed under his gaze which seemed to land on Caleb a fraction longer than anyone else. "Let's look at what Jesus has to say about impossible things. 'But Jesus beheld them, and said unto them, With men this is impossible; but with God all things are possible.' All things are possible with God."

Love. Bless. Do good. Pray.

Caleb tried praying. Again. He even tried to consider Jesus's command to love thine enemy. But that would mean loving Benton Calloway, and that thought sickened him. Calloway wasn't worthy of love, of any forgiveness. He deserved whatever judgment and condemnation could be dealt out to him.

But with God all things are possible.

As soon as the final amen was said, Caleb hightailed it out the door. Not that he had anywhere to go. He used to have a seat around the big table at the Double E for Sunday dinner. Then after a big slice of steaming pie, he and Mr. Roberts would mosey out to the front porch and sit in those big old rockers. They'd spend the afternoon rocking, and Caleb would be a student of Mr. Roberts's, soaking up everything he could about ranching and life. When Miz Elizabeth had dried the last dish, she'd come out and chat a few minutes with them. Then Caleb would stand and head over to the bunkhouse, leaving Mr. and Mrs. Roberts to spend time together. Every Sunday, it was that way, until her death. Then Caleb stayed on the porch all afternoon, feeling he was the one keeping Mr. Roberts company, instead of the other way around.

Those days seemed a lifetime ago, not just months. With the saddlery shop closed on Sundays, all Caleb could do was sit with his horse and eat a cold piece of meat for lunch.

He turned to head alone toward his shop without looking back. He knew what the congregation did after church. They gathered into little groups and buzzed like bees around honey, catching up with neighbors and news. Especially at potlucks—which it appeared one was being set up outside today in the temperate weather. No one, though, ever approached him. He even knew he was the topic of the buzzing. But today, with his aching leg, he hadn't moved fast enough. He should have ridden his mare instead of walking the few short blocks. Now, right in front of him, he had to witness Benton helping Callie into her carriage and bidding her and her family good day.

"Mr. Morgan—"

Caleb turned. Miss Roberts was hurrying toward him. He sucked in a breath. Her smile was so radiant. She seemed to glow with goodness.

"Ma'am." Caleb nodded.

"I saw you in church—"

Caleb scuffed a boot in the dust. How she must view him—sullen, disinterested. Bitter. That one was right. He didn't know what to do about it, though. Apparently, she was about to tell him.

"It looked as though you were leaving. Aren't you staying for the potluck?"

"No."

"Nellie cooked plenty of food to share. Won't you join us?"

How he would like to. Especially to get to know this interesting lady a bit more. But as kind as her invitation was, it was impossible to accept. He didn't socialize with the townsfolk. All they wanted to do was ask questions he didn't want to answer. But not answering didn't slow them down any. It added to their Sunday afternoon entertainment—gathered into their little cliques and speculating about him. Why did he live in town now? How did he get his bum leg? Why did Benton Calloway take over as foreman of the Double E? Why did Callie desert him?

"No."

Miss Roberts's forehead scrunched up with...disappointment?

"Thank you," he tacked on. There was no need to sound rude. "That's mighty kind of you. Thank you for asking." He slapped his hat on, then nodded again. "Good day, miss."

"Good day, Mr. Morgan. May God's peace go with you."

God's peace? Oh, he yearned to have a taste of that again. He turned quickly and strode off, trying to squelch the stab of wistfulness in his heart. Peace was something Miss Roberts seemed to have plenty of. Something he actually longed for. But for him, it was unattainable. One last look back confirmed it. Benton Calloway was leading Miss Roberts by her elbow toward the food tables.

Dear Lord, please...

That was his prayer over and over through the afternoon. As he walked back to his shop for his usual Sunday cold lunch. As he saddled Ruby, his only friend in town, for a ride. And as he stopped before a little knoll to let her graze, if she could find anything among the dried grass.

Sitting on the ground, his back against a tree, minding his own business, he heard something. Giggling. He stuck his head around the trunk, then, seeing no one, crawled to the crest of the hill. Who on earth was so happy out here? As he lay on his belly like a snake in the grass, he discovered who was making all the racket. Miss Eliza Roberts. And three little girls seated on the ground next to her. All four blond heads bobbed along with the laughter ringing on the hillside.

"Let's sing it again," one girl pleaded between giggles.

"Yes, please!" chorused the other two.

Caleb hadn't meant to eavesdrop. Not at first, anyway. But the scene was so enchanting...

Eliza reached out, and the three girls tumbled toward her. Two scrambled right next to her, both encircled by one of Eliza's arms. The little one found a place on her lap.

"'Jesus loves me! This I know,'" they all sang together.

"'For the Bible tells me so.

Little ones to Him belong;

They are weak, but He is strong.

Yes, Jesus loves me!'"

With each phrase, they got louder and louder. "'Yes, Jesus loves me! Yes, Jesus loves me! The Bible tells me so!'"

The laughing girls all ended up together in a heap on Eliza's lap.

"Now," Eliza was asking them, "why do you love Jesus?"

"Because He loves us, of course," the oldest girl said.

"Yes, He does, Lila. Virginia?"

The smallest of the girls smiled adoringly at Eliza. "Because he made the flowers!"

"And how beautiful they are. Rosita?"

The middle girl puckered her brow, then smiled. "I love Jesus because He's my friend."

"The best friend we'll ever have." Eliza reached over and tickled each of the girls, and again, they burst out into high-pitched giggles.

"Miss Eliza?" Virginia planted her hands on Eliza's cheeks and pulled her face close. "Why do you love Jesus?"

Caleb waited for her to say *because He loves me*. But she bowed her head and was silent a moment.

Then she gazed at the girls one at a time. "I love Jesus because I can trust Him and His love. I'll tell you a story. When I was a little girl not much older than you, Virginia—are you five?"

The girl nodded, setting her braids swinging. "But I'll be six next month."

"My grandfather would tell me how much he loved me and

started calling me his little angel. Then when I was about your age, Rosita—seven?"

"Yes."

"He moved far away, out here to build his ranch when Caldwell was just becoming a town. Mother and Father and my aunt Belinda said it was because he didn't love any of us anymore."

Anger clawed at Caleb, and he crawled a bit closer.

"They always said we weren't enough, that Grandfather loved his ranch more than us. More than me."

The oldest girl patted Eliza on the arm. "But did he still love you?"

Eliza gave a sad smile. "Yes, I believe he did. That's why I'm here. To at least see what made his ranch so important to him."

Caleb didn't get it. Because Mr. Roberts had loved his family.

"But"—and her smile brightened along with her eyes—"I clung to the promise that Jesus loves me and was always with me. I love Him because He loves me. Stand up and hold hands, and I'll teach you a song I made up. It's what I want everyone to know." The girls scrambled off her lap and formed a circle with her. Skipping to some tune, she sang, "'I love Him because He loves me. Glory to God in the highest. I love Him, He's always with me. Glory to God in the highest.'" Eliza pulled the girls to a halt. "Do you like it?"

Nodding heads answered her question.

"Can you sing it with me?" At more eager nods, Eliza led them in the song like an off-key choir.

"Girls! Here you are." A worn-looking woman approached. He'd seen her around town—Widow Billings, was it?

"Mama!" the girls chorused. "Miz Eliza was singing to us."

The woman looked as though she didn't have the energy to even smile, but she did. "That's lovely."

"And she told us a story," Virginia added.

Eliza gathered the woman into her arms and hugged her.

43

"Thank you for letting me borrow your girls for a bit, Mrs. Billings." When Eliza released her, she held the older woman's hands in her own. "Peace. That's what God wants you to have. Remember, God cares for you so much. He'll provide for your every need. Just ask Him. And"—she winked at the girls—"will you all join Miss Nellie and me at the Double E tomorrow for supper? We don't have very many to cook for, and I know Nellie is hankering to bake up some more pies for this week in the hope of having someone who will eat them all up."

Now how did Miss Roberts know Mrs. Billings already? Let alone that she needed help feeding her girls and raising them alone?

"Thank you, Eliza." Mrs. Billings looked at her daughters. "We'd love to come, wouldn't we, girls?"

"Oh yes!" they said practically in unison.

"Will we really get to see Miz Eliza again tomorrow?" Rosita asked.

"I love pie! I hope it's pum-kin tomorrow!" Virginia shouted.

Caleb couldn't listen to any more. He slid back down to where Ruby was munching on something. He grabbed the reins, surprising her. Of course, Ruby would want to stay in this peaceful place. Who wouldn't love to be near Eliza? But he couldn't afford to be seen out here. How he wished to be like those innocent little girls, like Eliza, loving to sing of Jesus and His love, to have a heart of peace and to worship again. To have a wife who offered to bring home hurting people. But he'd let bitterness burn too deep and too long in his soul for that.

Most of all, he didn't dare stay in her presence because he couldn't let his heart long to know her better. For, one day, even sweet Miss Roberts was bound to disappoint him.

CHAPTER 5

*E*liza sat at the kitchen table, cracking breakfast eggs into a bowl for Nellie. The potluck at church yesterday had passed pleasantly. She could barely keep straight all the introductions and names of the many folks who came over to welcome her to Caldwell.

"You doing okay over there?" Biscuits baking in the oven filled the kitchen with their warm scent as Nellie flipped sizzling slabs of bacon in her skillet. "You're mighty quiet this morning."

"I was just thinking about church and meeting the ladies of Caldwell yesterday. They're very welcoming."

"Welcoming—puh. That's one word for them. Busybodies, most of them are, if you ask me."

"Perhaps, but kind." Various women had volunteered their opinions on how to dress for ranch life and recipes she should try and the names of numerous eligible bachelors once they learned she was planning to stay to get the Double E back up and running again. But no one offered advice on how to save the ranch, not even any ideas of how to start.

So...it was beginning to look as though Eliza was just going to have to do it herself. She took a quick mental inventory of what she knew about ranching. Nothing. But she did know how to supervise. How much harder could overseeing a couple of ranch hands be than keeping order in a classroom or on the playground?

She cracked the last of the dozen eggs and handed them to Nellie, then pulled plates, forks, and spoons from a drawer.

In addition to helping Nellie keep the house, gardens, and chickens, Eliza would take over the recordkeeping while Benton and George continued to work the ranch.

But whatever she did, she needed to act quickly, before any more cattle had to be sold and the Double E lost even more income. After breakfast, her first order of business was to pen a letter to the school in Los Angeles, asking to postpone her position due to family matters in Idaho. Hopefully, they'd still want her when she was able to continue her journey. Or perhaps another school would have a position for her, as Los Angeles was a growing town.

This evening, she would be reaching out to a family in need as Mrs. Billings and her girls would join them for supper. Nellie had confirmed that Maggie indeed was struggling since Mr. Billings died two years ago in a farm accident and that Maggie was taking in sewing to keep the girls fed and clothed.

Yet long term, there was a problem. Double E money would eventually run out, and that meant not being able to minister to others through hospitality. And that's where Eliza had to do something.

George came in to breakfast as Nellie scooped the eggs and bacon onto platters and Eliza pulled the biscuits from the oven.

Eliza's brow knit as she took in George's long face. "Why are you so glum-looking this morning?"

"Well, Miss Eliza..." George sat, not meeting Eliza's gaze. "I don't aim to disturb you, ma'am. But I guess you got to know."

He glanced over at Nellie, but she hurriedly busied herself with scraping the iron skillet. "We're down another head of cattle."

"What happened?" A frightening image of a mountain lion or some other dreadful creature sneaking onto the ranch at night made her legs quiver.

"A heifer is gone. No sign of a critter getting it. I didn't hear any ruckus last night either. Same as last time."

"The last time?" Eliza sank onto her chair. "When was that?"

"About a week ago now, ma'am."

"Does Mr. Calloway know?"

"Yes, ma'am. He's out there right now still looking around. But it appears there's nothing to be found."

George and Nellie eyed her as if to ask what she was going to do about it. "There's nothing we can do right now. I'll ring the bell to call Mr. Calloway in for breakfast. You men will need full stomachs if you have to ride out in the fields to check."

With a quick meeting of their eyes, George and Nellie seemed to pass a silent message between them. Then George nodded and reached for an extra biscuit. Nellie hurried out to the porch and rang the bell herself, summoning Benton to the house. Eliza sighed with relief. Perhaps their immediate action signified that they accepted her as the boss of the ranch.

"Good morning, ladies." Benton tucked his cowboy hat under his arm as he entered the kitchen. "I guess you heard about the missing heifer." He directed the comment to Eliza. "I've searched all around the barnyard, but there's no trail of anything." He shrugged and frowned. "I'm sorry, ma'am. This is another hard blow to the Double E. She isn't going to be able to be salvaged if even another head or two of cattle disappear. We're that short now."

"I understand. That's why I'm sending you and George out immediately after breakfast. I want the entire ranch searched. Even if it takes all day. Nellie and I will care for the livestock."

Eliza didn't dare break eye contact with Benton. This was the moment that would determine whether he would accept her position as owner of the ranch, his boss. He was, after all, the foreman, the one with experience. She knew nothing about ranching—a fact he was well aware of.

Almost imperceptibly, Benton's eyes widened. Eliza counted the ticks of the clock in the otherwise silent kitchen as Benton weighed her request.

Six...seven...

Benton nodded. "Yes, ma'am. As soon as we finish breakfast."

"Eat up, men," Nellie said, placing another platter of biscuits before them.

Eliza smiled. They may not find the missing animal, but she'd found something even better—the tiniest hope that just maybe she could run the ranch—with her good employees, of course.

As the day progressed, Eliza helped Nellie take care of the livestock and ranch duties, all the while wondering if the men had found any sign of the missing heifer. When Benton and George finally returned for dinner, dirt-streaked, sweaty, and with downcast expressions, Eliza knew their search had been fruitless.

"Did you find any broken fences?" Eliza asked the men when she met them out on the porch.

"No, ma'am." George took off his hat and swiped his forehead.

Benton sat on the top step. "It's like she just up and vanished. We didn't find one single track of a wild animal."

"Thank you for riding out to check." Eliza nodded at both of the men, grateful for their loyalty. "Let's all be extra cautious and alert. Now, after you get washed up, our supper guests should be arriving. And Nellie has some delicious-smelling pies waiting for you." With a smile meant to encourage them, she turned and headed back inside the house.

But once inside, she dropped the smile. She had to do something drastic before she lost her grandparents' ranch—the very thing they had deemed worthy enough to make the trek across country to come out west. For if she lost the Double E, that would make their leaving New York and family all for naught.

And it would add one more failure to her list of shortcomings in the eyes of her family.

❧

The next morning, Eliza went to Grandfather's worn desk tucked in front of the bay window in the parlor and pulled out the ledgers. Apparently, Benton had been keeping the books. Eliza needed to familiarize herself with the expenses and general operation of the Double E. And to see how long any money they did have would last.

The ranch seemed to be in a steady decline but still hanging on. In order to get an overall view of the Double E's activities, Eliza pulled out a previous book from close to a year ago. Here the handwriting was different. She didn't recognize it as Grandfather's, and it definitely did not belong to Benton. Carefully, she went through page by page. Several entries were made of cattle sales. But the prices steadily dropped. Not by much. But there was a pattern. Had the Double E's troubles started eight months ago? While Grandfather was still running the ranch?

She kept reading, checking each entry—until there was a gap in dates. As if nothing had happened at all on the ranch for several days. Strange.

Why, when someone had detailed every transaction daily, was a whole week missing all of a sudden? As Eliza sat staring at the ledger, she gasped. Little tell-tale stubs of paper were stuck in the binding. A page was missing—torn out.

Eliza checked the next page of entries. She didn't spot anything significantly different in the entries from the previous page still intact. So maybe there was nothing of interest on the missing page. Except the handwriting changed after that. Benton's?

Eliza took the ledger and headed out to the kitchen where Nellie was baking.

"Nellie, do you know why a page would be missing from this ledger? It's from when Grandfather was still alive. And who was keeping the accounting then?"

"Oh, goodness, who knows, dear? Anything could have happened to it. Mr. Roberts was always fiddling with those books. Always had his nose stuck in one. The books, the books. You'd think nothing was more important than those books." As Nellie talked, she began rummaging around in the cabinets, banging the pots and pans, fussing and muttering. "Oh dear. I'm out of sugar already! How will I make any more pies for the men? Oh, what will I do?"

"Don't worry, Nellie. I'll ride into town and buy sugar. What else should I get while I'm there?"

Nellie wrote down a few items while Eliza went to saddle gentle Rosey. Had Grandmother ever ridden her into town or always taken the wagon?

Eliza was getting used to this ride to town now. She didn't miss the busy streets and noise of New York City. The openness, the smells of ranches and animals, even the coating of dust and the quietness of this land offered restfulness, a calmness for her soul. This strange land was intriguing. But why was it enough for Grandfather to leave his family behind forever?

She'd only gotten to know him through a handful of letters in the three months before he died. She wasn't sure what had even triggered that. Loneliness? The fact that Eliza had moved from her parents' home to live with Father's spinster sister across town to be closer to her teaching position? Aunt Belinda seemed to know a little about her parents' life in Idaho, whereas Mother and Father knew nothing of it—or at least never spoke about it. What could have happened that Grandfather no longer corresponded with his own son?

That was one mystery she was unlikely to solve, as Nellie was close-mouthed about Grandfather. If only there was someone who would talk. There had to be someone Grandfather had shared his secrets with. The man he had written that he had trusted, Caleb Morgan, certainly wasn't about to share anything with her, though.

The ledgers were her business now. Balancing the books was one thing she could contribute to keeping the ranch running. And something didn't set right. The books said cattle were sold. Though she didn't know livestock prices, the entries seemed like reasonable amounts. Enough so that the ranch hands were paid—ten of them. So why couldn't they afford to keep more men on now?

And strange about that missing page—when entries before it showed the ranch doing well. And the entries following showed a profit until there was a gradual but steady decline after Grandfather's passing. Why would anyone pull out a page randomly in the middle of the book?

Eliza knew enough about Grandfather to gather that he was a meticulous man. Even the neat, almost artistically penned letters he had written her spoke of this characteristic. His cursive formations were copybook perfect. His grammar was impeccable. And his words seemed specifically selected to give the most vivid pictures imaginable. So she couldn't envision that he would ever tear a page out of a book. And even if he had needed to take the page out for some reason, someone as fastidious as things indicated he was wouldn't have ripped it out, leaving a jagged, uneven edge.

No, someone else had torn it out. But who? Why? And where was it? Who had been keeping the books at that time?

Eliza had to stop musing then, as she arrived at the mercantile. She tethered Rosey and pulled out Nellie's list.

Eliza scooped up her skirt and climbed the steps to the store, knowing exactly who had the answer to some of her questions. Nellie—banging pots and pans, muttering. Starting a pie without having enough sugar.

Eliza opened the door only to find Mr. Jacobs, arms ladened, ushering out two ladies she'd met at church. She held the door open as he handed them their packages and bid them good day.

"And good day to you, Miss Roberts. Come in."

"Hello, Mr. Jacobs."

He took his usual place behind the counter. "Back again already? No one from the Double E used to come in more than once a month." He studied the list Eliza handed him. "How many pies is that woman out there baking? I've never seen anyone go through sugar this fast. If those pies are for you, miss, you'll be plumped up before you know it."

Eliza just smiled. Banging pots and pans, indeed. "No, Mr. Jacobs. I guess Nellie's just trying to keep the men happy."

Feeling someone watching her, Eliza spotted a gray-haired man sitting in a chair near the counter staring at her, a slight grin on his face.

"Howdy there, miss." He pulled himself up to stand barely even with Eliza.

"Hello."

"Couldn't help but hear you're here from the Double E. Heard Elliott's relation is in town."

"Yes, I'm Elliott Roberts's granddaughter—Eliza Roberts."

He stuck out a hand. "I'm Gus. Just plain Gus. Knew your grandpa."

Eliza politely shook hands with him. "Did you know Grandfather well?"

Gus burst out with a hearty laugh. "Did I know him well?" He winked at Mr. Jacobs. "As well as anyone in this town, I'd guess."

"Don't let him fool you, Miss Roberts," Mr. Jacobs said. "The two of them were in cahoots, best friends if ever I did see any."

Gus's eyes lit up with a twinkle, making his craggy face look years younger. "I welcomed Elliott to Caldwell back when him and his missus arrived in their wagon when the town was just getting built. Right here in this very store. One of the first structures in this town. We started yapping then and never quit until —" He stopped. The smile left his face, and he looked ancient once again. He cleared his throat. "Until they both passed on to glory." Then he blinked, the smile returned, and he took right off talking again. "Best friend I ever had. And the stories I can tell you..."

Hallelujah. Eliza had found the person who just might divulge why Grandfather had abandoned his family for Idaho life. And if Nellie wouldn't speak of the problems on the ranch, perhaps Gus would.

CHAPTER 6

*L*iving in town wasn't too bad most days. Caleb was able to get around pretty good with businesses relatively close to each other. At least the few places he needed to visit. Church. The train station. The mercantile—which was where he was headed now.

"Howdy, Caleb."

No one ever greeted him outside his shop or business interactions. He looked up at the man he'd almost ran into. "Reverend Thompson."

"It's good to see you." The preacher had a way of looking right into his thoughts—or maybe heart. "I didn't get a chance to say hello on Sunday."

No, because Caleb had taken off, stopping only when Miss Roberts had waylaid him with her invitation. Which was odd also, considering their encounter at the saddle shop a few days ago. "Uh, fine sermon, Reverend."

Pastor Thompson laughed. "Thank you, son, but I'm just the Lord's messenger. I try to let His Word do the speaking to hearts."

"Um, yes." Caleb resisted rubbing his hand over his own

heart. Could it be that the unsettledness weighing on him was God nudging him?

"Are you going to the mercantile?"

"Yes, heading that way."

Even the sight of the reverend brought back words from Sunday. Words Caleb did not want to think about. *But I say unto you, Love your enemies, bless them that curse you, do good to them that hate you, and pray for them which despitefully use you, and persecute you.* Caleb tugged his coat tighter, warding off any conviction that might threaten to seep into his soul.

The pastor rubbed his hands together. "Ah, yes, I just came from there, and it's quite toasty inside. I'm glad it was warm enough on Sunday to have the potluck outside, but a nice fire is certainly appreciated today."

"Yes, sir." Caleb edged a step toward the store.

"I hope to get over to your shop one day soon, Caleb. You have quite the reputation for your saddles."

"Thank you. Stop by anytime."

"Will do." Reverend Thompson finally doffed his hat. "May the blessings of the Lord go with you."

Those words settled like a benediction upon him. If Miss Roberts were standing here, she'd probably say it was God's peace. Could be, but it wasn't something he'd known for a long time. He nodded to the reverend. "Good day to you."

Caleb continued to the mercantile, up the steps, and had his hand on the door when he saw Miss Roberts inside. She was so attractive—not so much outwardly, he supposed. She was fairly plain-looking, rather tall and gangly, freckled, though her hair and dresses were always neatly kept. But her spirit was what intrigued him.

Maybe he could figure out some way to help her restore the ranch—without actually stepping foot on it. He scowled, hating the fact that he was unwelcome there. Most likely, Miss Eliza would allow him on the property, but he tried to be a man of honor. And Mr. Roberts had forbidden him on the land. Until he cleared his name, he would honor Mr. Roberts's order.

How sweetly Miss Eliza had sung and laughed with the little girls after church on Sunday as she had shared her joy of God with them. A year ago, he wouldn't have crept over the knoll, trying to hide his presence. He would have stepped out and joined in the merriment himself, singing joyfully off-key. He would have eaten the Sunday picnic with her and Miss Nellie, seated on the Double E blanket.

Caleb swallowed. Sentimental longings were useless. He pushed the door open only a few inches before he realized whom Miss Eliza was talking to. Gus. Caleb stepped back as quickly as his bad leg allowed, pulling the door toward him until it softly clicked shut. Through the window, he stole another look at Eliza, who had not turned his way. Neither had Gus nor Mr. Jacobs. They were too busy talking to have noticed him.

He could surmise just what—or whom—they were talking about. Miss Roberts's head was a-bobbing, her eyes wide. What lies was Gus filling Miss Roberts's ears with about him?

His heart churned. Head down, Caleb limped down the step to where the horses out front were tied. The Double E mare whinnied at him, and he stopped to rub her.

"Do you remember me, Rosey?" He dug in his pocket and pulled out the apple he'd been saving for lunch. He held it out, and the horse chomped it noisily.

"That'a girl, Rosey. Are they treating you good out there?" He gave her neck a couple of pats. "Now that Miss Eliza is there, she'll take care of you." He gave the mare one last pat and rounded the side of the mercantile. He'd wait a few minutes to see if Gus left before checking if it was safe to go inside again. Or maybe he'd just come back later to get his few supplies, though that would interrupt his day even more. Or he'd just go without.

One thing was certain—he couldn't risk running into Gus. It was too late to clear his name with Elliott Roberts, but if he could ever prove his innocence to Gus, it'd be almost as good.

~

*E*liza couldn't help laughing along with Gus at his stories. What a charmer the older man turned out to be.

"Yes sirree, your grandpa was the best man around these parts. Now there was a man who loved his wife, I'll tell you. Yep. But then again, Miz Elizabeth was one everybody loved. She may not have been the town beauty, but everyone'll tell you she had the town's most beautiful heart. Elliott was mighty proud of her. Broke his own heart when she died of the fever back, oh, when was it now, Daniel?" He turned to Mr. Jacobs.

"Reckon it's nigh about, let's see—eight, nine months ago now? Yes, it was right before Ca—"

"Uhkkukkuhkkuhkk!" Deep, quick coughs had Gus in a spasm. As his coughing increased, he cupped both hands over his mouth and bent over, his whole chest shaking. "Wa—uhkk —ter!"

"Gus! Are you all right?" Daniel Jacobs slapped him on the back a few times. "Miss Eliza, pour him some of that coffee."

"Uhkkukk!"

Eliza grabbed a tin cup off the counter and poured some of what smelled like cold, day-old coffee. She handed the cup to Mr. Jacobs, and he thrust it into Gus's hands.

Gus took a few sips, and little by little, the coughing subsided.

"I guess I'd best muster my way over to Doc's one of these days." Gus set the cup on the counter and patted his chest, then grabbed his hat and jammed it onto his head. He nodded at Eliza. "As I was saying about your grandpa, he was the most honorable, godly man you'd ever want to meet. You stop by my cabin your next trip to town, missy, and I'll tell you some stories. You'll feel like you knew your grandparents."

"Thank you, Gus. I'll do that." Yes, indeed, Eliza had found the person she needed. Once she learned the secret about her grandparents and got the ranch up and making money again, she'd be on her way to California to assume her teaching position. Just as she'd planned.

Gus stood and took his leave. Without any purchases. But maybe that was the way of life out here—that people came to town and the mercantile to talk, not necessarily for supplies. Mr. Jacobs followed him to the door, and they spoke in low tones before Gus exited.

Eliza waited by the counter until the proprietor returned to his post behind it. "Do you think he's okay?"

"Gus? Sure. A little coughing spell won't keep him down." Mr. Jacobs picked up the tin cup Gus had used and stuck it under the counter. "I'll wash that up later."

"Does he live in town?"

"Nah, he rarely even comes in. He lives out a ways—you pass his cabin on your way to and from the ranch. He and your grandpap go way back. Come to think of it, he used to come in quite regularly. But not since Elliott passed on."

"Do you think it'd be safe to visit him at his cabin?"

"Old Gus is as honorable as your grandfather was. And it'd be good for someone to check in on him. What with his cough and all." He winked. "Now, let me get you those items for Nellie. Though I sure don't know how many pies you all are eatin' over there—as it hasn't even been a week since you were here buying her supplies."

Exactly. Something was definitely going on with Nellie.

He bustled about, selecting her purchases and grouping them on the counter. "There you go. I'll just add this to the Double E's tab, and Benton can settle up with me later."

"One more thing." Eliza clasped the envelope in her pocket and took a deep breath before she changed her mind. "Is this where I can send a letter?"

"Yes, if you have it with you, I'll take it."

She pulled her letter out. How disappointed her parents would be when they read it. Even after several attempts at wording the missive, this was the best she could do in detailing the ranch and her decision. Not only would Mother and Father see Grandfather as a failure in running a ranch, but they would think the same about her. Delaying her plans for a teaching job in the up-and-coming city of Los Angeles to spend more time on the Double E would be considered yet another misstep for her.

"Here it is. Thank you." She handed the envelope to Mr. Jacobs. At least she wouldn't be present for their and Aunt Belinda's reactions when they read it.

Eliza gathered her supplies and bid Mr. Jacobs good day. Outside, Rosey was tossing her head, looking at or for something out of sight.

"What has your attention, Rosey girl?" Eliza walked to the corner of the building and peeked around, and— "What are you doing?"

Caleb Morgan sat on the ground underneath the mercantile's side window. He scrambled to his feet and dusted off his pants. "Miss Roberts. I—I—"

"Never mind." She held her tongue about how odd this town was. Or maybe it was just this certain resident. "Rosey gave away your hiding place, but I won't disclose it to anyone else."

"Ah, Rosey. See if I share my lunch with her again." His eyes twinkled, and again, there was that kindness in their depths, despite his words.

"Well, if you need a lunch replacement, I can help with

that." She set her purchases down, pulled some coins from her reticule, and held them out.

"Ma'am, no." He held up a hand. "It was just an apple. And my pleasure to give her what I had."

Hmm. If this man had been generous even to someone else's horse, maybe that said something for him. "I hope she thanked you, then."

"She did. How is the new saddle working out for you—and her?"

"Very well, thank you." She put away the coins and picked up her items from the mercantile.

"Let me help load your purchases if I may."

He bent and was picking them up before she got a word out. When he decided to be kind and gentlemanly, he was certainly captivating. The problem was, she never knew which aspect of him she would see—one to trust or one to fear.

He packed them into the saddlebag, arranging each parcel for balance as if he'd done this many times before. Then he held out a hand to help her mount. As his bare fingers closed around her gloved ones, she stifled the gasp that almost escaped. Men through the years—even Benton Calloway—had taken her hand to assist her. Firm, strong, gentlemanly hands. But no one had set off this reaction. Caleb's touch sent tingles right through the thin glove, straight up her arm, all the way to —somewhere. Surely, not her heart.

"Thank you." She fiddled with arranging her skirts, not daring to look at him. He'd probably see a silly schoolgirl blush on her cheeks. And silly it was. Indeed, he was simply being helpful, and the cold air would be the cause for any redness. Gentlemanly, that's all his touch had been.

He untied the reins from the hitching post and handed them to Eliza. She took care to not touch him in the transfer. "Miss Roberts—"

"Yes?"

"I just wanted to say..."

Staying still and quiet even as her heart pounded, she looked at him—into the depths of those deep brown eyes—as he seemed to tumble words around to find the right ones to speak.

After a moment, he shook his head and gave Rosey a final pat on her neck.

"Be careful traveling back to the Double E."

Oh. "I will." Eliza turned the horse onto the dusty road before he could glimpse whatever might be reflected in her eyes. Confusion? Disappointment? But she would not look back, even though she could feel his eyes on her.

Just what had he been about to say? He seemed a man of few words, so whatever it was, it must have been something important.

And then a curious thought occurred to her, and she laughed out loud at its absurdity. What if he had felt that same tingle too?

CHAPTER 7

*E*liza had plenty to do at the ranch—cleaning, mending, gardening, picking up some of Nellie's overflow since Grandmother's passing. And studying the ledgers in the evenings. She was carefully checking every addition and subtraction in the books, which covered a period of about eight months. But she could hardly wait until Nellie declared she was out of supplies again so Eliza could pay a visit to Gus on the way to town.

Or maybe she could make her own opportunity. Certainly, Nellie would much rather Eliza be gone for a while so she wouldn't be asking so many questions. And getting information from Gus might prove to be a lot easier than from tight-lipped Nellie. For all she knew, he might have insights on what kinds of questions she should be asking Nellie.

Eliza entered the kitchen, still pondering how to broach the subject without causing Nellie to ask her own questions.

Nellie turned at her entrance and pointed to the bowl and apples sitting on the counter. "Miss Eliza, would you mind riding into town again? This is dreadful, starting a recipe without knowing if I had all the ingredients. I must be getting forgetful. And how could I not have asked you to pick up baking powder the last time you were there? I need it for this apple cake tonight. Goodness' sakes, Mr. Jacobs will be spreading talk around town about my absentmindedness. And you might as well get some tea while you're there."

And her problem was solved. Eliza smiled to reassure Nellie. "I don't think you need to worry about that. Mr. Jacobs needs his customers. I do think the Double E might be one of his best, though." She glanced at the clock. The ride was only half an hour each way, so if she left now, she'd have enough time before Nellie needed to bake the cake to stop by Gus's cabin on her way back. "I'll saddle up Rosey and be on my way." She hurried out the door, leaving Nellie muttering to herself.

Within minutes, Eliza was on her way. This was the only activity out here that reminded her of city life, running to the mercantile whenever supplies got low and Nellie didn't have the item she required already canned or dried from her summer garden. Somehow, she'd thought that in the West, one had to plan ahead and make the journey to town only once a month or so.

Not that she minded. The mere act of saddling sweet Rosey, swinging her leg over the sturdy Morgan saddle, and trotting down the now-familiar road by herself gave Eliza a sense of triumph. She was a teacher, after all—and what did teachers do but learn new things? So with advice, determination, observation, learning—and of course, God's help—she could manage the ranch for a few weeks.

"Come on, Rosey," Eliza urged, nudging the mare with her knees, "let's hurry this time. I hope to learn about Grandfather today. And Grandmother. Do you miss her? Is this what the two of you used to do—go to the store together, though in the wagon? I imagine you'd have to wait patiently while Grandmother stopped to greet folks and chat a spell. And then end up with a heavy load to carry back to Nellie." She patted Rosey's neck.

When they stopped in front of the general store, Eliza swung down from the saddle and tethered Rosey to the hitching post.

"Good day, Miss Roberts."

Eliza looked up in surprise at the cheerful voice. Caleb Morgan, coming down the steps from the mercantile, was—of all things—smiling. At her. Her cheeks must be blazing, as she remembered her last encounter with him at this very spot. How when he took her hand—

"Is your saddle still working out for you?"

She pulled herself out of her stupor. "Hello, Mr. Morgan. Yes, very well, thank you. It's very nice."

"Are you comfortable"—his eyes twinkled as he glanced at her long, full skirt and then back to the Western saddle— "riding astride?"

She blushed again. Were the folks of Caldwell talking about her riding like this? "Yes, I do find it quite comfortable. And," she added with a feigned air, "I just might have to purchase a pair of man's dungarees, after all—or roll up Grand-father's."

Caleb Morgan snorted so suddenly that Rosey jerked her head at the sound. "That would be a sight to see. Though I've no doubt you would do it."

Oh the laughter in his eyes—it did something strange to her heart. Though it was probably just the unexpected pleasant-ness in place of his usual scowl. "Of course, I would."

He patted Rosey on the neck, his arm so close to her own. And that sweet memory of his touch galloped right through her heart again.

Rosey reached her head over and nuzzled at his shirt pocket. "Is this what you're looking for, Miss Rosey?" He pulled out an apple and offered it to the horse. He lowered his voice, and Eliza barely made out the next words. "It's your favorite kind."

"That's sweet of you to share with her again, but how did you know that's her favorite?"

An innocent question, but instantly, Mr. Morgan's smile vanished. With a tip of his hat, he mumbled, "Good day, Miss Roberts," and stalked off.

Eliza stared after him as he kicked up dust down the street. What an odd man Caleb Morgan was. She shook her head and headed into the mercantile.

"Howdy, ma'am," Mr. Jacobs called out from behind his counter.

"Hello, Mr. Jacobs." Eliza crossed the room, squashing any lingering daydreams of Caleb Morgan with each step. "I just need two items today. Baking powder and tea."

"Now don't get me wrong, miss, but what is Nellie doing out there? In all the years she's been working for your grandparents, she never needed to send for supplies more than one time a month. First of every month—unless it fell on a Sunday. If she didn't have it, she did without. Now you're here every few days or so with a need for this and that. All these little items could be planned for ahead, you know." He wagged his head, whether in confusion or a scolding, Eliza wasn't sure. "As far as I can count, there are only four of you out there. Isn't that right?"

"Yes, Mr. Jacobs."

He squinted and appeared to be measuring her from head to toe. "And it don't look to me like you're the one eating Nellie out of supplies. Why, even back when the Double E was swarming with ranch hands, they didn't eat this much, even with Ca—" Mr. Jacobs stopped talking and marched over to a shelf. Grabbed the baking powder and weighed out some tea without even asking how much she wanted—maybe Nellie always bought the same kind and amount?—and plunked them onto the counter. "There you go." He studied the baking powder a moment. "I'd say you'd best be hurrying back to Nellie if she's a-needing this."

Just like Nellie banging pots and pans when she didn't want to discuss something.

What had Mr. Jacobs been about to say that he didn't want her to know? Mr. Jacobs had made it sound as though he was talking about someone who had lived at the Double E. Caleb? Could Caleb Morgan have been a part of the ranch? If so, why had no one mentioned it?

There was one person who might not only know the answers—but might be willing to give them to her. And this time, she was determined to find out what this town was hiding.

≈

*O*nce Eliza exited the store, she looked up and down the road, making sure there was no sign of Caleb Morgan before remounting Rosey. She then headed back in the direction of the Double E, stopping only when she came to the cabin she had determined must belong to Gus. Set back from the road a ways, it looked both sturdy and tidy. And there was Gus himself on the front porch.

Gus rose from his rocker as Eliza rode up to his cabin. "Howdy, lass."

"Hello, Gus. I hope this is a good time to visit. I'm on my way back from town."

He nodded. "Yep, I seen you go by earlier. I've been 'spectin' you'd stop one day now. Any relative of Elliott and Elizabeth Rose is welcome here anytime. Just put Rosey out to graze in the yard, and you come up and visit."

"You mean to leave her loose?"

"Of course. She's been here before. She knows what to do."

Eliza gaped at the yard that merged into scrub and openness. "But if she runs off, I won't have a way home."

Gus guffawed as he turned to go inside. "She won't run off."

"Well, all right, then." She slipped down from the saddle and looped the reins loosely so Rosey wouldn't trip on them but could still get her head down to eat. "Don't leave without me," she whispered as a last admonition.

When Eliza entered the cabin, the smell of coffee heating on the stove greeted her nose. The wide-plank table was set with two china plates. Towering over them was a bouquet of dried wildflowers.

"Goodness, you really were expecting me."

"Like I said, I try to stay ready." Gus got a faraway look in his eyes and walked over to the counter where a pie was sitting. "When my missus was alive, she kept the table looking real pretty. And baked a pie once a week, just in case. 'You never know,' she'd say, 'when an angel unawares might stop by and need some coffee and a slice of pie. Or just an old friend.'" Tears formed in his eyes as he brought the pie to the table.

"And she loved flowers?" she asked gently.

Gus nodded and ran a hand over his eyes. "She had the prettiest garden in these parts. Maybe in the whole state. Every day, there were flowers of some sort on the table—fresh, dried, whatever she had that day. Even when it was only her and me."

"She sounds like a lovely lady."

Gus smiled and looked up toward heaven. "She was. So—won't you sit in her chair and have some apple pie with me?"

Eliza took her seat. "Thank you. I'd love to."

Between cups of coffee and bites of pie, Gus spent an hour talking. Within that hour, Eliza learned more about her grandparents than she had all her years growing up. And what wonderful, godly people they were—in the community, to their neighbors, and in their home at the Double E. So why had her own parents never wanted to talk about them? And when they had mentioned their names, it was always with disdain.

Eliza stared at her empty cup.

"Ah, I can see you're thinking. Perhaps about the rift in your family?"

"Yes... Grandmother and Grandfather sound so wonderful. Yet growing up, all I knew about them—until the letters Grandfather wrote to me the few months before he passed on—was that they had abandoned our family."

Gus gave a sad smile. "Yes, that's what Elliott told me his family thought."

"But it's not true, is it?" Eliza leaned forward, eager to hear the explanation for the terrible misunderstanding.

"That's a hard question to answer, lass." He was silent for a moment, seeming to consider something. "Perhaps it was true...in their minds, anyway."

"What do you mean?"

"Elliott begged your parents and aunt Belinda to travel to Idaho with them, to trust God to provide for their needs in this vast land. But you must remember that by the time Elliott and Elizabeth headed out West, their children were grown, with their own lives. They weren't adventurous souls like Elliott, and they were all sure that life out here would kill their mother—Elizabeth. Also, they weren't willing to give up city luxuries for a life of unending hard work on a ranch. So your parents and Belinda refused to come with your grandparents. It broke Elizabeth's heart that her children would no longer speak or even correspond with them. Belinda did, eventually. But then again, this happened when you were a child. Your parents had to consider the life they wanted you to have. So, you see, everyone did what they thought was best...perhaps without considering the consequences. But what is done is done."

Eliza sighed. "Yes. But it didn't have to be like that."

"No," Gus agreed. He reached over and patted Eliza's hand

with his gnarled one. "But you're here now. And you can see—and hear—for yourself how your grandparents' lives turned out. How loved they were here."

Eliza nodded. "Thank you for telling me this, Gus. Now I have one other question that concerns Grandfather and the Double E."

"Ah, you're an inquisitive one." He poked at his pie crumbs with his fork. "What is your question?"

"Was Caleb Morgan one of Grandfather's ranch hands, and—"

Gus was on his feet. "Lass, I've already talked way too much today. Now I'm tuckered out and need a nap."

"But—"

"Thank you for visiting with me. Good day, miss." With that, Gus headed away from the table to the back of the cabin, leaving Eliza to see herself out the door.

At least Rosey was still here, contentedly grazing.

Though Eliza had learned much about her grandparents—and even what prompted the problem between them and her parents—her mission had ultimately failed. She was no closer to learning the truth about the Double E and Caleb Morgan than when she'd arrived in Caldwell.

Except now she was more certain than ever that there was a connection. One she desperately hoped left him in a good light and honorable, as those schoolgirl tingles and fanciful wishes refused to stay at bay, even after the way he had stalked off at the mercantile.

But what if she was simply a horrible judge of character?

CHAPTER 8

The week was off to a good start. In the quiet of his shop, Caleb put the finishing touch on another saddle that had been special ordered. Though this wasn't the life he would have chosen, it seemed the good Lord was blessing his business. Blessing him.

"Hello, Caleb." The purring voice sent shivers up Caleb's spine.

He should have locked the door. For a moment, he buffed the saddle, giving it an extra shine when it didn't need any more. How he dreaded turning around, having to acknowledge the owner of the voice. How much more could he endure from her?

Lord, please give me some grace for this...

He set aside his polishing cloth and slowly turned. "Callie. Hello."

She beamed at him. He just stared back. It'd been an effort to even muster up enough of his manners to acknowledge her presence.

A year ago, he would have been pleased to see her. A year

ago, they were planning on a future together. Until she turned traitor, abandoning him the moment trouble hit him square in the face. Once he was forced off the Double E, he was of no use to her.

Still, the unanswered question weighted his heart. Had she only wanted to marry him because he was the foreman, the man closest to Mr. Roberts—perhaps in line to become its next owner? It didn't matter now, because he could never trust her again—not after Benton Calloway stole her affections, just as he'd stolen everything else from Caleb.

"What can I do for you?" He struggled to keep his voice even. A tone he would use for any customer.

Callie seemed surprised at his lack of pleasantries. "Well, Caleb..." She walked over to his new saddle and ran her hand along the leather, letting it rest on the horn. "I came to pick up my saddle."

His jaw dropped. It'd been some eight months and—

"You said you were about finished with it months ago. Now I want it."

Caleb clenched his hands into fists. "I sold it."

"You sold it?" The smile on Callie's face changed to a deep scowl. "A promise is a promise, Caleb. Or aren't you a man of your word? You promised me a new saddle. And that's what I'll have. One with all of this fancy etching."

Oh, so she did remember that a promise was a promise, that pledges carried weight? Did she also remember her own promises? That she loved him and wanted to marry him and be with him through the years, through even the hard times?

"I said I'd make *my wife* a saddle." He remembered his words, not knowing at the time he said them they'd become a technicality.

Callie tossed her head. The motion made the dark tendrils escaping her bun flap across her face. Caleb used to think the stray wisps were beautiful. Now they reminded him of dried-up sagebrush.

"I'll have my saddle by next month. You owe it to me. Have it ready by then, or"—she narrowed her eyes and formed a stiff smile—"you'll wish you had. Good day, *Mister* Morgan." She twirled around and, with head high, strutted out of his shop.

Caleb kicked a pile of sawdust. She was wrong, so wrong. He owed her nothing.

He was about to turn back to work when something thudded against the door. He strode to the front window but shrank back out of view once he realized who was outside the door.

"Oh, excuse me! I didn't mean to run into you." Miss Roberts's usual lilting voice seeping into his shop sounded horrified.

"Well, watch where you're going next time, then!" Callie said scornfully.

"Certainly. I do apologize."

Caleb snuck a peek out the window. Miss Roberts was bent over, retrieving her hat off the ground. When she stood, she extended her hand to Callie.

"I'm Eliza Roberts. I don't believe we've met yet."

Callie seemed to grow before Caleb's eyes as she pulled herself up tall and squared her shoulders. "I'm Miss Browning-ton." She accepted Miss Roberts's hand but dropped it almost as soon as contact was made. "I have important business to attend to but was just checking on the status of my new saddle. A Morgan. Surely, you've heard how expensive they are. But Caleb is giving one to me as a gift."

Caleb groaned. What if he had married that woman?

"How wonderful. I'm sure you'll enjoy it. I know I do mine."

"You—what? You have a Morgan saddle?" Callie's voice dripped with venom.

"I bought one recently." Miss Roberts pointed to the saddle atop Rosey, who was hitched near the door.

"You b-bought that? That's a stock saddle. A man's saddle."

"It's a working saddle. Much more suited to my needs, I've discovered." Miss Roberts grinned, and his respect for her went up knowing not only could she hold her own with Callie—but she could do it and still be pleasant.

"Well, I never heard of such nonsense!" Callie huffed.

"I won't keep you from your business any longer, Miss Brownington. May we glorify God, and may His peace go with you."

Callie's only answer was to lift her nose into the air again and turn on her heel. The cloud of dust wafting toward Miss Roberts was probably kicked up on purpose, knowing *Miss Brownington*.

Caleb waited. Was Miss Roberts coming in? Why in the world had she stopped by the saddlery? But that must have been her intent, what with Rosey hitched out front, seeing as how there were no other businesses on this side street. Maybe the delay was due to the fact that she was regaining her composure.

After a few moments, the door opened, and she entered.

"Ah, Mr. Morgan. Just who I was looking for."

He moved over to the door. "Miss Roberts."

"Oh, please." She gave a sweet smile. Especially surprising after the way he had stomped off from her the last time he saw her. "You may call me Eliza."

"Eliza." He tested the name, savoring the sound of it, reveling at her invitation to use it. "Eliza..."

She cocked her head, eyes wide.

What was he doing? He was acting like a— He didn't know what, as he'd never acted in this fashion before. "Is it short for Elizabeth, after your grandmother?" That sounded suitable, even if not clever.

"Indeed."

"Very appropriate, as she was a lovely lady." He caught himself from adding his thoughts about her granddaughter as well.

"I certainly hope I do her and her name justice."

Oh, she did. More so than he had the right to say. "She was the loveliest lady."

"So you knew her well?"

He hadn't meant to give that away. "Everyone in town knew her. And that she was one of the kindest people anyone could hope to meet."

"I'm so happy that people speak so highly of her."

"Yes. So, Eliza"—he repeated her name simply to again taste the sweetness of it on his lips—"how may I help you today?"

She looked around the open area at his saddles on display. "I just met Miss Brownington as she was exiting your shop. A friend of yours, I gather? As she said you're making a special saddle for her as a gift."

Why would she want to know more about Callie? And she hadn't yet answered his question. "So she said. But no, I can't say yes to either. She's neither a friend, nor am I making her a saddle." And perhaps that came out harsher than intended, based on Eliza's raised brows.

"Oh?" But the glimmer of light that flitted across her eyes might have been relief.

And though he could practically hear the multiple questions behind that one word, he refused to elaborate.

"I'm sorry." Eliza's shoulders relaxed. "I didn't mean to be intrusive. As a teacher, it's my nature to pursue learning." She laughed. "That's what I call it, anyway. Though both my mother and my aunt call it being nosy."

She was so guileless. So utterly charming. And so very unattainable. He had to remember that—in case he had any longings to the contrary.

"About your purpose for visiting my shop today?"

Eliza blinked. "Oh. Yes. My purpose. I had visited a widower on my return to the ranch the other day and wondered if you had any insight into...um, how I might help him in any fashion."

"You want my advice on helping someone?" What a strange request.

"Well, yes. You're one of the few people from town whom I know. And you've been kind to me. And you're a man." She shrugged. "So I thought maybe you'd have some insights."

Caleb certainly wasn't following her line of thinking. Why would she ask him? Had no one yet set her straight on not talking to him? "And who is this widower?" His suspicions were growing, as he knew of only one offhand. He moved over to the saddle he'd been interrupted polishing, keeping his back to Eliza in case it was—

"Gus."

Of course. "No." And this time he knew his tone was harsh.

"Do you know him?"

"I do."

"Don't you think he might need some help?"

"I do not."

"Why? He's a nice gentleman, once you get past the...crusty part." Eliza stumbled over the last words.

Caleb set down his polishing cloth and faced her. "He's very self-sufficient. He's more apt to refuse any help or advice than accept it." Especially from him.

"I visited him, and I think he's lonely." She crossed her arms as if daring him to contradict her.

"Just don't believe everything he says."

"Why not?"

"My advice to you, Eliza, is to stay away from him." He turned back to his saddle until her steps crossed the floor and the door clicked shut behind her.

Eliza and her questions might be gone, but he'd behaved toward her as rudely as Callie had.

Which proved exactly why Eliza would never see him as anything other than a curmudgeon. Never consider him a gentleman like Gus after getting past the crusty parts. For crusty was all that was left of him now.

~

*A*fter supper, once Nellie retired to her room and the men returned to the bunkhouse, their stomachs full of stew, biscuits, and rhubarb pie, Eliza wandered out to the wide porch. Choosing the slightly smaller of the two rockers, she sat bundled in her coat and a blanket and put the chair into motion. Had this one been Grandmother's, where she sat with her husband after a long, hard day of activity on the ranch, watching the sun set together? Chatting into the evening, giving thanks to their Savior? She sighed. Wouldn't that be such a precious gift, to share her life with a man after God's heart? One who could love a simple woman?

Eliza gazed off into the distance, surveying this land Grandfather had loved. She cherished the stories of her grandparents here, learning to see the land through their eyes. But she didn't belong permanently to this kind of life. So, once she got to California and settled, made a life for herself there, maybe someday God would bring along the man she could now only dream of. Someone exactly like her grandfather.

"Excuse me, ma'am."

Eliza jerked, startled. She hadn't heard anyone come up the porch steps, let alone walk right up beside her.

"Please pardon me. I didn't mean to startle you." Benton Calloway, hat in hand, spoke in a low tone.

"Oh—that's quite all right. I guess I was daydreaming. I didn't hear you approach."

"I don't mean to be forward, Miss Roberts, but I couldn't help but wonder if perhaps you were missing your life back in the East. So I wondered if...that is, if you don't mind...if I might keep you company for a while. To enjoy the sunset together." He glanced down at his boots, then raised his eyes toward Eliza.

"Not at all, Mr. Calloway. Please, sit in the other rocker."

"Thank you, ma'am. And if you would, call me Benton."

"Why, thank you...Benton. And since I'm part of the ranch for now, you may call me Eliza."

"Thank you for that privilege, Miss...Eliza. It sure is a beautiful evening, isn't it?"

"It is. The sunsets out here are lovely." She waved toward the last remnant of lavender in the distance.

"Mr. Roberts used to sit out here in the evenings with his missus before she passed on. Sometimes I'd watch them from over at the bunkhouse. They'd be holding hands, smiling at each other, I guess surveying their land. Made me want to have that for myself someday." He glanced down again, as if the admission embarrassed him.

That was Eliza's longing also. "That sounds like a wonderful life, having someone you love to share it with."

"Do you have a beau back East, Eliza? Or perhaps in California that you're on your way to meet?"

Eliza blushed. She had no one. Though it was flattering for Benton to even think it possible. "No. I haven't found a man yet to share my life with. I would want someone with my grandfather's character, though."

Benton pursed his lips. "Someone strong and commanding?"

"No—a godly man."

Benton rocked silently for a few moments, then stood. "Well, I won't intrude any longer. I just wanted to check that you were faring well."

"Thank you, Benton. Good evening."

He stepped off the porch and after a few steps, stopped and turned around. "If you ever get lonesome for someone to talk to at sunset, I'd be glad to keep you company." He put his cowboy hat on his head, tipped the brim to her, then headed toward the bunkhouse.

Eliza tugged the blanket closer and continued to rock a few more minutes, as the sky darkened. How considerate of Benton to show concern about her. And being strong and handsome didn't hurt either.

But what she had said to him was true, even if she hadn't fully thought it out in detail yet. The man she would give her heart to would be much like what she'd been learning Grandfather was like. A God-fearing man to start with, first and foremost. Then one who doted on his wife. A hard worker, kind to all. And one who enjoyed sunsets at the end of the day alongside his wife as they sat quietly or talked of their day or simply worshipped God through the beauty He'd provided. As of yet, no one had met these standards.

And one other thing she'd add to her list—someone to laugh with.

Deep brown eyes that crinkled up in merriment, whether he actually let it drift to his mouth or not, danced before her. Teasing banter that made her want to be witty and to laugh out loud. Definitely, she could think of someone who would meet that last qualification.

But Caleb Morgan was not the man for her. Callie Brownington had intimated there was something special between them with the gift of a saddle made for her. Though Caleb firmly denied that.

And just look at how rude he'd been to her today when all she'd been doing was trying to help Gus. Or maybe that wasn't all she'd been trying to do, and Caleb had seen through her. He certainly wasn't kind to all. Though time and again, she had seen his kindness and gentleness, not just with her but with the horses when he didn't know she was looking.

She was pretty sure there was something deep to him. Something worth discovering.

But she was also sure Caleb Morgan could not be the man for her.

CHAPTER 9

*C*aleb rubbed his leg, trying to ease the steady throb starting out the morning.

It was doubtful Eliza would come to town again today, but he needed to see her. To apologize for his rudeness yesterday. If life had been normal, he'd ride out to the ranch to do it posthaste. But he couldn't.

Even if he'd been welcome, on days like this, with the cold of December infiltrating the air, his leg bothered him more than ever. Gone were the days when he could ride the roundups and spend the nights under the stars, the hard ground his bed. Some days he couldn't even stand on his feet all day working on a saddle. He had to stop and sit, like now. Nor could he trot over to the mercantile to pick up his supplies. He had to saddle up Ruby or hitch her to the wagon for anything heavier than an ordinary armload. At twenty-four years old, he already felt like a decrepit old man. Why, even when Mrs. Roberts had taken ill, she was able to get around better than he could some days.

Things had been great back at the Double E when Mrs. Roberts was there. She had been a true lady. So godly and stalwart, standing by her husband's side even through hardships. He could see so much of her in her granddaughter, though Eliza probably had no idea how much she was like her grandmother in spirit, let alone her looks.

But after Mrs. Roberts died, things changed on the ranch within a few weeks. Almost as if the culprit had waited for his deceit out of respect for Mrs. Roberts, not wanting her to witness his true character. The memories of those days could choke him as he relived them, one by one. If only he could go hand to hand once more with that—

"Howdy, Caleb."

Caleb looked up. He had almost wanted to voice a prayer of thanks for the interruption until he realized who his visitor was.

"Gus." The word came out at least cordial, though not welcoming.

Gus ran his hand over the saddle Caleb was working on and nodded. "Nice work."

The affirmation wove around the rough edges of his heart a bit. "Thank you."

"I see you're still paying attention to detail. What's this bulge you've done to the fork?"

Heat rose in his face. "It's a new technique I'm trying out. The wider swell's meant to give a smoother ride up steep terrain with somewhere for the rider to put his knees."

"Hmm. Talk has it that your saddles are quite the ones to own."

Caleb shrugged. "I have plenty of orders."

"Boys from over in Owyhee County?"

"Mostly from there. Some from Oregon." He couldn't tell what Gus thought of his departure from typical construction to experimenting with this wider fork. Should it even matter anymore what Gus thought? "What brings you to town?"

Gus walked over to the other chair and pulled it close to the work area and seated himself. "Someone's asking questions about you."

Caleb groaned inwardly. Of course, Gus hadn't dropped by to discuss saddles. The days of quiet camaraderie between him and Gus were over—thanks to Calloway. "People in this town are always gossiping."

"It's *who's* asking—and what's being asked—that should interest you."

"And you came to tell me?"

Gus nodded. "If you have a cup of coffee that isn't a day old, then I'm here to tell you."

Caleb stood and headed to his coffeepot in the back. "It's barely warm and not quite a day old."

"Good enough for me."

Caleb poured two cups of the awful-tasting stuff, handed one to Gus, and sat down again. "Who's asking?"

"Elliott's granddaughter."

Caleb all but spit out the mouthful of tepid coffee he'd been about to swallow. Eliza Roberts was asking about him? That did not bode well.

"What's she asking?" He was almost afraid to know.

"She wanted to know if you ever were one of Elliott's ranch hands."

Caleb swallowed hard.

"She's full of questions, that lass. Reminds me of Elizabeth."

She reminded Caleb of Mrs. Roberts, too, in so many ways. But he didn't have time to be thinking about her gentleness and lovely spirit. "Go on."

"Well..." Gus tipped his chair back on its legs. "Over at the store the other day when she came for supplies, old Daniel started to blabber about when you—" He averted his gaze from Caleb. "About the past."

His heart was pounding. "What did you tell her?" Oh, the questions—and probably fury—Eliza would have once she heard the talk around town about him. He had to guess she had no idea yet. But once she did, he would most likely know within the hour, as she'd mount Rosey and ride up to his door here and burst inside—

Gus bellowed with laughter. "Miss Roberts must think I'm a peculiar, sickly codger." He chuckled again. "I started hacking away to cover up anything Daniel said before Eliza could get in any questions. Then out at my place, once she started asking, I up and told her I needed a nap." He burst out laughing again.

Caleb couldn't help a small smile. Gus didn't need naps. But another thought quickly cut off any merriment. He was also certain that Eliza Roberts wouldn't give up asking until she had her answers. Why, just yesterday she'd been by here to tell him she'd visited Gus. Yep, he'd known right then there was more to her story than merely wanting advice on helping the old widower.

Gus stood. "Just thought I'd drop by and let you know." He stuck out his hand in parting.

Caleb stood also. "Much obliged, Gus." He shook hands with the gray-haired man. But as Gus walked out of the saddle shop and headed in the direction of the mercantile, Caleb had a few questions of his own.

Was it possible Gus had stopped by to show his support? Could he maybe believe in Caleb's innocence? Or was he just hoping to keep things stirred up and seek his own retribution on behalf of Elliott Roberts?

~

The sun had set, yet Eliza still sat on the front porch in the dimming light. Slowly, she rocked back and forth, mulling over the ledger books she'd been trying to understand all day long. Wouldn't Grandfather have mentioned if there was a problem, especially in light of the fact that he was planning to bequeath the Double E to her? Yet his letters only spoke of the glorious land and the mountains in the distance and the vibrant sunsets. Of his hopes and dreams for this place. How could he have had those hopes and dreams if the place was falling apart?

Everything in the ledgers was accurate so far, except for a few minor errors on Benton's part. But anyone could make mistakes, especially if they weren't schooled in bookkeeping. Records certainly weren't her best subject, either, but she continued tediously making her way through each of the entries.

The rocker made low whispers of squeaks as she kept it at a steady rhythm. Back and forth. Back and forth. It was enough to lull her into the world of peacefulness about the ranch...almost.

She slowed the chair as something seemed out of place. The evening was calm except for...something.

There it was again. What was that noise?

Eliza brought the rocker to an abrupt halt and strained to listen. It sounded like shrieks coming from the barn. The horses! This time, shrill neighs were followed by pounding against wood.

Nellie opened the back door and stepped out onto the porch. "Miss Eliza, did you hear that?"

Eliza stood. "Yes." She grabbed the broom leaning beside the door. "You stay here. I'll go see what's going on out there."

"No. I'm coming too."

Together they ran across the yard with Nellie clinging to Eliza's arm. Just as they opened the barn door, a loud crack of splintering wood reverberated through the air. And headed right toward them at a mad run were all four of the Double E horses.

Shoving Nellie hard, Eliza pushed the cook against the open barn door. But the second it took to get Nellie to safety left

Eliza standing right in the path of the oncoming stampede. Sweet Rosey, eyes blazoned with fear, was in the lead. She dodged Eliza, but the other carriage horse caught Eliza's shoulder, knocking her to the ground. Curling up into a ball, arms wrapped tight around her head for even the slightest bit of protection, Eliza let out a cry that was drowned out by more flying hooves.

Then...silence. Except for her thudding heart and a soft whimper. And a wet tongue on her cheek.

"Eliza! Eliza!" Was that Nellie standing over her shouting?

She squinted one eye open. Kep was right there, checking on her. She ran her fingers through his fur, grateful for his presence.

"Miz Eliza!" A man's strong arms reached around her, helping her to sit up. "Miz Eliza, are you all right?"

She sat, and suddenly, she was weeping, trying to focus on George.

"Shh, child." Nellie wrapped her arms around her. "It's all right. We're all safe. You're safe."

Benton appeared in Eliza's view. He looked from Eliza to Nellie. "What happened? Are you all right?"

He barely waited for Eliza's nod before he disappeared.

"Wha-what happened?" Eliza grasped Nellie's hands. "Did the horses hurt you? Are they safe too?"

"We're all fine, Eliza," Nellie said.

"Something spooked them." George nodded to where the four horses now stood in the yard, snorting and glancing around. "I'll go see if I can find out what scared them." He stood and had strode into the barn only a few steps when Benton came out of a stall with a rattlesnake dangling from a pitchfork.

"It was this. Looks like it crazed all the horses."

Kep growled and circled him.

George peered down the aisle of the barn and scratched his

head. "But only one stall is kicked down. How did all four horses get out?"

"I was working late mucking out the stalls and only put them together for a few minutes. I thought they'd be fine." Benton shook his head. "I'll work on fixing up the stall tomorrow. The horses can spend the night in the paddock." He gazed at Eliza. "They'll be safe. Why don't you and Nellie go inside now and get cleaned up?" He raised the pitchfork, watching the snake wriggle. "I'll take care of this here thing."

"Yes." The suggestion seemed to spark action in Nellie. "I'll heat up some water for you to wash with. Then I'll set out some pie and tea. That's just what we need to settle ourselves."

Still shaken, Eliza allowed Nellie to help her to her feet. Kep followed as far as the porch, then trotted over to the horses. Herding them into a close circle, he nimbly darted between their feet.

Leaning heavily on Nellie, Eliza went inside and slowly climbed the stairs to her room. Her head seemed to pound to the rhythm of her heart, both asking the same question.

How had Grandmother Roberts ever stood this horrid place?

CHAPTER 10

"*H*ow are you this morning, Miss Eliza? You're looking mighty peaked." Nellie looked up long enough from transferring eggs from the skillet onto plates to peer at Eliza.

Eliza shuddered, thinking about the night before. Of course, she must look terrible. She'd lain awake for hours reliving the terror. Just the thought of ever stepping into that dark barn again petrified her. And what if a snake should ever slither right inside the house?

"This place has too many dangers. We could have been trampled to death!" She rubbed her sore shoulder.

"Mercy, we could have. But the good Lord spared our lives. Now don't go forgetting that."

Eliza picked at her breakfast, then excused herself. Sitting at Grandfather's desk, she had no urge to pick up the ledger. What was the use? She didn't fit in here. She would never get used to the perils of ranch life. Suddenly, she longed to be surrounded by people and the everyday luxuries that city life offered. This ranch was secluded and beyond salvaging. If Benton—who loved the ranch—hadn't been able to save it, what had made her think she could? Even if she sacrificed and scraped by for years, it might not ever be profitable again.

She'd never known Grandfather Roberts beyond dim childhood memories and a handful of letters in recent months. So why should she risk her life for his dream? Maybe her father was right about Grandfather, after all—he was an adventurer, a dreamer, who never counted the cost to himself or others.

Eliza pulled a sheet of paper from a desk drawer and began mentally composing her letter to the Los Angeles school. She'd sell the ranch now and wash her hands of this whole place, of Grandfather's dream—and what had even started to become her own dream. She'd continue on to California to teach and start a new life. Perhaps last night's catastrophe was God's way of getting her to move on. Except who would buy the Double E now with all its troubles? Benton might be interested, but he wouldn't have the money after the sacrifices he'd made to keep the ranch running until she'd arrived.

"Excuse me, miss."

Eliza peered at Benton as he approached. "Yes?"

"I just wanted to check on you today, following the ruckus last night. Are you all right? You're bound to be bruised up a bit. Not to mention the fright you took."

Eliza sighed. There was no easy way to tell him of her decision. "Thank you for your concern. I am bruised a bit, but I'll be fine. And you're right—it was very frightening. So I'm sorry to tell you this, but I think I'm going to sell the ranch and continue my journey to California." There, she said it.

Benton's eyes widened. With disapproval? Surprise?

"Well, Eliza...I can't say I blame you." He shook his head. "To be honest, ranch life is no place for a single lady. You did a mighty fine job of running it during your stay. But it's a hard life for a man, let alone a lady by herself. Why, in California I reckon that in no time, a man will come to realize what a lovely lady you are...just as I have." He lowered his gaze as if afraid he might have offended her.

"Thank you, Benton. For understanding."

He gave a slight nod. "Yep, a mighty fine job. Just let me know when you decide it's time to leave. I'll bring the wagon around and get your belongings all loaded up." He turned and headed to the door, then stopped and took a couple of steps back toward Eliza. "If your intention really is to sell the Double E, I would like to make an offer. Though it may be rather feeble."

Eliza would gladly consider anything Benton could manage. She didn't need an excess amount of money, and it would be only fair for Benton to be able to own some land, especially a place he loved and had invested his all into.

"I'll take into consideration whatever you offer. We'll talk about it after I've made more definite plans."

"Thank you. If you'll excuse me now, I have morning chores to finish up."

With that, he left the living room and headed toward the kitchen. Eliza followed his progress by the sound of his whistling as he went out the back door, onto the porch, and then off through the yard.

Slowly, she rose and went up the stairs to her room and sat in the chair overlooking the window. As soon as she could muster the energy, she'd ride into Caldwell to speak with Grandfather's attorney.

"Child, what are you doing?" Nellie stood in the doorway, frowning.

"I didn't hear you approach."

"Are you truly fixing on leaving us already? I didn't mean to eavesdrop, but I couldn't help but overhear Benton Calloway practically running you off."

"Nellie, he did no such thing."

"Sounded to me that he did." Nellie crossed her arms.

"Offering to buy the Double E. Ready to load your belongings up as soon as you say the word."

"No, Nellie. I told him I was leaving, heading on to California, and was going to sell the ranch. And I would have told you too. As soon as I found the words, as I know how you love this place and it's your home."

"And it could be your home too." Nellie's face softened and she roughly swiped a tear.

"I had hoped so. Dreamt so. But it is not." Eliza dabbed at her own eyes. "I don't belong here."

"But you—"

"I'm sorry, Nellie." She stood and crossed the room. "I'm going to ride into town and talk with Grandfather's lawyer in person. Mr. Taylor will guide me as to how to go about this."

"Miss Eliza, it's not my place to ask you, but for Miz Elizabeth's sake, won't you reconsider? You are strong, so much like her."

"That's the problem, Nellie." Eliza gave a sad smile. "I am not strong like her. Shall we go downstairs now?"

Nellie opened her mouth, then shook her head and headed down the stairs, Eliza close behind. But instead of following Nellie to the kitchen, Eliza veered off to the barn. Too scared to actually step inside, Eliza called out for Benton and asked him to saddle Rosey for her.

As she headed into Caldwell, she made her plan. After talking with Mr. Taylor, she would go to the train depot and inquire about continuing on to California. Hopefully, the next train headed west would be coming through within the next few days. If Mr. Taylor could work out the details that quick, she'd be on that train. The sooner she was out of here, the better.

Upon reaching Caldwell, Eliza trotted Rosey directly to Mr. Taylor's office. After dismounting and tying the reins to the hitching post, she gathered her skirt and climbed the steps to the boardwalk. Just as she was about to enter the lawyer's office, she stopped to read the sign nailed to the door.

Due to a family emergency, this office is closed for a few days. Please refer any immediate problems to Mr. James Milbrook in Boise.
Matthew Taylor, Esquire

Eliza placed a hand over the sign and leaned her head against her arm. What was she going to do now that she had to stay even longer on that awful ranch?

∼

*C*aleb was headed back to his shop when he spotted Eliza standing at Mr. Taylor's door as if in distress. He was careful to keep his distance by Rosey at the hitching post but called out to her. "Good afternoon, Eliza."

Eliza whirled around. "Oh. Good afternoon, Caleb."

"Were you looking for Mr. Taylor?"

"Yes, I was."

"I hope there's not an urgent problem, because, as you can see, he's away for some time. But may I be of assistance to you in the meantime?"

Eliza met his gaze. "Thank you. That's most kind of you. I—I was hoping to speak with Mr. Taylor about selling the Double E."

Caleb's jaw dropped. "You wish to sell it?"

Eliza nodded.

"Does that mean you're moving away from here?"

She nodded again, as if getting words out required too much effort. In the moment of silence between them, she studied him. Hopefully, she couldn't see how disappointed he was at the thought of her leaving the Double E. For even though he wasn't the man for her, she was exactly the woman he longed for. And being in her joy-filled presence was what gave him comfort in his lonely days.

"Eliza..." Caleb rubbed Rosey's neck and murmured little nothings to her. It was so much easier talking to Rosey than to Eliza. Even back on the ranch, Rosey had always liked him. He glanced up at Eliza. She looked so downcast, as though she could use a friend. And how he'd like to be that friend. Except he didn't know how to go about it. He had nothing to offer her. He'd been downright rude to her and had told her point-blank that he would not help her.

So how could she trust him now? The truth was, she couldn't—not after he'd covered up his past from her. And she was going to find out one of these days. Maybe he should just forget about trying to hide it from her and tell her himself.

Except...he couldn't. But he could apologize. "I—I don't mean to be brash in asking, but—I know I was inexcusably rude to you before when you asked for my help, but—please forgive me. I would like to ask if I might help you save the Double E. I have some ideas on how we could do it."

Eliza gave a sad, slow smile. "Thank you, both for your apology and your offer to help. It's very kind of you. However, something happened that changed my mind. I now have no desire to live there any longer. I came to town to find out how to sell the Double E and to inquire about continuing on to California."

His heart thudded. Just with those words, the town already felt bereft of Eliza Morgan's goodness, her sweetness. The way she spread smiles and joy and words of encouragement to those in her path.

"May I ask what happened?" He couldn't imagine any true danger on the ranch. Yet as he looked deeper into her eyes, there was no question about the fear lurking there.

"Last night..." She stepped off the boardwalk and stood in

front of Rosey. His heart lurched at the shudder that passed across her shoulders. "Something spooked the horses. Nellie and I went out to check on them. When I swung the barn door open, all four horses came stampeding out, and—and—" She patted Rosey's forehead. "You were terrified, weren't you, Rosey, girl?"

She stopped speaking, but was she finished telling the story?

"Did you get hurt?"

She rubbed her shoulder. "Biscuit knocked me down accidentally. I—I just was so afraid we were going to be trampled."

How he wished he knew how to comfort her. But all he could do was to keep on asking questions. Questions which she probably didn't want to answer.

"But you were safe?"

She gave a slight nod.

"And Nellie?"

Eliza looked over at him. "Yes. I pushed her out of the way."

That didn't surprise him. It proved she was exactly the kind of lady he thought her to be—one who would care for others before herself.

"Did you discover what spooked the horses?"

"Benton Calloway did. He found a rattler in the big stall— where he'd put the horses for a few minutes."

Why had he ever put them together? "Was it dead?"

"No. It was still wriggling when Benton brought it out to show us."

Eliza's whole body trembled, and rage ignited in Caleb's heart. "Where was Kep?"

"He was right beside me, licking my face. No—wait." She puckered her forehead, as if reliving the scene in her memory. "That was afterwards. I—I don't know where he was during all the commotion."

Caleb shook his head. Either one of the ladies could have

been seriously injured—or even killed by the frightened horses. And leave it to Benton to show the women a live, wiggling snake on top of this.

The horses all together in the big stall. A rattler in that very same stall. Benton the hero. It all added up to a terrifying and very suspicious experience. No wonder Eliza wanted to leave the ranch. Except one thing was terribly odd. Just where was Kep during the ruckus? With that dog on patrol, there hadn't been a rattler around the barn or yard in all the years he'd been there.

One thing was sure—this had been no accident.

"Eliza..." Caleb swallowed hard, suddenly knowing the words she needed to hear. But would she accept them from his mouth, knowing the hypocrite that he was? "I don't really know much about giving good advice, but I once heard a wise lady tell someone these words. 'Remember, God cares for you so much. He'll provide for your every need. Just ask Him.'"

Eliza's eyes widened. She squinted at him, obviously puzzled. Then, after a moment, a soft glow settled in her eyes, and she smiled. It was a bit shaky, but it was indeed a smile. And as that smile landed on him, warmth spread through his soul.

"A wise lady, you say?"

He nodded. "Yes. Very wise." *And lovely inside.* But he didn't dare add that.

"Thank you," she whispered. "For reminding me that God will take care of all of us—of me."

"You're...welcome."

Yep, that was him—a hypocrite, spouting off godly sounding words as though he believed them. And yet, as the beginnings of peace replaced the fear in her eyes, he wondered... Could God actually have given him the words she needed to hear? If so, then that meant God was still talking to him, didn't it? And since Caleb had passed on the words, he was being obedient, wasn't he? So maybe God was still taking care of him too.

Now that was something to ponder.

"Miss Eliza! Miss Eliza!" The three little Billings girls came running up the street, dust flying beneath their shoes.

Eliza bent down to scoop them into her arms. "Hello, Lila, Rosita, Virginia. Where's your mother?" She stood, looking up and down the street.

"She's at the mercantile," Lila, the oldest one said.

"Buying what she can for the month," added Rosita, the middle child.

Something about the girls, maybe the way they were dressed in frayed dresses or the forlorn expressions on their faces as they glanced back toward the mercantile, touched Caleb. He dug around in his pocket until he found three coins.

"Here." He thrust one into the palm of each girl. "Buy yourself something sweet at the mercantile."

Four pairs of big blue eyes stared at him. The girls were all smiles and giggles, chattering about what stick candy they would buy. Eliza's eyes clouded with tears, and she seemed not to know who to smile biggest at—the girls or him.

"Oh, thank you!" The girls suddenly seemed to remember their manners.

The smallest one reached up and touched Eliza's hand. "Your beau is very nice."

Eliza opened her mouth, but before she could utter a denial, the girls ran back toward the mercantile. She looked at him. "That was very kind of you."

Caleb shrugged. "They looked like they could use some happiness."

"Well..." Eliza scuffed at the dirt with the toe of her boot. "I reckon until Mr. Taylor returns, there's nothing I can do except stay in Idaho." She reached for Rosey's reins and untied the mare. "I'll return in a few days to see if he's back."

Caleb took the reins and held Eliza's hand while she mounted. And with their hands clasped, there it was again. That warmth winding farther and deeper through him. What was he doing? He couldn't pursue her. And he couldn't release her hand either. The hand she had yet to pull away even once she was secure in the saddle.

"Caleb?"

That brought him out of his stupor.

"Thank you again for reminding me of God's care." And this time her smile lingered on him.

All Caleb could do was nod.

She pulled her hand away and reached for the reins. "Good day, Caleb." Her sweet voice was a song in his ears.

All he could manage was a wave as she turned Rosey to the road. He stood watching the cloud of dust Rosey kicked up behind her as she and Eliza trotted away from town. Yep, he had some thinking to do. Not only about God—but also some other puzzling questions. Such as, why did he care whether Eliza Roberts stayed in Idaho or not? And though he had no claim on her—never could—why did it please him that she hadn't put into words the denial of him being her beau? Neither calling after the girls to set the record straight nor clarifying it with him afterward.

For if he ever thought about having a wife, the face of Eliza Roberts was the one that popped to mind. With a sudden, sweet thought, he smiled.

Just maybe—what if—he found her truly trustworthy?

CHAPTER 11

*E*liza slowed Rosey to a walk as soon as she was out of town. What was God trying to tell her through all of this? To leave Idaho and head out to Los Angeles? Or had He used Mr. Taylor's absence—and Caleb Morgan's appearance—as signs to tell her to not be afraid but to stay put at the Double E? But how could she even think clear-headedly after the way Caleb held her hand, as if he never wanted to let go? She certainly hadn't wanted to. That in itself was another matter for prayer. As he was not the man for her. Not a godly man like Grandfather.

But Caleb's words had certainly surprised her. The way he sat glowering, hunkered down in the last pew at church, she never would have expected him to be the one to bring a message from the Lord. Yet he had spoken so forthrightly about trusting in God. And oh, the sweetness of what he had done for the little Billings girls. His simple act of kindness had brought such delight to their faces.

It was all beyond her. She shuddered, remembering that wriggling snake dangling at the end of the pitchfork. Benton Calloway was such a brave man. And his offer to buy the ranch gave her peace that someone who knew her grandparents and loved the ranch would continue her grandparents' dream.

So what should she do?

Upon arriving back at the ranch, Eliza declined Nellie's offer of pie. Though Nellie looked like she was bursting with curiosity about the trip to see Mr. Taylor, she refrained from any questions. Thankful for that, Eliza headed up to her room. The chair by the window beckoned her, and she sat, immediately pulling her Bible onto her lap. What did God want her to do?

"This place has too many dangers. We could have been trampled to death!" Her words spoken this morning came back to her, as well as Nellie's reply.

"Mercy, we could have. But the good Lord spared our lives. Now don't go forgetting that."

Yet she had forgotten. She'd let the terrors shove aside the promises of God's word. The good Lord had even sent a second messenger in Caleb Morgan, of all people, to remind her of His goodness. She gave a little smile—for God had used her own words to do it too.

"Remember, God cares for you so much. He'll provide for your every need. Just ask Him."

Hadn't she spoken those very words to Mrs. Billings to encourage her at the church gathering not only a week and a half ago? And how was it that Mr. Morgan had come by those words? Her exact words, as near as she could remember. Now that was something to save to think about another time. But if he'd been eavesdropping, then he'd most likely also heard her tell the girls about Grandfather abandoning her.

Eliza looked up at the ceiling, wishing she could look up into heaven itself. Oh goodness—how many reminders did she need?

She opened her Bible to the book Psalms, where she so

often found comfort. And there before her she found yet another reminder, words spoken right from God.

> For thou art my rock and my fortress; therefore
> for thy name's sake lead me, and guide me.
> Pull me out of the net that they have laid
> privily for me: for thou art my strength. Into
> thine hand I commit my spirit: thou hast
> redeemed me, O Lord God of truth.

Eliza slipped from the chair and knelt beside her bed.

"Dear Lord, thank You for Your reminders over and over. Please lead me and guide me, for You are my rock and fortress and strength. Show me the way, please, and help me to follow it. In the name of the Lord Jesus, I pray. Amen."

She arose and headed downstairs, ready to face the world again—or at least to start with a piece of Nellie's pie. Maybe it'd be blueberry—from the canning jar of berries that had been sitting by the stove earlier. "Show me the way, Lord, please show me the way" was her prayer as her feet barely touched the steps on her way down.

By the time she entered the kitchen, she was sure of a little seed of hope—or peace—in her heart, a quiet assurance that she should at least try to save the ranch. For Grandfather's sake. For now, she'd cling to that. But Benton's words—that ranch life was no place for a single lady—still rang in her ears. Was that the only way to save the ranch? Find someone to marry? Now that'd be an awful hard thing to do, seeing as how no one had ever come courting—unless perhaps he'd been hinting?

"Glory be, child!" Nellie looked up from chopping carrots at the table. "Have you decided to join the land of the living? What have you been doing up there all this time?"

"Praying."

"Oh. Well, that's a mighty good way to spend your time."

She smiled as if in satisfaction. "Now sit, and I'll get your pie if you're up to that now?" Nellie stood and wiped her hands on her apron.

"I believe I am. But I can get it."

"No, it's my pleasure." She ushered Eliza into a chair and brought her a plate with a generous slice of blueberry pie. "I'll put the kettle on. Eat, child."

Eliza grinned, enjoying the fussing and mothering of Nellie.

"So you're not a-fretting about last night anymore now, are you? I tell you, those horses are as tame as can be, wouldn't ever intentionally hurt us. And that old snake—he just slithered in from who knows where. Never has there been one in the vicinity of the house or the barn in all the years I've lived here. Nothing gets past Kep or wants to tangle with him."

Hadn't Caleb basically implied the same thing—that Kep was the protector of the property? Except, where *had* he been last night? As best as she could recall, she hadn't seen him at all until after the whole incident, when he was suddenly beside her, licking her face. And then he had seemed ever underfoot—running back and forth between her and Nellie and the horses.

"My advice, Miss Eliza, is not to go fretting about an old snake or anything else out here. We're safe in God's hands alone."

"You're right, Nellie. Safety is in God's hands." Yes, another reminder—and with it, the little seed of hope had just been watered a bit more. And by God's grace, she would be—could be—strong like Grandmother had been in this land.

She let those thoughts grow the next day as she helped Nellie with chores. There must be something—maybe a mistake made and compounded—that had sent the Double E into its spiral. Maybe she could find ways to cut costs even more. But more than that, she needed a new idea, something big, to not only get the ranch back on its feet but for it to grow.

She went to bed weary and in the morning continued her

ponderings. And then as she fed the chickens, she knew exactly what to do. She finished up and hurried into the kitchen.

"Nellie, I need to go into Caldwell today. If you need anything, make me a list while I'm saddling up Rosey." She'd be bold and step into the barn again, as she didn't have time to find George or Benton.

Nellie stopped peeling potatoes at the counter and turned, brows puckered. "No, I don't need a thing. But why are you going in again?"

"I need to see if Mr. Taylor has returned."

"Eliza..." A look of concern crossed her eyes. "I thought you had that settled. That you're not selling the ranch."

"I'm not. But I had an idea and hope to take care of the details."

"How long do you expect to be gone?"

"If Mr. Taylor is there, it could be a while. Plus, I have other business to see to." She barely kept a smile from breaking out at the thought of where that business would take her. To Caleb's saddlery. But no need to mention that. "I'll hurry back to help you—don't worry."

Nellie waved her hand. "Once I have all the vegetables cut up for my soup, I'll be in good shape. Besides, you need to be making some friends in town. So take your time."

"You're such a godsend to this ranch, Nellie. I hope you know that." Eliza gave her a quick hug and headed out to the barn.

Within minutes, Eliza was galloping Rosey down the road, not minding the dust billowing around them. But when she arrived at Mr. Taylor's office, tethered Rosey, and climbed the steps, the notice of the temporary closure was still nailed to the door. Only now, *for a few days* was crossed out and *indefinitely* handwritten above.

While disappointed, she wasn't dismayed, as her visit with him was of a different nature now and not at all urgent. She turned to her next—and most important—item of business. The one that made her previously contained smile burst into a full grin as she relived the last time she'd been at Mr. Taylor's office—her conversation with Caleb. Then, at her departure, the way he'd kept her hand enclosed in his far longer than was necessary. As if he, too, had been lost in unexpected feelings.

Eliza unhitched Rosey and mounted easily. "Let's go see him, shall we?" She patted the horse on the neck. "Maybe he'll be happy to see us again today."

And who knew where this encounter might lead?

~

*C*aleb had his rhythmic hammering down to an art. Some days, like today, he could hammer saddle tacks while thinking about other things—such as Eliza Roberts. Good thing he had this secluded work spot plus the back room —so no one was likely to interrupt his muddled thoughts or question the furrow those thoughts surely put on his brow.

That last encounter with Eliza Roberts still had him befuddled. And pondering. And—another reason he was glad no one was around—smiling. She truly seemed to believe God could use him, of all people. That alone gave him a glimmer of hope. And as he again pictured the obvious way she cared for those little Billings girls, a warmth fluttered across his chest. What a mother she would make to some precious children someday. Truth be told, she'd be a wonderful wife to whatever lucky man she would consent to wed. And of course, she would be very particular about who that—

"Caleb?"

His thoughts of her were so vivid, he could actually imagine her voice calling out to him. He shook his head, wiping clean the slate of any longing. That'd be the day, that she'd ever come seeking him. He'd better pay attention to his saddle making, concentrating on each blow of the hammer.

"Mr. Morgan!"

Her voice rang out again in the momentary silence between blows. A real voice. He lost his grip on his hammer, and it clanged to the floor as he jumped up. She was here, calling out to him? He strode out to the front of the work area.

"Eliza!" She stood before him, gloves dangling from her hand. Perhaps she planned to stay a while. "Uh, good morning —or afternoon." He'd lost track of time.

She smiled sweetly at him. "Good day, Caleb."

Swiftly, he wiped his hands on his work clothes. "May I help you?" If only he were witty, but his words came out as all business.

She smiled broader. "I just wanted to come by to thank you."

"To thank me? Whatever for?"

"Yes. For your words the other day outside Mr. Taylor's office. I was being hasty in declaring my intentions to leave the Double E. I thought God had forsaken me on the ranch, that He was showing me it was time to move on. But I do believe now that He has some real purpose for me here. God arranged for Mr. Taylor not to be available." She gave him a shy look. "And He brought you just when you were needed."

Now she'd gone and muddled his thinking up more. And yet she had said what he'd been pondering—that God had used him. A smile was trying to get past those muscles that were so unused to forming the shape, of being stretched this much in one day.

He hadn't had much to smile about in the past eight months. And now within moments, something strange was happening. He wasn't dwelling on his bitterness but actually thinking about God—and, of course, the spunky Miss Eliza. So maybe it was the other way around—that God had brought her to him when he needed to hear from God.

"You said you had some ideas about saving the ranch." When she continued speaking, he realized he hadn't yet said anything in response to her. "Would you really help me?"

Caleb gulped. She'd remembered. He let his eyes linger a moment on her face, her earnestness as though she was hanging on to some fragile thread of hope. Yes, he had offered assistance. And he would keep his word. Though he still couldn't step foot on the Double E, he would aid her to the best of his ability from here.

"Yes. I'll help you."

At the glorious smile Eliza gave him, he wondered why he hadn't offered this solution sooner. But he knew the reason. Beyond honoring her grandfather's edict, he'd been stubborn. Proud. Angry. All things he wanted to change. "I'd be glad to do what I can."

"Oh, thank you!" She clasped her hands, her eyes sparkling at him as if he were the answer to her prayers. "What should we do first?"

"Could you bring me the ledgers so I can look through them and see how things stand? I'll need to know how much money you have to work with."

"Sadly, there isn't much. But, yes, I'll bring them my next trip to town. Or you can come to the ranch and see them if you'd like. Nellie always has pie to share."

"No!"

Her eyes widened at his outburst.

"I mean"—he toned his voice down—"if you're able to bring them to me, that would be best. So I don't have to leave my shop unattended." And until he could get the courage to tell her why he couldn't go to the ranch.

"Oh, of course." She smiled again, her eyes a perfect match

with the cloudless sky outside. "You're right, that's the best plan."

"I'll see which of my ideas will work best once I go through the books."

"God did send you just at the right time." She took a step closer to him and—mercy—laid a bare hand on his arm. His shirtsleeve wasn't enough to stem the heat of her touch. He could barely think, much less find any words to respond. "So thank you so much, Caleb."

He managed to nod. Maybe words weren't necessary, as her sweet smile again fixed on him.

Too soon, she removed her hand, put on her gloves, and headed to the door. "And," she called over her shoulder as she exited his shop, "Grandfather was right about you."

Caleb's head was still spinning from her touch and the fact that she truly believed God Almighty had sent him to help her. He was almost starting to believe it himself. So much so that he'd almost missed her last words. Now she was gone and all he could do was stand in the doorway staring after her.

If she agreed with Elliott Roberts's opinion about him—that he was a worthless scoundrel—why in the world was she still asking for his help?

CHAPTER 12

*H*ope filled Eliza's heart the whole ride home. And God had used Caleb Morgan to bring that about with his promise to help save the Double E.

But in her exuberance, had she been too bold, touching Caleb as she had? If only she had a lady friend to discuss matters such as those with. But one thing was certain—Caleb hadn't pulled away. And even if that meant only that he was a gentleman, she had the lovely memory to accompany her on the ride back to the ranch.

Before the men came in for lunch, Eliza filled Nellie in on her trip and how Caleb was willing to help. Minus, of course, her daydreams about him that went beyond business.

"So I'm going to take the ledgers to him to check over."

Nellie turned to the stove and gave the soup a stir. "Hmm."

Eliza waited for further comment, but none came. "Don't you think that's a good idea?"

"If he agreed to it." Nellie shrugged but didn't turn around. "If it helps, it helps."

"Well, I certainly hope it helps. We have to do something."

"Yes, I suppose so. Can you dish up the soup while I ring the bell for the men?"

"Of course." Eliza filled the bowls and set them on the table to the clang of the bell calling Benton and George in. But another bell was clanging louder in her head.

Nellie wasn't giving up on the Double E, was she?

In the afternoon, Eliza worked on mending—alone, as Nellie claimed she didn't need help today preparing supper or completing any of the yard chores. After the evening meal, Eliza moved to Grandfather's old desk before night settled in. Carefully, she chose the books she thought Caleb would need. What a kind man Caleb Morgan was behind his sometimes rough demeanor. Underneath, she was discovering, there was a tender heart. Perhaps a heart that had been wounded some-how, but he was someone of integrity, she felt certain. A man God could use to speak to her own needs.

"Dear Lord, please show Yourself in a mighty way to Caleb. If he has a hurting heart, please heal it and make him the man of God You yearn for him to be."

Eliza took a deep breath and smiled to herself. Within just a few days now, once she delivered these books to Caleb for his perusal, the ranch would be on the road to being saved.

"But, please, Lord, guide me—as well as Caleb. Don't let us rush ahead of You."

At the thought of delivering the ledgers to Caleb, Eliza's smile grew broader. And it wasn't just because the possibility of saving the ranch seemed within reach. Yes, if she truly was honest, the smile was in anticipation of being in his presence. She didn't know a lot about men, mostly because none had ever looked her way. And neither had Caleb Morgan, exactly. Yet in his quiet manner, the way his eyes met hers and looked into her soul, and his offer to help, he had told her he cared. And he came with Grandfather's endorsement. She closed her eyes, letting herself dream about what life could hold.

"Oh, and Lord," she whispered, amending her earlier prayer, "especially don't let *me* rush ahead of You."

She opened her eyes. Maybe she'd take a look at these awful books one more time before turning them over. What frustrated her was that they simply stumped her. Opening the top volume on the stack, Eliza stared at the latest entries again.

One last time, she checked the numbers, adding them carefully. As usual, they came out the same as the figures entered into the columns. And still, the amount wasn't the same as the money on hand. It was almost as if—

The thought was too horrible to consider. Yet it was her responsibility to see that things were in order.

Eliza's heart hammered. What if someone had stolen the money and tried to cover it up? She'd heard Father talk of people doing that. But that was in New York. No one on the ranch would do that. They all loved the Double E.

But what if that person was no longer on the ranch?

Eliza picked up her pencil and jotted down tidbits of information on a blank piece of paper. Grandfather had written of the glories of the ranch, so the ranch must have still been doing well when he was alive.

Eight or nine months...

She tapped her pencil. Who had said something about eight or nine months? The only places she'd been were the ranch, church, the saddlery shop, Gus's cabin, the mercantile, and—

The mercantile. Mr. Jacobs had said Grandmother had died eight or nine months ago when—

When what? He never did say, because Gus had started coughing and they'd rushed to his aid. But what had he been talking about? She scrunched up her face, trying to remember the details from that day.

"...eight, nine months ago now? Yes, it was right before Ca—"

Yes, that was exactly the moment poor Gus had had his

coughing spasm. Or...could it be that he had his coughing fit because of what Mr. Jacobs was about to say? Perhaps he was going to say *right before Caleb*—?

Eliza let out a soft "oh!" as another memory surfaced. When had talkative Gus gotten so tired when she had visited him? Right when she asked if Caleb Morgan had ever been part of the Double E.

What if he had been on the ranch up until eight months ago? That would explain a lot of things. But it would also break her heart. For Grandfather had trusted him.

"Eliza."

She jumped in her chair, then sighed in relief as Benton crossed the room to her.

"I'm sorry, Benton. I didn't hear you come in." He certainly had a way of sneaking up on her. She put her pencil down and closed the ledger.

"I didn't mean to frighten you. Pardon me for interrupting your work." He nodded at the book still beneath her hand.

"No, no. I was just finishing up."

"Thank you for taking over the books for me. I—" He looked down at the floor. When he met Eliza's eyes again, he gave an apologetic half smile. "I'm not real good at numbers, as I guess you've probably seen."

"No—your work was fine. Oh, there were a few minor errors, but that's not the main problem."

His jaw went slack. "The main problem?"

"Yes. There's something very wrong." As the frown on Benton's face deepened, she hastened to add, "But it started before you took over the bookkeeping. So it's not your fault. I haven't figured it out yet, but I won't give up until I do. I'm getting the ledgers ready to deliver to Mr. Morgan in town. He's going to help me go over them."

"I...see." He scuffed a boot on the floor. "Miss Eliza?"

"Yes?"

"I beg your pardon as it's likely not my business to say. But perhaps he's not the best one to help you. I mean, I'm not a book man myself, but even I'm aware there's a lot of difference between managing the income of a good-sized ranch and that of selling a few saddles here and there."

Eliza bit her lip. Perhaps he was right, but then again, numbers were numbers, clear-cut and straightforward, for the most part. Folding her hands atop the desk, she focused on her foreman. "I know you took over after Grandfather died, and he took it over from someone else—someone he must have trusted with it. What I need to know is, who was doing the book-keeping before Grandfather?"

Benton shifted from one foot to the other. "Miss Eliza...it's really not for me to say."

She stood, now eye to eye with Benton with what she hoped was an *I'm-the-boss* look of authority. "Mr. Calloway, the Double E is at stake. Tell me, who was in charge of the records before Grandfather?"

He stared at her a few moments, as if deliberating. Eliza held his gaze, not daring to even blink.

"It was the foreman at the time."

"What do you mean? You haven't always been the foreman?"

"No, ma'am. Your grandfather dismissed him when he discovered an altered page. Then he gave the position to me."

Eliza stifled a gasp. Of course—if someone had altered entries, then that made all the sense in the world. "Who was it, Benton?"

He took a deep breath but still did not speak.

"Tell me. Now."

"Well, ma'am...it was Caleb Morgan."

Caleb? No. Her chest ached as surely as if it'd been stomped on. Was the love of money burning so deeply in his heart that he could betray her grandfather, the man who had trusted him?

No wonder he so willingly offered to "help" with the books. And here she'd been preparing to hand them right over. How convenient that would have been for him to do whatever he wanted, to change even more entries, however that might be possible.

Eliza's face burned along with her heart. He'd tried to make a fool of her, leading her to believe he was concerned about her and her troubles, even assuring her of God's care. Now she knew how he had heard the words she'd spoken to Mrs. Billings that day. He'd been spying on her. Maybe he had even planted that rattler in the horses' stall that night. She wouldn't put it past someone with such a deceitful heart.

"I see," she choked out.

"I think I'd best be heading over to the bunkhouse, ma'am," Benton said.

"Yes."

Eliza followed him outside and stood alone on the front porch. The sky had quickly darkened, and the chill in the air caused her to wrap her arms around herself. Was this the same view Grandmother had admired, standing on these very planks beside Grandfather, watching the evening stars appear?

Kep came up beside her and rubbed against her leg. Eliza reached down and gave him a pat. He leaned in a little harder in his show of thanks.

"Good boy, Kep. You were loyal to Grandmother and Grand-father, weren't you?" She scratched him between his ears.

At last the mystery of those ledgers was solved. Altered figures. She should be elated to know. She should have figured that out by herself—except how could she have done that without questioning the loyalty of Grandfather's employees? She clenched her fists. Foolish. That's what she'd been. And even more so when she considered how she'd fallen for Caleb's charms. Well, her eyes were wide open now.

Eliza turned to go inside. She needed a good night's sleep

for the day ahead tomorrow when she made yet another trip into town.

"Caleb Morgan," she said as she started up the stairs to her room, "if you're a praying man, you'd better start saying your prayers right now."

~

"*O*h, Caleb—yoohoo!"

Caleb lifted his head from the leather he was working on in the back room and sighed. What did Callie want now? He had come in to work on his saddles in the quiet of the morning as the sun was still rising. So what was she doing here so early?

"Are you here?"

He stood. "Yes."

"Well, come out here, then. I didn't know you were so rude."

Something he hadn't known about her either.

"Give me a moment. I'm coming."

"Oh, of course, Caleb. I forgot. It takes you quite a while now."

And who did he have to thank for that? Fury rose inside him before he could tamp it down.

Peace...peace...

He gulped in a couple of breaths. If only he could find the peace Eliza had spoken of. If only she were here to offer encouragement as she had done with Mrs. Billings. To calm his spirit with words of God's love.

When he reached the front of the shop, Callie was rubbing a white-gloved hand over a special order saddle. Oh, the tantrum she'd throw if any of the polish came off on her pristine glove.

"What can I do for you?" His customary words sounded uncharitable, coming through gritted teeth.

"Now, Caleb..." Callie inspected her glove, then stood straight. "There's no need to act so unpleasant. I thought you would want to congratulate me."

"For what?"

"Why, haven't you heard?" She giggled. "I'm about to become Mrs. Benton Calloway."

Perfectly aimed, her dagger thrust right into his heart.

"And..." She paused dramatically. "I'll be making my new abode at the Double E." She smiled in triumph as she delivered the final twist of the blade.

He turned and limped back to his saddle work, leaving her standing there with a gloating smile on her face. She could consider him the rudest man in the West for all he cared. Picking up his hammer, he put a tack in place on the leather he had been working on and raised his arm, gathering momentum for a hard wallop.

"Well, good day to you, too, Caleb Morgan! Teeheehee." The giggle of that silly woman reached him mid-strike.

And the blow meant for the tack struck his thumb, strong and sure. Clenching his teeth, he sat on the nearby stool and squeezed his eyes shut. He refused to let out the bellow of pain about to erupt from him. For it wouldn't be for the throbbing in his thumb but a cry from the pain in his heart.

"Caleb Morgan, if you're in here, come out right now!"

Now who in the world could that be? This high-pitched, angry voice wasn't Callie's. Caleb opened his eyes. Finally, the initial shock and pain were beginning to subside. And the throbbing—at least in his thumb—was lessening.

"I know you're here. Now come out like a man."

That did it. He pulled himself slowly to his feet, steadying himself against a wall.

"I'm here." He walked to the open area out front and stopped.

Eliza stood there, but something was wrong. Arms crossed,

she glared at him. Sweet Eliza Roberts? Fire had replaced her sweetness, and he was in its path.

"Eliza? What's wrong? How may I help?"

"Help? You've already done more than enough."

"Ma'am?"

"Don't you try to deny it, Caleb Morgan."

"Eliza...I don't know what you're talking about." He stood still, talking softly, the way he calmed wild critters. No sudden movements. Gain their trust.

"You know very well what I'm talking about. You just don't know that I found out."

Oh. This was the day he had known would come. He should have told her from the beginning. Of course, she was going to find out.

He hung his head. "I should have told you." He looked up.

She blinked. Paused. Then she seemed to regain her momentum. "Yes, you should have told me that you're nothing but a—a—thief and a crook."

A thief? A crook? He took a step forward, reflexively reaching out to clasp her arms.

She moved out of his reach. "Don't you touch me."

He stopped. What was he doing? He took a deep breath. She wasn't the one he should be angry with.

Calm. Gentle. Don't frighten her.

"What are you"—he lowered his voice another notch—"talking about?"

"You know what I'm talking about."

"You found out that I was the foreman at the Double E."

"Oh, yes, the foreman. The most trusted man on the ranch. The person my grandfather put in charge of all that he owned."

Caleb scratched his head. Something didn't make sense. She made it sound as though there was something wrong with all those things. He admitted he had made a mistake by not telling her he knew the Double E inside and out. And how well he had known both of her grandparents, how he looked up to them and loved them. Had been included in their lives as though he was family.

But the anger she possessed meant only one other thing. Someone had told her of the scandal at the ranch.

Who? Not her grandfather, or she would never have spoken to him in the first place. Not Miss Nellie, for she had always believed in him. Probably not Gus, or she would have accused him days ago. Daniel Jacobs at the mercantile? Doubtful. He mostly liked to gather gossip, not spread it.

That left only one other person he could think of...

"Benton Calloway tried to protect you," Eliza said, "but I forced him to tell me the whole story."

Protect him? That sorry, low-down, lying, thieving—

"How could you alter the ledgers after my grandfather trusted you? How? *You* led the ranch into disrepair and stole his money." Eliza advanced toward him with raised hands, fingers extended, as though she was going to claw him. Then she seemed to think better of it and halted mid-step.

"Eliza, I—"

"I don't want to hear your excuses, blame, or any explanation, Mr. Morgan. I wouldn't be able to believe a word from you. I do, however,"—she paused for a breath, then jabbed her forefinger at him with each word—"insist that you repay what has been stolen. I'll be in contact with Mr. Taylor as soon as he returns from his absence." She whirled around and stormed out the door.

Caleb stared after her. He let out a long, low moan, the sound of his breaking heart. So he had been right, after all. Eliza Roberts was just like the rest of this town.

CHAPTER 13

*E*liza was out of options.

Back at the ranch, she sat at the wide desk with her chin propped on her clasped hands. No money meant no ranch. Had she been wrong, thinking God was leading her to stay and fight for the ranch, to keep Grandfather's dream alive? Apparently, she'd been mistaken. And even now that she knew what had happened to the ledgers, had confronted that awful Caleb Morgan, she didn't feel any satisfaction with the knowledge. She felt empty. And abandoned.

"Eliza?" Benton stood in the doorway, twisting his hat in his hands.

"Yes? Please, come in and sit."

"Thank you." He advanced a few steps until he was in front of her, but still he stood.

"Is something wrong?"

"No, miss. That is...well..."

Eliza studied him more closely. She didn't spot trouble in his eyes, but something clouded them, something more like—

She blinked hard, scarcely believing her assessment. Why, he looked bashful.

"Yes, Benton?" Perhaps a soothing tone would put him at ease. He'd never acted like this around her before.

"Miss Roberts...that is, Eliza...I'd-like-to-ask-you-to-do-me-the-honor-of-marrying-me."

He'd blurted out the words in such a rush that there was only one she was absolutely certain of, and her heart was thumping wildly at that. Marry? He wanted to marry her?

"I know I'm not the kind of man who deserves a lovely lady such as yourself. But, as I hope you've guessed, I have feelings for you." He met her gaze briefly before looking away nervously. "I know you wish to stay on the ranch and do your best to salvage it. But, as I told you before, it's a hard job for a man, let alone a lady by herself. So, if for no other reason, Miss Eliza, perhaps you would allow me to be your husband to work the ranch on your behalf, so that you might still keep it."

Eliza was speechless. Of course, she'd heard stories of people marrying for practicality, but even so, someone chose her to marry? Was this God's answer, sending along this offer from a good man so soon after she discovered Caleb's betrayal? She wet her lips, searching for words. Surely, she needed to pray about this astonishing proposal.

She blinked as Benton hurried on. "I know you need to know me a bit better first. Will you allow me to court you toward that purpose?"

Eliza smiled at last, relieved. Yes, she'd get to know him better—though he'd been nothing but kind—and see how God was leading. She hardly needed any silly tingles or the dreams she'd indulged herself with over Caleb. That had all been calculated to sway her, anyway. "Yes, Benton."

At a gasp from the doorway to the kitchen, Eliza turned her head in time to see Nellie ducking back into her domain. So now that her friend knew of this private matter, how wonderful that she had someone with whom to discuss it.

And what could make Nellie happier than Eliza marrying someone from the Double E, ensuring that the ranch be kept running?

"Thank you, Miss Eliza," Benton said. "I know I took you by surprise, but I'll bid you good night now and give you some time by yourself to consider this. You've made me a mighty happy man." He backed away to the door, a grin on his face.

"Good night, Benton." Once he left, Eliza stood too. God was answering her, after all. And in a very unexpected way.

Nellie didn't come out to congratulate her, which was fine with Eliza. So she headed up to bed, relishing her time alone to ponder this new turn of events. She would read her Bible, pray, and write to Mother and Father and even Aunt Belinda. They would certainly be most surprised that someone counted her worthy to court.

Eliza woke early the next morning, the Lord's day. Eagerly, she dressed in her finest dress for church.

Sunday was special each week it came around, as she loved to worship God with other believers. But she also certainly enjoyed the chance to chat with the dear people in Caldwell. Maybe she would have a moment privately with Benton before they left for church to discuss how he wished to make known their courtship today. But when neither he nor Nellie mentioned it at breakfast, neither did she.

Upon their arrival at church in the wagon, Benton helped Nellie off the bench. When he assisted Eliza down, he continued to grip her arm. Ah. Eliza smiled up at him, touched that he was stating to the churchgoers his intentions toward her even without words.

Nellie hurried off to greet some of her lady friends headed into the church building. No doubt she was as eager as Eliza herself to share the good news of Eliza's courtship.

"Good morning, Mrs. Billings," Eliza gaily called out. "Hello, girls!"

The girls stared curiously at Benton's arm on her in such a possessive way.

Little Virginia came up and tugged Eliza's hand. "Where's your other beau, Miss Eliza? He's awfully nice."

"Virginia!" Mrs. Billings sharply reprimanded her daughter. "Eliza, please accept our apologies."

Before Mrs. Billings could tug her daughter loose from Eliza, Virginia slipped a piece of red-and-white candy into Eliza's hand. "I bought two peppermints. I ate mine, but here—this one is for your other beau."

Eliza stared at the candy in her hand. To give it to Caleb, she'd have to speak to him—and that she wasn't about to do. "Virginia—"

But Mrs. Billings had pried the little girl loose from Eliza and was herding her troop toward the church door. Virginia squiggled free and turned around mid-hop. "Don't forget, Miss Eliza!"

Benton gave Eliza a tug on her arm and led her toward the church. "What was that all about?" He was staring down at her hand clenching the candy.

Eliza looked at him, surprised at his tone of offense. "Oh, just a little girl's gift."

"Well, it's going to get your dress sticky." He reached into his suit pocket and extracted a white handkerchief. "You can wrap it up in here."

"Thank you." Carefully, she covered the candy and tucked it into her own pocket.

Several ladies whom Eliza now knew greeted her warmly and nodded to Benton. Benton tightened his grip on Eliza's elbow and marched her up the steps. "We best be getting on in before the singing starts."

Though Eliza missed sitting down front on what folks still called the Roberts's pew, she followed Benton without question into the seat he chose midway down the aisle. If she did become Mrs. Calloway, she would be expected to follow her husband's leadership—so what better time to start than now?

Only once while standing for the singing did Eliza turn around. And then she wished she hadn't. Glaring at her from the rear pew in his usual spot was Caleb Morgan. How dare he even show his face in God's house? He should be so ashamed of himself, too embarrassed to be seen worshipping a holy and just God. Unless he was here to repent—which, by the look on his face, he was not. With the slightest lift of her head, she hoped he understood her message. *Stay out of my way, you scoundrel.* His shoulders slumped even lower, and he could not even meet her gaze. Benton turned and glared in Caleb's direction too.

Pastor Thompson read the Scripture verses, then waited for the congregation to settle back in the pews before he began his sermon. When she realized what the message was on, Eliza leaned forward eagerly. Repentance. Good. Hopefully, Mr. Morgan would pay attention and humble himself before God Almighty. But Pastor Thompson didn't stop with that. He went on to his next point. Forgiveness. Well, perhaps she did have a problem there.

When Caleb Morgan repented from the wrongs he had done, then she'd ask God to help her forgive that deceitful man. But since it wasn't likely that the cheat would ever repent...well, she didn't have to worry about him asking her forgiveness.

Eliza shifted uncomfortably on the pew, suddenly feeling squashed between Benton and the lady next to her. Not to be irreverent, but it'd certainly be nice if the minister could hurry along a bit and end his sermon early.

*C*aleb had to force himself to stay seated until the very end of the sermon. *Repentance. Forgiveness.* Hmph. That Benton Calloway would never repent from his sins nor ask anyone for forgiveness. Not that Caleb would let that belly-crawling snake off the hook even if he did ask. Fury smoldered in his heart. Calloway needed to be brought to justice, that's what he needed.

And Eliza... Caleb stared at the back of her golden hair. Why was she sitting with the enemy? Except the look of daggers she had given him when she had turned around told him exactly whom she considered her enemy.

"The Lord says that vengeance is His, not ours," Preacher Thompson was saying. "The Word of God, Romans chapter 12, verses 19 through 21 says, 'Dearly beloved, avenge not yourselves, but rather give place unto wrath: for it is written, Vengeance is mine; I will repay, saith the Lord. Therefore if thine enemy hunger, feed him; if he thirst, give him drink: for in so doing thou shalt heap coals of fire on his head. Be not overcome of evil, but overcome evil with good.'"

Coals of fire. That's exactly what Caleb would love to put on Benton Calloway's head. And even that wouldn't be enough punishment for him.

As soon as the sermon was finally over, a hymn was sung, and the final amen said, Caleb stepped into the aisle. He'd hightail it out of this church and—

"Good afternoon, Caleb." Old Mrs. Ramsey blocked his path to the door. "How's your business doing these days?"

Caleb blinked. No one ever spoke to him at church. He was the last in, the first out.

"Um...fine, Mrs. Ramsey. Thank you for asking."

"I might just be by one of these days soon. My nephew should be arriving in Caldwell with his family by the end of the month, and I'd like nothing better than to give him a gift, get him started off on the right foot as he takes over some of the duties out at my place."

"Yes, ma'am. Stop by anytime."

"He'll be right proud to own a Morgan saddle."

"Thank you, ma'am." He edged away a step. Finally, Mrs. Ramsey stepped aside, and Caleb reached the back door, anticipating a breath of fresh air.

"Here!"

Something was thrust into his hand. He turned his head. Eliza? She was emptying a white kerchief and dumping something sticky onto his palm.

"Thank you." Manners sprang to the forefront even before he had a chance to see what it was—and to figure out why she sounded so gruff.

"Don't thank me. It's from Virginia." Eliza brushed past him out the door, with Calloway trailing along behind, glaring at Caleb as he passed.

Caleb opened his hand and looked down at the red-and-white object—a peppermint candy. That sweet little Virginia. But he didn't have a moment to let the girl's love touch him before he was pushed along with the crowd, out the door, onto the church steps. Just yards away, Calloway aided Eliza and Miss Nellie into the wagon. People bumped Caleb as they tried to hurry around him, down the steps, home to their dinners. But his sinking heart rooted his feet in place on the landing. Even the fresh air he had been longing for now felt stale against his face.

"Mister Caleb! Mister Caleb!" Virginia came skipping up to him. "Did Miss Eliza give you my present?"

"She most certainly did." Caleb took a deep breath to absorb the pain and knelt on one knee next to her. He opened his hand and showed her the candy he still held. "This is going to be my dessert after my noon meal. So I thank you very much."

Virginia giggled. "You're welcome. Mama says we should always share with our friends. And because you're my friend and Miss Eliza's other beau, I chose you."

He nodded, though the little girl had no idea how untrue her last words were. "Then I doubly thank you, Miss Virginia. I'm honored to be your friend."

"Goodbye, Mister Caleb!" She turned and ran off, back to her mother and sisters.

On the side of the yard, Benton slapped the reins against Rosey and Biscuit, and the Double E wagon started down the road, heading out of town. Caleb managed to stand upright without groaning out loud, and right then, he made up his mind. He accepted the fact that Eliza Roberts wanted nothing to do with him. But he would not allow her to be led blindly into trusting Benton Calloway. Knowing Calloway, he had some plan up his sleeve, and Caleb intended to stop it.

Slowly, he descended the steps, then walked over to Ruby.

"What was that all about?" The whiny, demanding voice just behind him belonged to only one person.

"Callie." He sighed. When would she ever leave him alone? She was a good match for Benton.

"Why was Benton sitting with that uppity girl instead of me?"

Why, indeed? Given the choice, anyone clearly would choose sweet Eliza over Callie. But with Benton, one never knew his reasoning.

He shrugged. Why Benton would do it today, he had no idea. Except, clearly, Benton had made a statement to the entire congregation by holding Eliza's arm.

"I'll fix him," Callie muttered. Then she slipped her arm through Caleb's, pulling him away from his horse. "Come on, Caleb. Won't you have lunch with me this afternoon?"

He jerked away from her. "No, Callie. Not today. Not ever."

"Well! I never!"

Caleb didn't bother watching her stomp off to her buggy. He was still staring after the wagon carrying the only lady he ever wanted to have lunch with. Except that would never happen, as she was about to be feasting with his enemy.

~

"Nellie..." Eliza turned to her on the wagon ride home from church. "Since Christmas will be on Saturday, how did my grandparents celebrate here on the ranch? I hadn't thought about it until now, but I'd like to continue their customs."

"Ah, Christmas Day was very special when Miz Elizabeth was with us. First, we'd plan a big feast. It'd include all the ranch hands and their families. And anyone from church who had no one to eat with. The table would be overflowing with food. And Mr. Roberts and Miz Elizabeth would make sure to find a family in town with children who had hit hard times and needed a little extra. Of course, they'd be invited to the dinner. But there would be new—and well-fitting—clothes for each of the children."

"Your grandparents made the day memorable for so many," George added from the back. "I always looked forward to it myself."

"Yes," Benton broke in, "but this year, with the ranch doing so poorly, I'm afraid we won't have the money to spend for the fancy dinner or on clothing for poor people." He shook his head. "I'm sorry to have to say that, Eliza. Maybe next year will be different."

Nellie's spine stiffened, and her face took on a hard look, but she said not a word. Nor did George.

"We'll find a way." Eliza patted Nellie's arm. "If my grandparents did this each year, I'll do the same..."

They rode in silence for a bit as Eliza thought through solu-

ANGEL FROM THE EAST

tions. Of course—if she used her travel money to California, she'd have enough. And she wouldn't be needing it right away, anyway—if ever. "I'll pay for our Christmas celebration out of my savings."

"Hallelujah," George called out.

Nellie gripped her hand and Benton's mouth dropped open. "Don't worry, Benton." Eliza smiled at him. "The Double E won't need to pay for a thing. And I know just the family on hard times whom we can invite. Nellie?"

Nellie released her hand and gave a firm nod. "Yes. The next time you ride in to town, you invite Mrs. Billings and her sweet lasses. And I'll prepare the longest list Daniel Jacobs has set eyes on."

Eliza laughed. "And I'll do a little shopping for them as well. I think they'd each love a new pretty Sunday dress. And a bag full of candy."

"But, Eliza..." Benton looked her full in the face. "I can't ask you to do that, generous as it is. It's the Double E's responsibility to carry on this tradition of the ranch. And, sadly, there is no money for it. As foreman, I must advise against it. For the sake of the Double E. And we need to think of our own family as well, to leave a solid legacy for those to come."

Eliza frowned. She did appreciate his caution. He might even be right. Did she dare override Benton, as she was still the owner of the ranch and his boss? Or submit graciously, practicing now what she would need to learn to do once they were married? At the firm set of Nellie's mouth, Eliza knew better than to ask her opinion or even George's.

She drew in a long breath. "You're right, Benton. It should be a gift from the ranch, as it has been in the past. So"—she gave a schoolmarm clap of her hands—"we'll sell one of the cows and reap the benefits before another goes missing and we lose the income, anyway."

"What? No! You can't do that." Benton seemed to realize his

125

voice was rising and tempered it with his next breath. "That'd be foo—unwise, Eliza."

"I'm sorry, Benton. But this is a tradition that must be kept."

"Very well. But surely, a smaller meal and used dresses will suffice."

Eliza sighed, tired of arguing. "Nellie, plan your meal exactly how you and my grandmother did. And the girls shall have new dresses. The prettiest Mr. Jacobs has in his store."

Benton nodded, though his jaw was clenched tight. As they continued down the road, he stared straight ahead and spoke not a word more.

Eliza half listened as Nellie and George made plans for selling a cow and what dinner would consist of. Obviously, she had offended Benton, but to what extent? From overriding his wishes? Or maybe he was simply embarrassed that she had what he might consider wealth, coming from New York with her traveling money.

She darted a glance at Benton's ramrod back and lips tightened into a straight line. Hopefully, his posture and silence were only from the burden of financial problems weighing so heavy on him. Though she hadn't expected this testing of their apparently different ideas for running the ranch to occur this soon in their courtship, perhaps it was good to sort things out early. They could speak privately once they reached the Double E. As they deepened their courtship, they would work out their differences, come to an understanding about their roles should they marry, and she'd learn how to be a good helpmate to him.

With that thought, she laid a hand on top of his. But his hand remained stiff beneath hers, and he didn't look at her all the way back to the ranch.

CHAPTER 14

*S*undays came around too often to suit Caleb. At least he could get out of the saddlery this morning after spending Christmas Day alone. For months, he'd asked himself why he still bothered attending the church services. And week after week, he recited the same answer to his question—it was ingrained in him from his mother and from Mr. Roberts. Even though both were gone, he couldn't bring himself to let either of them down. So here he was again, trudging in and slumping onto the back pew as the pastor stood to welcome folks.

He tried to avert his eyes from the honey-gold bun three pews ahead of him and just to his left. She shifted in her seat, as if suddenly aware someone was staring at her. This Sunday, she and Benton were even closer to the back. In another week or two, he might actually have to arrive early to get this seat nearest the door.

Feelings of betrayal by Eliza and envy toward Benton warred in his heart. How did Benton end up with everything Caleb wanted? That didn't require any actual pondering—Benton just stole it. But even so, couldn't Benton tell how much Eliza missed sitting down front in church? Couldn't he tell that the farther back they got, the duller her eyes grew? Hadn't he noticed how her smile had faded in these two Sundays of sitting together? Or how her singing had no lilt to it anymore? Of course, he hadn't noticed, for his bellowing was louder than ever, drowning out Eliza, as well as everyone else.

Didn't Benton realize how Eliza enjoyed chattering away with the other ladies both before and after the service? Not just idle chitter, but from the times Caleb had overheard her, she was encouraging the women, urging them toward peace and joy. He knew because he had actually hoped she would talk to him about her peace.

And now that the service was over, she was smileless once again as Benton took her elbow and hurried her out the back door—so fast this time that they even beat him.

Caleb stood and followed. Who was he to judge? He didn't belong here any more than Benton did. They were both hypocrites, still bound by Mr. Roberts's rule of the ranch. Caleb cringed, hating to think they had anything in common. But apparently, they did. Two hypocrites longing for the same lady. Except Caleb was smart enough to know he was undeserving of a lovely, godly wife like Eliza.

Sadly, the only thing Caleb had learned in church this morning was that not one single hair of Eliza's silken bun was out of place.

He stood on the steps and watched Benton lead Eliza straight to the Double E wagon, with Miss Nellie trailing behind.

Silently, Reverend Thompson appeared beside him on a step and clapped him on the shoulder. "I'm always glad to see you, Caleb. You know, I don't always have the right words, whether in a sermon or just talking, but God does. Sometimes they seem loud and clear, yet other times, merely a whisper." The preacher followed Caleb's gaze to where it hadn't left Eliza. "And when you hear God's words in a whisper, listen hard. And follow them. He's the one who changes hearts." He clapped Caleb again. "Love isn't easy, but it's worth pursuing, son." And with that, he walked over to another parishioner.

All this talk about whispers and love. He wasn't counting on ever having either.

Caleb headed toward Ruby and was stopped again.

"Excuse me, please." Mrs. Billings looked nervously at her three girls skipping around a tree a ways off. "I just wanted to thank you for your kindness to my girls."

"Ma'am?"

"Someone left money Friday before Christmas as a gift at the mercantile for penny candy whenever the girls come in. Mr. Jacobs would not say who had given it, but I know it was from you. You have a kind heart, Caleb."

At least one person thought so. "Thank you, Mrs. Billings. It's my pleasure to bring smiles to their faces. You have three lovely girls."

"Thank you. And though I scolded them for speaking out of turn last Sunday that you were Miss Eliza's beau, I do agree that you two seemed to fit together so nicely." Her eyes lifted to Eliza riding off in the wagon with Benton. "You may be too much of a gentleman to interfere, but God has a way of making crooked paths straight."

"Ma'am?"

"Mama! Mama!" Little Virginia shrieked as she raced up to her mother and skidded to a stop behind her skirts with the other two girls chasing her.

"Caught you," Rosita said, and Lila giggled as she wrapped Virginia in a hug.

A longing lodged in Caleb's heart at seeing them laugh and play, loving each other. "You girls sure look pretty this morning. And do you have new Sunday dresses?"

"We do." Lila twirled to show hers off. "Miss Eliza invited us to her ranch for Christmas dinner yesterday and gave us brand new dresses."

"The prettiest in the whole mercantile," Rosita chimed in.

So that's how Eliza had spent Christmas Day. The thought of her continuing the tradition of Miz Elizabeth and Mr. Roberts of having a dinner for the ranch hands and inviting someone who needed it sent a warmth through his heart, counteracting the emptiness of missing out this year.

"It was Miss Nellie and Mr. George and us and Miss Eliza," Virginia said, then made a face. "And that Mr. Calloway. I don't think he likes us."

"Hush, Virginia." Mrs. Billings held up a finger, a clear warning to the girl to watch her words.

The little girl frowned. "But, Mama, he doesn't—"

"Shh. It doesn't matter. He also was Miss Eliza's guest, and we're to be kind to everyone, whether they like us or not."

"Yes, Mama."

"Come, girls. We need to be getting home." She held out her hands to her girls and gave Caleb a meaningful nod.

"God has a way of making crooked paths straight." He half wished she hadn't been interrupted from whatever she'd been going to say beyond that.

As they walked away, Caleb stood stock still a moment. Two people had spoken to him this morning, had sought him out even. And they both hinted at hope. He didn't see any future for him and Eliza, but the words of the reverend and Mrs. Billings sparked the slimmest glimmer that they did. And they certainly were praying people.

So maybe they were God's whispers to him this morning.

"Mister Caleb, Mister Caleb!" Little Virginia came tearing back to him and wrapped her arms around him. "Mama said I could come back to give you that." She looked up at him and grinned.

"Thank you, Virginia. That's the sweetest greeting I've had all day. Please thank her for allowing you to deliver that."

"I was going to give Miss Eliza one, too, but she's already gone."

"I'm sure she would have loved a hug from you. Maybe you can catch her next week." But she'd have to be fast to get to Eliza before Benton escorted her off the church property.

Though Caleb had missed out on the preached part of the sermon, God was still sending him home today with words of wisdom.

"God has a way of making crooked paths straight." From Mrs. Billings.

And from Reverend Thompson—*"When you hear God's words in a whisper, listen hard. And follow them."*

And maybe a third. *"Love isn't easy, but it's worth pursuing."*

Surely, God was speaking to him. And this time, he was going to listen hard even for the whispers. If he could hear them.

~

The wagon ride home after church was pleasant enough, if Eliza considered only her conversation with Nellie and George. Benton sat quietly, guiding the horses. Not sullen or tight-lipped as he'd been on last Sunday's ride home. Even their conversation that day in the privacy of the parlor had been cordial, and Benton had accepted the fact that Grandmother's Christmas dinner and traditions would go on.

And yesterday, Christmas dinner with the Billings family had been joyful. So maybe he was just quiet today after the busyness and work of the whole past week. And sometimes quiet was welcome and peaceful.

As soon as Benton pulled the horses to a stop at the ranch

house, George helped Nellie and Eliza down. Then the men took the horses and wagon to the barn.

Nellie hurried inside straight to the stove. "Eliza, let's get our meal going since I'm sure everyone is hungry. If you can do that, I'll just throw these scraps out to the chickens."

"Of course." Eliza was grateful for the quiet of the house as she could continue mulling over the unsettledness in her heart. She put the already-made soup on a burner and absent-mindedly stirred as it heated.

She'd never had any experience courting, so she didn't know exactly what to expect. Benton was gentlemanly and mannered, so that wasn't the problem. Yet it seemed something was missing. Perhaps it was the giddiness exhibited by her friends back East who had courted and become betrothed. The only giddiness she'd encountered was from her misplaced trust in an untrustworthy saddlemaker. But her friends had eagerly elaborated on the wonderful attributes of their beloved whenever someone would listen. Here, she had only Nellie to confide in, and Nellie was distant around Benton.

Perhaps that was the only thing bothering her—she had no lady friends to share her joys or anxieties with.

She stirred the broth again, watching Nellie out the window as she scurried amongst the chickens, tossing tidbits to them. Why didn't Nellie like Benton? Even Kep never tagged after him or wagged his tail in greeting when Benton came around. Occasionally, she'd even heard Benton speaking a bit gruffly to the faithful dog. And dear old Rosey seemed nervous whenever Benton hitched her up on Sundays, as if anticipating a strenuous slap of the reins on her back.

Sundays. Eliza sighed. She used to love Sundays, sitting with Nellie in the same pew her grandparents had worshiped in through the years. Sitting almost at the feet of Pastor Thompson as he taught from the Word of God. But each week with Benton, he chose a seat closer and closer to the back.

Farther from the family pew and a sense of closeness to her grandparents. Farther from sitting at her teacher's feet. Benton rushed her in and rushed her out of the services. She supposed they needed to hurry back to tend to ranch duties. But she sorely missed the special time of fellowship afterward when she and Nellie longed to spend a few minutes catching up with other ladies and their needs.

Was Benton truly the man God had for her?

The door slammed shut in the wind as Nellie reentered the kitchen. "Ah, those chickens. If I don't keep them all fed, there'll not only be no eggs but no roast chicken either. Is the soup ready?"

Eliza gave it one last stir. "Yes. I'll ring the dinner bell."

She stepped outside, and no sooner had she rung the bell than George and Benton appeared. Once everyone was washed up and seated, Eliza turned to Benton.

"Would you like to ask the blessing?"

He shrugged, then bowed his head. "Lord, we ask that You bless this food. Amen." He picked up his spoon and slurped his soup.

Eliza's heart sank further. How she longed for a man who loved to speak to his Lord, who would pull out the family Bible after a meal and share with her what he had been learning. She moved her spoon idly around her bowl. She wanted someone who would share his heart with her.

"Eliza?"

She looked over at Benton, eager to hear his thoughts. Perhaps about the sermon?

"More rolls, please."

That was what was missing. Benton had never once shared his longings, his dreams, his heart with her.

She passed the baskets of rolls to him and stirred her soup again.

George grabbed a roll as the basket went by and looked

over at Nellie. "Nellie, this meal is delicious. Just right for the day. A good sermon, a good meal, good company. You always provide this. I just meant today's is very tasty as usual."

"Why, thank you, George."

"I was remembering how Miz Elizabeth would have us say something we learned from the sermon or were thankful for at the Sunday meal. And while I learned from Reverend Thompson's words this morning, I sure do appreciate your cooking and staying on at the ranch with us, Miss Nellie."

Nellie chuckled. "What a kind thing to say. And you're absolutely right. We've gotten away from that custom over the last few months. It's time to start it up again. I'm thankful for God's protection over us and His daily provisions. And to you two men for keeping the Double E running in the absence of Elliott and Miz Elizabeth."

This was exactly what Eliza was longing for. "I loved Reverend Thompson's points about listening to God. And I pray for wisdom to hear the Lord's voice when He does speak. And as far as being thankful—oh my. I'm so blessed to be here and have a glimpse into Grandmother's and Grandfather's lives all these years. Thank you to each one of you for being so faithful and kind to them. And even now during these harder times of keeping the Double E going."

George's face turned red, yet he smiled and nodded. And Nellie's eyes filled with tears, which she discreetly wiped away.

Eliza, George, and Nellie turned to Benton for his words.

He cleared his throat and set his spoon down with a clatter. "Yes, I agree it's been a struggle. I'm just not sure how long the Double E can continue."

Silence met his words, and Eliza worked hard at not breaking it. Surely, this conversation had revealed clearly what she should do. And what she needed to say now should be said in private.

As soon as Nellie's apple cake was eaten and the dishes

washed, Eliza found Benton in Grandfather's rocker on the porch.

"Benton, may we talk in the parlor?"

He grinned. "Of course, Eliza."

Please give me the words, Eliza prayed silently as she led the way inside and took her seat across from Benton.

"What would you like to talk about?" He leaned back and crossed one leg over a knee.

"The Double E."

He sat up straight and smiled.

Eliza clasped her hands in her lap. "We need to have a plan to save the ranch. If we are to keep it, we need to make it profitable again. What are your ideas to do this?"

Benton frowned. "Well, like I said, I don't know if we'll be able to keep it going for long. I figured we'd sell everything that's left. The cattle. Some of the acreage to start with. Selling the land—if anyone will buy it—is the only way to get a decent amount of money. And lastly, the horses once we don't need them."

"What are you saying?" Her voice rose in alarm. "Are you giving up?"

Benton shrugged. "Eliza." He stood and knelt by her chair. "I don't see any other way. Caleb Morgan ran it into ruin. I tried my best to salvage it for your grandfather's sake, but there's nothing more I can do." He took Eliza's hand. "But when we get married—"

"No!"

Benton dropped her hand. "What do you—"

Gathering her courage, Eliza jumped up, almost toppling Benton over. "No, I won't marry you."

By this time, Benton also stood. "You agreed—" It sounded almost like a snarl.

"No. I never agreed to marry you. I only agreed to courting to see if it might lead to marriage. And now I know it won't."

Benton's eyes narrowed, and before she could move, he took a step toward her and grabbed her wrist. She tugged, but his fingers were as strong as a vise.

"Benton, let go. You're hurting me."

He looked at his hand on hers, as if shocked he was holding it so tightly. He relaxed his grip but still didn't release her. "Please, Eliza." His tone was softer, pleading.

"No, Benton, I cannot marry you, nor even court you any longer. Grandfather had dreams for the Double E, and so do I. And I'm glad I discovered the truth today—that you don't." And he'd also shown his true character as another deceiver.

"Eliza, I'm sorry. But the truth is, the ranch isn't worth trying to salvage. Even if you won't marry me, I'll still buy it from you. I don't have much money, but it's more than anyone else will be willing to pay. Then you can travel on to California and teach. You won't have to worry about this place."

"No. I'm also sorry. Now please let go of me." She tugged her hand, but his fingers clamped down hard.

He stared at her for several seconds, then his mouth curved up cruelly. "Gladly." With a hard twist to the side, he released her wrist.

Eliza grimaced from the pain shooting through her arm but dared not back down. "Benton, you are no longer welcome here. You're fired."

He glowered at her. "You'll be sorry. I promise you, I'll get this ranch one way or another."

Eliza swallowed. She wouldn't let him see her fear. Where was Nellie? George? Or Kep? "Get your horse and leave."

"Right after I get my belongings from the bunkhouse."

"No. You'll leave right now."

"Ma'am?" Thankfully, George poked his head into the parlor, with Nellie peeking out from behind him. "Do you need help?" He looked from Eliza to Benton and back again.

"Yes. Benton is no longer an employee here. Will you please escort him immediately off the Double E?"

"But I have something—some items—in the bunkhouse I need!" Benton shouted, his eyes blazing with hostility.

"George can pack them up tomorrow and drop them off at the mercantile."

"No! I need it—them—now!"

George shoved Benton toward the door. "You heard the boss lady—tomorrow. Now get a move on."

"Benton..." Eliza called after him, then waited until he turned around. "I don't want you ever stepping foot on my property again."

His only response was a chilling smile before turning on his heel.

Once Benton and George walked out of the house, Eliza collapsed into Nellie's arms.

"There, there, dear," Nellie said over and over as she stroked Eliza's hair. "He's gone. But"—she tilted Eliza's chin up so their eyes met—"we have to keep a watch out for him. If he threatened you, believe him. He means his threats."

Eliza rubbed her wrist and shuddered. She had no doubt he did.

CHAPTER 15

"What brings you by today?" Gus asked as Eliza pulled Rosey to a halt in front of his cabin the next morning.

"I wanted to talk to you." Eliza dismounted and left Rosey loose in the yard.

"Come in out of the cold, then."

Together they walked into the warm kitchen. Gus motioned for Eliza to sit while he ambled to the stove and poured two cups of coffee. After handing one to her, he took the chair across from Eliza. "I've only got the coffee going this morning, haven't made pie for the week yet. But I can scrounge up a cookie if you want one."

"No, thank you."

"So what do you want to talk about?"

Eliza let the warmth from the cup seep into her hands. "Benton Calloway."

Gus studied his coffee. "What about him?"

Eliza swallowed. Maybe she'd been wrong in coming to Gus. What if she had misjudged him, and he was actually a friend of Benton's? She sipped her coffee, trying to decide whether to ask or not.

"Spit it out, lass."

"Why did Grandfather ask him to be foreman of the ranch?" There, she said it.

Gus nodded slowly. "That's quite a question. But I'm not the one with the answer."

"Who is?"

"Ahh, that would have been your grandfather. So I'm afraid none of us will have the real answer now, will we?"

"But you know something. You were Grandfather's closest friend, I hear."

"That I was. But that doesn't mean he shared everything with me."

Riddles and evasion, that's what Gus was the master of. "Can't you tell me how Benton became foreman? I already know Mr. Morgan held that position once."

"Then all I can say is that there was a private matter between Elliott and Caleb. Apparently, Calloway was the one available to take up the position when Caleb—when Caleb moved into town."

Eliza pondered this. So many questions. What kind of a private matter? Why was Benton the one picked? Had Grandfather ever discovered the altered ledger page?

"So Grandfather trusted Benton?"

Gus pushed his coffee away. "Trust and position are two different things."

"Well, Benton no longer works for me. I dismissed him yesterday."

"Why was that?" Gus's words seemed carefully selected and measured.

"He betrayed my trust."

"Then you did right by firing him."

"But...Grandfather trusted Caleb Morgan." Even as she said it, it didn't make sense. But that was what Grandfather had written. So perhaps he never knew that Caleb had betrayed him.

"Aye, he did at one time."

"No, when he was dying, he still did."

Gus's eyes widened ever so briefly before he quickly looked down into his coffee. "And how do you know that, lass?"

"Because Grandfather wrote me that he did."

"When was this?"

How had Gus become the interrogator? But Eliza dutifully answered. "In his last letter to me. It was attached to his will which I received shortly before my arrival here."

A smile spread slowly across Gus's face. "Well, I'll be." He stood. "Will you excuse me, Miss Eliza? I have something to do."

She stood also. "Certainly. But—"

But Gus was right on her heels, hand on her back, escorting her to the door. He walked her outside and held Rosey's reins while Eliza mounted. "I'll be," he muttered again, giving Rosey a slap on her flank, sending her off at a trot back in the direction of the Double E.

What a strange, close-mouthed man Gus was. Eliza shook her head. He seemed to have more secrets than a graveyard. She rode a quarter mile, wondering about those secrets all the way. Well, maybe she could find the answers somewhere else. Pulling the reins gently, Eliza turned Rosey around and headed straight for Caldwell herself.

She let Rosey set the pace at a leisurely walk. The sweet horse was getting on in years, and there was no hurry to get to town. Except—right up ahead, coming out of Gus's yard, was Gus riding bareback. Already his horse was galloping, stirring up a cloud of dust behind them. Now where was he going in such a hurry?

Eliza pressed her knees against Rosey, asking her to speed

up just a little bit. If Eliza followed Gus, she just might learn one of his well-kept secrets.

Gus was heading right toward Caldwell, and so far, he hadn't seemed to notice her trailing him in the distance. When she and Rosey reached town, it was easy to figure out where Gus had gone, as his horse was tethered in front of Mr. Jacobs's store. That figured. Those two were more than just friends—they were in some kind of cahoots together.

Eliza pulled Rosey next to Gus's horse, slid off her, and looped the reins around the hitching post. She'd march onto the elevated boardwalk, throw open the door, and demand to know what they were up to. On the other hand, if she crept quietly up to the door and put her ear up close to it, she might learn more.

One thing was sure, though. If she wanted to find out what Gus and Daniel Jacobs were about, she couldn't let them distract her by a coughing spell or any other diversion. She hated being sneaky, but that looked like her best option at the moment.

Checking to make sure no one else was headed toward the store, she stepped lightly over to the window first. The two old heads were bent together, nodding and shaking, as the men talked. Ducking low, she scooted over next to the door and leaned up against it, straining to hear the voices inside.

"There you are!" Iron-like fingers digging into her arm and a low, harsh voice in her ear made her lose her balance, and she went sprawling onto the boardwalk in front of the door. Eliza looked up into the unshaven face of Benton Calloway as he still held on to her.

"Let go of me." She jerked her arm to wrench it free, but he dug his nails deeper into her skin. "You're hurting me."

His sneer, close to her face as he bent over her, sent shivers up her back. "You don't mess with me and get away with it. I promised you trouble, didn't I?"

"What do you want?" She tried again to break away, but he twisted her arm.

"What do I want? All I want is the Double E. You should have taken my offer of marriage or to buy it from you."

"I wouldn't ever sell it to you. And where did you get money? Did you cheat Grandfather too?"

"Ah, you're the smart one, aren't you? I'm giving you one last chance—"

"Get away from me!" With all the strength Eliza could muster, she yanked her arm from Benton and scrambled to her feet.

"You ain't going far!" Benton lunged at her and caught her by her sleeve, tearing it loose from her dress.

"What's going on here?" Gus burst out the door with Mr. Jacobs right behind him. "If you harmed Miss Eliza—"

Eliza scurried next to them, clutching the torn sleeve that now dangled from her wrist.

Mr. Jacobs stepped up to Benton, toe to toe. "I'm telling you now, get out of here. This is a peaceful town. If you come back and threaten people, you'll land up in jail—probably a good place for you, anyway."

Benton glowered at the three of them, jumped off the boardwalk, and mounted his horse. "I'll get you!" His threat hung in the air as he kicked his horse and thundered down the road.

"Thank you, Gus, Mr. Jacobs." Eliza looked from one to the other.

"Off with all of you." Gus waved his arms at the crowd that had gathered until they'd all dispersed.

Mr. Jacobs reached for her elbow. "Come inside, Eliza. I'll fix you something warm to drink. You need to sit down."

Just before she followed him into the store, she looked back. A cloud of dust on the horizon verified that Benton had left town. But now standing on the boardwalk was Caleb Morgan, watching her, fists clenched at his side.

~

*W*hat had happened?

Caleb had leapt onto the boardwalk too late to help. Or even to know what was going on. But with Benton Calloway riding his horse hard down the road and Eliza's dress torn and sleeve hanging down, it didn't take much to deduce that Calloway had attacked her.

His insides churned at that thought. Benton was surely a madman. If word around town was to be believed, Eliza Roberts was a spunky one for sure, standing up to Benton and firing him. But it did no good to make an enemy of Benton Calloway. If he'd made a threat, he'd keep it.

What Eliza needed now was protection. Gus and Daniel would do their best, but what could these two do against the wiles of Calloway? Eliza might not want Caleb's help, but he would do everything he could to keep her safe. Even though he'd have to do it from a distance.

Caleb edged over to the store's window and peeked in to assure himself Eliza was safe. Gus and Daniel were fussing over her, one patting her arm, the other handing her a cup of something to drink. She was in good hands. He started to walk away, but as he passed the door, he heard voices. Not muffled, indistinct words, but a conversation. Caleb stopped. He shouldn't listen. He should just keep walking. He should—

"...take good care of you, Eliza. Don't worry." He could picture Gus still patting Eliza's arm, reassuring her. "You must never be left alone out there."

Then Daniel's voice snuck through the door crack. "Things will work out. As Gus said, Nellie or George must always be there with you."

Silence. Eliza must be talking, but he couldn't hear her.

Then Gus again. "Let me tell you a story about your grandmother, Elizabeth Rose. You're named after her, are you not?"

Caleb glanced around, desperately hoping no patrons would come to the mercantile during the story, during his eavesdropping.

"Miz Elizabeth was much like you when she first arrived in Caldwell. Life in New York is much different than life on the range, as you well know. Now I've never been east, but I hear things. I know she had things easy in the city and many a hardship here. No friends when she came. No place to wear her fancy clothes that got ripped and worn from her working out in the garden or riding down cattle. And no family, because she'd left them all behind to follow her husband, who was following God's call. Now, let me ask you, which is more important? Following a husband God gives, or staying put with the love of family if that's not where God chooses to keep you?"

If only Caleb could hear Eliza's response to that. He leaned closer to the door.

"So, here was Miz Elizabeth, feeling alone in a land of tumbleweed, dust, and sagebrush. And the bitterbrush." Never had he heard Gus talk so much. "That plant is appropriately named. Bitterness. During the winter months after their arrival, it was growing right in her heart. But sometime during that first winter, Miz Elizabeth allowed God to show her His mercies and faithfulness. Come spring, Miz Elizabeth had determined to make friends in town."

A momentary bit of silence. Maybe Eliza commenting or asking a question.

Then Gus's voice again. "She took her fancy dresses and made them into work clothes and into baby dresses for the little ones born to poor mothers in town. And a quilt that had patches of each dress in it as a reminder of God taking her drab, bleak-looking life out here and turning it into a life of beauty.

Anyone who knew her talks only of her godliness, of her unselfishness, of her love to everyone."

More silence followed before Gus resumed.

"When it came time to plow and plant the fields for their first crops, she looked out the window one day, and what she had thought was a dreary, bleak sagebrush was bursting with yellow blossoms and giving out a sweet-smelling fragrance. Ah, the bitterbrush. Often mistaken for sagebrush. Until spring-time. Just like her life. So one day when I was out helping Elliott plow up the field, she came a-rushing out, insisting that one bush be left as a testament to God's power and grace. So come this spring, look out the back window. You'll see your grandmother's bitterbrush—the very one—in bloom. That's her legacy to you. To remember God's goodness and faithful-ness. You are so much like her."

Caleb had seen Miz Elizabeth's bush in full bloom. Had even seen her sitting out beside it on the ground with her Bible in her lap. But he'd had no idea what it meant to her.

What did Eliza think of the story? She probably couldn't wait until springtime to see it for herself. Caleb wanted to dart over to the window and see Eliza's expression, hear her response. Was she nodding her head, brushing away tears? If only her soft, gentle voice would penetrate this old door, then—

Thwump. He landed in a heap on the threshold of Mr. Jacobs's mercantile.

"Caleb Morgan, what are you doing?" Eliza's voice was neither soft nor gentle.

When he looked up, Eliza was stepping around him, stomping down the boardwalk. And Gus and Daniel were standing near the counter. Laughing.

CHAPTER 16

*P*romise or not, Caleb was about to step foot on the Double E.

For a week, he'd been mingling more at the mercantile, actually listening to town gossip about the ranch and Eliza and any sightings of Calloway. But over an hour ago, he had passed George driving the ranch buggy toward town with Nellie perched beside him. Mounted on Ruby on his way to deliver a saddle to a customer in the direction of the Double E, Caleb had nodded a greeting as he passed them at the edge of town. He had even been close enough to see what Nellie was holding on her lap—a pie basket. Likely, she was planning on visiting while George did errands.

Why had they let their guard down only a week after Benton's threats? If the two of them were together, Eliza must be out at the ranch. Alone. He tried not to worry, as Kep was with her.

Then, on his way back home, Caleb had stopped to give Ruby a rest while he sat by a stand of trees to take a drink from his canteen. That was when he had seen Benton running his horse hard down the road leading to the Double E. He could be going anywhere—except at that speed and given the deep scowl on his face, wherever he was headed, trouble was brewing.

Caleb looked back toward Caldwell. Beyond Benton's dust cloud, none other was being stirred up. If Nellie and George had returned to the Double E, he would have seen them as they passed the sheep farm where he had just delivered a saddle. Which meant no one was at the ranch still except Eliza. And he could not allow Eliza to be alone out there if Calloway showed up.

Before the dust settled, Caleb capped his canteen and pulled Ruby away from her grazing. Within moments, he was on his way to the ranch. Not only would Mr. Roberts have understood the necessity of following Benton onto Double E land, especially if he had known the truth about that mangy coyote, but hopefully, he would have approved of Caleb's actions.

"Lord, I'm trying to listen to Your whisper. And I think You're saying to go. This isn't about my revenge. I have to protect Eliza. Please, help me for Eliza's sake."

Ruby brought Caleb closer and closer to the Double E. The day was mild and still, unlike the day months ago when he had left in shame. On the heels of Benton, Caleb barely had time to register the faded and tilted Double E sign. When had that happened? And why had Benton allowed the fences to start graying beneath the once-gleaming white paint?

He slowed Ruby at the rutted entrance road. No one had bothered to smooth out the gouges made by wagon wheels being sucked into thick mud during the rains. Now dried, the ground was uneven and dangerous to the horses.

No cows were visible in the pastures, no horses filling the air with neighs. All was quiet, except for faithful Kep bounding out, barking.

"Hello, Kep."

The herding dog barked again, looking back toward the house, ears alert. Caleb glanced toward the outbuildings just in time to see Benton coming out of the bunkhouse, patting his coat pocket. Then the trespasser headed toward the house.

"Kep, come. We have to get to Eliza." He urged Ruby forward, but with the uneven ground, he dared not go faster than a walk. Plus, there was no sneaking up on Benton now that Kep's barking would have alerted him to Caleb's presence.

There was no sign of or sound from Eliza. If Kep had barked at Benton's arrival, too, maybe she'd been able to barricade herself inside the house. As if even that would stop him from getting in. But it could keep her safe until Caleb got there, maybe slow Benton down enough that Caleb could jump him. He aimed to do whatever was needed to protect her. Even if Calloway had a gun.

God, please protect Eliza.

Caleb pulled Ruby to a halt. Benton wasn't inside. He sat rocking on the porch in Mr. Roberts's chair, as if anticipating a social call.

"Well, howdy, Caleb. I can't say I'm surprised to see you." Benton smirked.

At least he was still outside. Maybe if Caleb kept Benton distracted long enough, Eliza could sneak out the back and hide or saddle Rosey and go for help.

Caleb dismounted and walked halfway up the steps with Kep at his heels. "Kep, sit." Kep obeyed but kept his head cocked toward Caleb. "Why are you here, Benton?"

"Morgan." Benton said the word as if he were spitting something disgusting from his mouth. "If you're such a man of honor, as you seem to think yourself, seems to me you're the one who'd better be hoofing it off the Double E. Or don't you remember the boss's order—that you never step foot on his property again?" His laugh seemed to cloak the ranch in evil.

Please, Eliza. Get out of the house. He didn't hear anything from within, but if he kept Benton talking, that would give her more time to get out and help cover up any noise of her own.

"You know as well as I do, Calloway, if Mr. Roberts had known who changed the ledger page who would be unwelcome here."

"Roberts had his proof."

"No. He didn't. He had what you wanted him to see."

Benton shrugged. "It was harder than I thought it'd be convincing the old fool, but he knew numbers don't lie. He was getting just weak enough by then. See—timing is everything."

Timing. Now was the time to grab hold of Calloway. How would it feel to have his hands around that varmint's neck? Caleb clenched his hands into tight fists, fighting to keep them at his sides.

"A battle is not won by fists..." Of all the times to remember Mr. Roberts's words.

"The old man made his decision about you clear. A man of *honor*"—Benton snorted—"would abide by it."

"I'm not here for my sake." Caleb kept his voice as even as he could. "I have abided by his wishes. But you also were fired and told to leave and not come back." Oh, he hoped the town gossip was accurate this time. "So I'm here to protect Eliza from you."

"From me." Benton laughed again, then jolted the rocker to a halt, his eyes hard. "You think I'm going to listen to some woman bossing me? I'm glad she won't be my wife. I'll get the ranch another way."

Caleb bounded up the rest of the steps, feet away from Benton's throat and—

A soft answer turneth away wrath. Words from Proverbs that Caleb had learned long ago filled his mind, seeping down into his heart. His feet stopped right where he stood on the porch, as if God Himself held him back.

Caleb drew in a deep breath. Was that God whispering to him? A whisper he heard?

"I'm telling you to get off the Double E, to leave Miss Roberts with what's left of her ranch. To leave her alone."

Benton hooted. "*You're* telling *me* to get off? Seems to me you still have it all backwards, Morgan. You were dismissed as foreman by the boss *man*—that's whose word counts—and I was chosen."

Chosen. *Ha.* Caleb glared at him. "I know you were behind the stampede of the horses—and had to have locked Kep up while you did it—and the stealing, then selling, of the cattle. You ran the ranch into disrepair so Miss Roberts would become desperate and then you could rescue her by buying it. Am I right?"

"You have no proof." Benton smiled, baring his teeth. "Don't deny that you wanted the ranch yourself. But you won't get it, Morgan. You lost your job, your woman, your precious honor. Everything."

"Only because you stole them from me."

But the truth was, Calloway was right. Without that ledger page, there was no proof of what Benton had done, nor was there any way Caleb could prove his own innocence. The proof was probably just a smattering of ashes now, long ago blown into the fields.

Sucking in a ragged breath, Caleb stared at the rough planks of the porch. There was no getting the truth out of this devil. But how to get him to leave before he went in search of Eliza? Pounding him and hauling him off to the sheriff was his solution. But if God was whispering to not fight, what could he do? Didn't God know Benton Calloway wasn't listening to Him, either, much less to Caleb?

"This is your last warning, Calloway. Leave peacefully on your own, or when George returns, I'll send him to fetch the sheriff. Then you'll not only be off the ranch but will land right where you belong. In jail." Caleb wasn't going anywhere until he knew Eliza was safe.

Benton smiled and rocked, not budging.

Oh the days of plunking down in his old rocker just a couple of yards away. There, at the end of a hard day, he used to listen to Mr. Roberts's dreams. He'd had dreams himself, long ago. Hopes that one day he could buy the ranch, if Mr. Roberts ever wanted to sell it. That he'd be the one sitting side by side in those rockers with a devoted wife, someone like Miz Elizabeth, watching the sunset together, talking about the trials and joys of the day. Now those dreams were just empty longings. There would be no ranch for him. No wife to share his life with. And worst of all, there would be no peace in his heart.

"I'll give you my advice, Morgan. I'd suggest you turn tail and leave. Or you'll end up getting worse from me this time than a few broken ribs and a bum leg. If Roberts hadn't interfered that night I showed him the ledger page, I would have finished you off then. But I guess the good ol' boss fixed you even better than I could, didn't he? What could be worse to an honorable man than to be considered *dishonorable* by the whole town?"

Benton's sneer almost did him in. Caleb focused harder on the boards under his feet.

God, if You want me to only use soft words, then please give me some.

More Bible words he'd known from long ago settled in him. *Glory to God in the highest, and on earth peace, good will toward men.* Except maybe they weren't words from so long ago. Hadn't that been Eliza's message to Caldwell all along?

A seed of hope, of assurance, sprang to life in his chest. God was right here with him, for Caleb could feel Him whispering to his heart, could hear Him this time. Little by little, his anger faded, his heartbeat going back to normal. He could stand his ground as a gentleman and speak courageously, for God was with him.

If God be for you, who can be against you? Another verse he remembered from the Bible. Indeed, if God was for him today, he'd be the victor. He could overcome Benton Calloway this time...not by his fists, but with the power of God's words. The seed of hope was flourishing. He lifted his head and looked up.

Right into the barrel of a Colt .45.

~

*E*liza had had enough of those two men. When had Benton dared return? And what was Caleb doing here? She'd taken a short nap while Nellie had gone to town with George. Now, walking into the kitchen to pump some water, she had stumbled upon the makings of a brawl. She edged closer to the window Nellie had left ajar to air out the kitchen. The coldness in Benton's voice stopped her from bursting out onto the porch and demanding that they act like civilized gentlemen.

"So..." Benton had an ugly sneer to his tone. "Unless that snoopy cook found the ledger page, you can't prove anything."

What? Who had hidden the ledger page? Eliza clasped her hands tightly in front of her chest as if to still her thundering heart.

Caleb's brows shot up, but he remained silent. Why didn't he move? Or say something? He just stood there staring. She followed the line of his gaze and sucked in a breath.

Benton was pointing a gun at Caleb. What was he doing? Surely, he wouldn't use it—would he?

Benton gave an exasperated grunt. "She's had enough opportunities to search for it."

When had Nellie ever had time to search for anything? Eliza had been with her day in and day out except—

Except when Nellie sent her to Caldwell to pick up supplies. Numerous trips, because they were always needing something. Maybe it was more than simply a tactic to evade Eliza's questions.

"She knew the consequences," Benton ranted on. "Her time's up. And so is that nuisance Eliza's."

What did he intend to do to Nellie? Or her? So the times Benton had been sweet and shy and kind—all an act. Because she was nothing more than a nuisance to him.

"Now I'm going to own this ranch one way or another. So you can forget any hopes you had of getting your hands on it. Seems I beat you again, didn't I?"

Mockery laced his words, but they went deep into Eliza's heart. So Caleb, too, had been pretending all along. Just another ruse for him to possess the Double E.

Benton sprang up from the rocker and walked to the door. Leaned against it. "Now I think it's time I go inside and find my little Eliza darling."

Chills crawled up Eliza's arms. What was she doing standing here? She should run.

Caleb moved a step closer to Benton, hands out, legs bent as if ready to spring. "I wouldn't try anything."

Benton raised his gun higher, aiming it level with Caleb's eyes.

She couldn't stand by and let him shoot a man in cold blood. No matter what Caleb had done. With no thought beyond a quick prayer, Eliza ran the few steps to the door and jerked it open. "That's enough!"

Benton fell backward into the kitchen, and a shot exploded as the gun flew out of his hand and onto the floor. He jumped up and grabbed Eliza, pinning her against the doorframe.

"Let go of me!" She kicked him, but before she could land another, Caleb and Kep were there.

With a roar, Caleb grabbed Benton, dragging him off Eliza. Benton's fist smacked Caleb in the face, but even as Caleb crumpled onto the porch, he took Benton down with him. With Kep growling and barking as he circled them, the men rolled and punched.

"Stop!" If this was the kind of wildness her parents thought existed out here, they were right. And she'd wound up in the middle of stealing, shooting, and fighting on what should be a peaceful ranch.

When they bounced down the steps, she grabbed the porch broom. Swinging it overhead, she ran down the stairs. "Stop!"

With the men twisting back and forth in the dirt, neither she nor Kep could get a clear aim at Benton.

Suddenly, Caleb was on top of Benton and rammed his knee into the heavier man's stomach. With a grunt, Benton went still, his eyes wide. Caleb let out a low growl filled with a smoldering sound of revenge such as she'd never heard before. He raised his fist high above his head.

"No, Caleb!"

He glanced her way, arm still raised.

"Please. Don't." Maybe talking calmly would help more than screaming. *Please, God.*

Caleb turned back to Benton, his arm lifting higher.

Eliza pressed her hands over her eyes.

But the yard was silent. There was no sound of breaking bones. No howl of pain from Benton. No cry of victory from Caleb.

Eliza peeked through her fingers. Caleb had removed his knee from Benton's belly and was holding Benton's arms to his sides with Kep standing guard.

"Eliza. Grab the lasso off the post." Caleb kept his eyes on Benton.

She scrambled to the fencepost and grabbed the rope, quickly delivering it to Caleb. He rolled a dazed and groaning Benton over, tying first his hands behind his back, then his legs together.

"Caleb..."

He finished the last knot and stood. Brushed his hands on his pants before looking her way but not meeting her eyes. "What?"

"He's bleeding."

"It's just his nose. Can you get a towel? Kep, stay. Guard. I'll hitch up your wagon and take him in to the sheriff."

She couldn't get her feet to move. When she thought of all that could have happened...and the two men who had both seemed like they had cared...

She took another look at Benton tied up and moaning. Yes, he had shown his true character today. But Caleb? She'd seen him fighting with her own eyes, but she couldn't believe that was who he was. In truth, he was a defender. Defending her.

"Eliza, a towel. Please."

"Oh. Yes, I'll get one."

She hurried back into the kitchen and grabbed the first one she saw. When she returned with it, Caleb stood with his head bowed, Kep licking his hand. Almost a reverent moment.

"I brought the towel." She took a deep breath, dreading getting close to Benton to care for his nose, even though his hands were tied.

Caleb raised his chin, still not meeting her eyes. "Thank you." He took the towel from her and bent over Benton himself, mopping the blood off his face. Then he stood and finally looked at Eliza. "I should have asked sooner—are you hurt at all?"

She was shaky and weak-kneed but unhurt. "No. Thank you for rescuing me."

He nodded, then gave his command again to Kep. "Stay. Guard." And headed to the barn.

Eliza retreated to the porch steps, keeping an eye on Benton and Kep from there. Not daring to even glance behind her at the gun lying on the kitchen floor. She had no idea what to do about it. But if Caleb also had been after the ranch, she knew what she had to do about him. Even if he had rescued her.

CHAPTER 17

"What have I done?" Caleb spoke softly to Ruby as he fit the Double E harness on her. Since George and Nellie still hadn't returned in the buggy, he'd have to use the larger wagon.

It looked as though he had his revenge on Calloway, who was tied up tight, about to be hauled off to jail where he belonged. But where was the satisfaction he should have felt? The feeling of righting a wrong?

It plain wasn't there. Instead, he felt battered. Not just his leg and his ribs, which screamed silently in pain with each movement, but beaten in his heart.

He led Ruby over to Benton and dared a peek back at Eliza. All she had witnessed was ugliness, though today had also proven what a low-down skunk Calloway was.

But what did she think of him? He didn't know how much of Benton's jabberings she'd heard. Or believed. Did she still think he was responsible for running the ranch into hard times? That he was trying to steal it out from under her?

Regardless, she had seen him battering Calloway. Maybe overheard that he and Benton had gotten into a fight before.

She'd view him as a man of violence. Not someone trying to do right.

But she also needed to know how God had used her calm words to quiet his hand, his anger. *"Please. Don't."*

"And when you hear God's words in a whisper, listen hard. And follow them. He's the one who changes hearts."

Only her quiet admonition today had kept him from delivering that final blow to Benton Calloway straight in the face. What if he'd killed the man? It'd been too late to stop the momentum even as Caleb had tried to change his trajectory. But that moment had given Benton time to turn his head, avoiding a punch full force right in the face. But the ground hadn't been any softer.

"I didn't mean for it to turn out like this, Ruby. I really didn't."

He patted her on the neck and walked over to Benton. Gritting his teeth against the pain that would knife through him, he leaned down and lugged Calloway up. Now that he was more alert, his groanings turned into threats. Perhaps Caleb should gag him as well. Ignoring the rants, Caleb hoisted him up to the wagon and plopped him in as gently as he could. "Kep. Come." Obediently, Kep leapt into the wagon and took his post next to the prisoner.

Caleb walked over to Eliza, where she sat on the steps, head down. "Eliza."

She didn't look up.

"I'm sorry."

Again, no response.

"I'll be taking Benton to Caldwell to the jail. He won't be bothering you again. I'll return your wagon by evening."

Finally, Eliza raised her head. "I'm sorry too. And I do thank you for intervening. But I don't want anything to do with Benton Calloway—"

"You needn't worry. I'll make sure he doesn't bother you ag—"

"Or you, either, Caleb." She stood, brushed off her skirts, and headed inside, closing the door firmly behind her.

He should have expected that, but all the way into town, Eliza's words seared his heart, each rut and bump the wagon wheels hit hammering the words deeper. And Benton's bellows added to the cacophony as he yowled and rolled in the wagon bed with each bump. Caleb bit back a howl a few times himself as each jolt shook his ribs, leaving him gasping for breath.

Finally, Caldwell was in sight. Spectators gathered in clusters, turning their heads and whispering as the wagon paraded through town, stopping at the Canyon County Courthouse. Caleb eased himself as gingerly as possible down from the wagon.

"Kep, stay. Guard." He then strode into the first-floor offices. "Sheriff Flint."

The gray-headed lawman looked up from his desk, eyes dark and shadowed, though kind. "Howdy, Caleb."

"I've brought Benton Calloway in. He's bound up in the back of the Double E wagon."

"Benton? What's he done?" Jerome stared at Caleb.

"He attacked Miss Roberts out at the ranch."

"Hmm. Do you have witnesses?"

Caleb should have known what justice was like in this town. People were suspicious of him, assuming his guilt in whatever matter came up. "Yes. Miss Roberts herself."

"Tell me your account, then, and I'll talk with Miss Roberts later."

Skipping the parts he deemed personal, Caleb stuck to today's events of following Benton out to the ranch and ended with Benton attacking Eliza, the gun going off, and the fight.

"All right. That's enough for now." The sheriff stood. "Pull the wagon around to the jail, and let's bring him on in. I'll meet you there."

Caleb returned to the wagon and drove Ruby to the four-cell stone jail at the corner behind the courthouse. Sheriff Flint met him, and they stood at the wagon rail on the side Benton's head was facing.

"So, Benton, you have anything to say for yourself? Attacking a lady is a mighty serious charge."

Benton just glared at him.

"Untie him so he can walk." Sheriff Flint nodded toward Caleb. Caleb did as he was bid while Benton continued glowering. "I have a cell waiting for you, Calloway. Let's go."

Finally, Benton was where he belonged, locked up behind bars. For a moment, Caleb observed the villain slumped atop the cot like a mangy animal.

Sheriff Flint gave the cell door a shake. "That'll keep you in there good and tight." He turned to Caleb. "And I'll be speaking with Eliza. You might tell her to come see me if you see her first."

"Of course. I'm headed out there right now to return the wagon." He wouldn't dishonor Eliza's request that he leave her alone, but if she would allow him to speak to her this once, he had much to say. While the trip back might not be long enough for him to rehearse any eloquent words, he'd speak forthrightly. And let her know how her words had changed his heart. Used by God. What could make Eliza Roberts any happier than that?

Caleb returned to Ruby and the wagon and climbed aboard.

"Come on, Ruby, girl." She pricked her ears forward at his soft clicking. "Time to go. It's time I told Eliza the entire story."

And when she heard it, maybe he'd witness again today the truth of Reverend Thompson's words—that God was the one who changed hearts.

At the Double E, Kep jumped down at the ranch sign and ran alongside the wagon. Once Caleb reached the yard, he went to the barn, unharnessed Ruby, and took care of the wagon. Rosey wasn't in her stall nor the buggy in its spot, so George and Nellie still weren't back.

"All right, Ruby." Caleb let her loose in the yard. "You rest up before we head back."

He walked up the stairs to the porch, Kep at his side. When he stopped at the door, the dog wagged his tail and sat beside him. Caleb knocked, rehearsing his words. First, an apology, then to make sure Eliza was fine, then to tell her the whole story of his time as foreman on the ranch and his friendship with her grandparents. And to answer any questions she had about them. About him.

He knocked again with no answer. And a third time.

"Eliza? It's Caleb. May I speak with you?" She must be inside. Could she hear him through the door? "I want to tell you again I'm sorry." Still no response, not even a sound from within. "Eliza?"

He had to find a way to prove himself to her. But if she wouldn't answer the door...

He turned away and Kep stood. Caleb bent and rubbed the dog's head between his ears. "Stay." He was Eliza's, and he didn't need divided loyalties.

Caleb retraced his steps to the barn and searched his saddlebag for a scrap of paper and a pencil. At least Eliza could hold in her hand the words he had wished to speak out loud.

When he finished writing, he propped the paper against Eliza's new saddle in the tack area—in plain sight where she would find it the next time she saddled Rosey.

Caleb saddled Ruby and left the ranch. But unlike the time he'd left in shame months ago, this time, he was leaving with hope.

Hope that Eliza would see his heart. And even a bit of hope for them.

~

*E*liza stared out her bedroom window at Caleb and Ruby as they rode off. She'd been tempted to answer the door when he'd knocked, but what good would have come from it?

If only Nellie had been here. What could be keeping her and George for so long? She had said she'd be late, stopping to deliver a pie to a sick friend and visit. But Eliza needed her too. She longed for Nellie to wrap comforting arms around her, needed her wisdom to somehow make sense out of the horrid fight she'd witnessed and been a part of.

When Caleb returned the wagon, she would have told Eliza to get on down to speak with him. To hear what he had to say. But on her own, she hadn't had the strength to talk to him. He probably was rejoicing that his enemy was locked up in town. What rowdies, both of them. Except, Caleb had come to her rescue. She had to remember that in spite of everything else that man had done.

She'd been so foolish, letting Benton blind her with his practiced charm. Her cheeks burned just thinking what a good laugh he must have had at her expense. Why, she had actually believed him when he had told her he cared for her. When had she become that desperate, believing the first man who flattered her with his attentions? If God wanted her to stay a maid like Aunt Belinda, then she would. Gladly. For she didn't know a single man with a trustworthy heart. And maybe that was why her aunt had never married also.

When she'd seen Kep walking alongside Caleb, then sitting next to him as he knocked, she almost softened her resolve. Especially when Caleb rubbed Kep on the head and told him to stay with her rather than follow him. To stay and protect. She remembered too well how tender he was with animals. How he had been the same with her. How, though he seemed to harbor deep wounds, he could be so gentle. How he had so unexpectedly encouraged her with God's truths when she'd been ready to give up. But none of that mattered, because he, too, had been after her ranch, not her heart.

Now that he was gone, she ventured out onto the porch and sat in Grandmother's rocker.

Billows of dust signaled someone was coming up the lane to the house. She stood, relieved once the buggy got close enough to see that it was Nellie and George.

Nellie stepped down the moment George brought Rosey to a halt. "Merciful heavens!" She trotted up to the porch and engulfed Eliza in just the hug she'd been needing. "Are you all right, child?"

"Yes, yes." Eliza nodded against Nellie's shoulder.

Nellie released Eliza and took her arms, holding her at arm's length. "Let me look at you and decide that for myself." Her eyes traveled up and down, then she gave a nod and released her.

George hopped down from the buggy and took the steps two at a time. "We met Caleb out on the road, and he told us what happened. I never should have left you here alone."

"None of us could have known. And everything"—her voice caught a moment—"worked out."

Nellie planted her hands on her hips. "I'm just glad Benton Calloway is where he belongs and can't bother us anymore."

"Amen to that," George added with a vehement nod.

"Let's get you inside and I'll put the teakettle on. You, too, George, once you get Rosey unharnessed and settled." Nellie hooked her arm through Eliza's elbow and marched her inside.

Once they were all seated, Eliza warming her hands around a cup of tea, she turned to Nellie. "It sounded as though Benton was threatening you to find a missing ledger page."

Her gaze darted to George, and he gave a barely perceptible

nod. "Yes, but I've had no luck. It doesn't matter anymore, as he's behind bars and has no hope of a claim on the ranch."

"I'm certainly not selling it to him."

"Of course not. And we don't need any piece of paper to prove anything about Caleb. We know he's an honorable man. He'd be the best one to have come back and be foreman."

"That's right." George grinned. "Sure's a shame what he went through, but he was the closest to a grandson Mr. Roberts had."

Eliza choked on a sip of tea. He what?

"He and Miz Elizabeth treated him exactly as if he were blood kin to them."

Had Grandfather considered selling—or even giving— Caleb the ranch if the problem over the ledger had never occurred? Before he willed it to her, she who knew nothing about ranching and didn't even live on it? Is that why Caleb and Benton had returned today when they'd both been banned, to battle it out over who would get it?

George set his cup down. "Eliza, now that Benton is in jail, what are your plans for the Double E? You can run it as you wish and bring in ideas you might have from out East."

Both he and Nellie leaned forward as if anxious to hear her plan.

She squared her shoulders as they waited, their eyes full of hope.

One thing was sure as the day was long. She wasn't about to sell the ranch to either of those two, let alone allow them back on the property for any reason.

All she had to do now was to think of some way to keep it herself.

CHAPTER 18

C. Morgan Saddlery was making a fine profit. Caleb had enough orders to keep him busy for quite some time. But hours, then days passed with his rawhide, leather thongs, wood, brass tacks, and silver all sitting neatly organized along the back room wall, basically untouched. He couldn't concentrate on his craft. All he could think about was Eliza. Being attacked. Her words that still stabbed his heart, that she wanted nothing to do with him. Her utter forlornness.

He had meant to help. But he'd gone wrong right from the beginning. He'd known he never should have let her thread her way into his heart. First of all, she was a godly woman, deserving of someone who would walk by her side and lead in the things of God. He had shown her none of God's love, insisting on stubbornly clinging to his soul-devouring bitterness. In essence, he was no better than Benton, responding with vengeance and retaliation. Instead of stepping in and helping Eliza salvage the ranch as he should have the first time she asked, he let false accusations embitter him.

"Oh, Lord God, what have I done? I've ruined everything."

Caleb sat with his head in his hands in the workroom. Then Mrs. Billings's words whispered to his heart.

"God has a way of making crooked paths straight."

Even his?

And the answer settled in his heart. Yes. Was that not His specialty? Caleb slid out of his chair and knelt, beseeching God out loud. "I've been bitter and unforgiving. Disobedient." He drew in a ragged breath. "Humbly, I ask for mercy. Please forgive me. Help me to forgive Benton Calloway. Most of all, I beg You, please make my crooked path straight. Make me into a godly man."

"So now you're holy, Caleb?" The shrill voice of Callie jerked Caleb to his feet. How had she gotten back here without him hearing her? "Since you're a forgiving man now, will you forgive me for being so foolish for having broken our engagement? Will you propose to me again?" She had her hair down and stood twirling a dark curl around her finger. Trying to look captivating?

"You—" Anger seared from Caleb's heart up his throat. How dare she spy on him, trespassing into his sacred time with God, especially as he was asking God for forgiveness for his bitterness?

Forgive.

Was he required to forgive her too?

Forgiving one another...even as Christ forgave you, so also do ye. Another verse he'd learned long ago.

He sighed. "Callie." Could she even hear him over his pounding heart? "I...I can forgive you, yes. But no, I cannot propose to you again. Our marriage would not have been right. But I will pray for you, that you find the peace of God."

"'The peace of God'?" Callie's face turned red. "No thank you, Caleb Morgan. You're spouting words from that holier-than-thou Eliza Roberts. Perhaps you two deserve each other, after all." She scooped up her skirts and stalked out to the front.

When the door rattled closed, he sank onto his stool. "Thank You, Lord. I think You just gave me a victory." He didn't dare pray that Callie's comment might someday be true—that he truly would be deserving of sweet Eliza.

Now there was one more person he had to forgive. And this would be the most difficult act of obedience of all.

He put up the *Closed* sign over the shop door and headed to his quarters, ready to start on his task.

By morning, Caleb rubbed his eyes and gulped down another cup of leftover coffee. His vision blurred, and his knees ached from the hours he had spent in prayer throughout the night. The old fight had waged in his heart—vengeance versus forgiveness. Every time he'd felt God's spirit drawing him to obedience, the flesh put up a fight anew. Only in the early hours of the morning had peace settled in his heart. Wonderful, sweet peace. Something he hadn't felt in nigh to a year.

"Thank You, God." He felt like stepping outside and half shouting, half singing as Eliza and the girls had done, but he settled for raising his eyes upward and saying it for God alone. "Glory to God in the highest, and on earth peace."

As he ate a bowl of lukewarm porridge, the wonderful smell of tender beef and herbs, potatoes, and carrots wafted over from the stove, tempting him. The stew, made with the best cut of meat he had, had been simmering overnight. Now it was tender, and the aroma almost made him give in to his own appetite. But as delicious as the stew smelled, it wasn't for him.

Once his bowl was washed and his modest dwelling readied, he hitched Ruby to his wagon for the four-block trip. Back inside, he lined his market basket with a feed sack and carefully placed the hot pot into the basket. Finally, he held his canteen underneath the pump and primed the handle, letting cold, fresh water fill the container.

Now he was ready. *Go with me, Lord.*

Over and over, for strength to make this journey, he recited the passage Reverend Thompson had preached on, words he'd spent the night memorizing.

> Dearly beloved, avenge not yourselves, but
> rather give place unto wrath: for it is written,
> Vengeance is mine; I will repay, saith the
> Lord. Therefore if thine enemy hunger, feed
> him; if he thirst, give him drink: for in so
> doing thou shalt heap coals of fire on his
> head. Be not overcome of evil, but overcome
> evil with good.

Too quickly, he arrived at the jail. Balancing his load, he limped inside where the sheriff was handing a cup of coffee to Benton.

"Morning, Sheriff." Caleb cleared his throat. It wouldn't do for his voice to shake. "I'd like to have a word with Benton."

The lawman frowned. Understandably so, as the entire town doubtlessly knew of the enmity between Benton Calloway and Caleb Morgan.

"What do you have there?"

"I've brought Benton some cold water and a pot of stew."

"Water and stew? Why? We feed him here."

"As a..." How could he explain how he was sure God had pressed this on his heart? "It's the least I could do. There's plenty for you too."

The sheriff lifted the cover and sniffed the food. "Well...I don't know why you're doing this, but it ain't poisoned, is it?"

"No, sir."

Benton banged his cup on the bars, splattering coffee on the floor. "Take it away! I don't want it!"

"Settle down in there," Sheriff Flint commanded. "If he's brought it already, we're gonna eat it." He turned to Caleb and motioned with his head toward the cells. "Go on."

"Thank you."

"Keep him away from me!" Benton hollered.

"Benton." Caleb spoke softly. "I've come to... I'm here to tell you I forgive you for the wrongs you've done to me."

Benton hooted. "You're forgiving me? I told you, you're of no account!"

"And to ask you to forgive me for the wrongs I've done to you."

There was silence for a moment as Benton's mouth hung open. "What are you really here for?"

Caleb smiled. The answer to that was simple. "'Therefore if thine enemy hunger, feed him; if he thirst, give him drink... Be not overcome of evil, but overcome evil with good.' That's why. Out of obedience to God."

Benton turned his back on Caleb. "Get out of here."

"I just have one more thing to say to you, Benton." Caleb's heart was beating hard. "May God's peace be with you." With that, he complied with Benton's order and turned to leave.

"Morgan." The sheriff stopped him as Caleb headed for the door. "Thank you for bringing the food. Even if Calloway won't eat it, I will." He stared at Caleb, then shook his head. "You're a real man of God."

Surprised, Caleb nodded at the sheriff. Once the door closed behind him, Caleb leaned against the building. Benton hadn't accepted his water or his stew. Or his forgiveness. Maybe he had misunderstood what God meant for him to do. Because this mission had failed. Benton still considered Caleb his enemy.

Therefore if thine enemy hunger, feed him; if he thirst, give him drink...

He had done that. As hard as it had been, he had offered his enemy food and drink.

Dearly beloved, avenge not yourselves, but rather give place unto wrath... Be not overcome of evil, but overcome evil with good.

Could that be all that God had asked him to do—simply obey His word? And then to let God Himself deal with Benton's heart? The words from Reverend Thompson that day after church came to him.

"When you hear God's words in a whisper, listen hard. And follow them. He's the one who changes hearts."

Breathing deeply, Caleb tried to get his heartbeat to settle back to normal. Once it slowed, a peacefulness enveloped him, as though God was whispering to his soul. *Well done, thou good and faithful servant.*

With a smile, he walked over to Ruby. "So, girl," he said, rubbing her neck, "perhaps I didn't fail, after all."

Grimacing, he boosted himself up into the wagon. "Let's go, Ruby." Just as he raised the reins, he let them drop into his lap. Barely fifteen feet away stood Eliza, watching him.

He hadn't seen her since the brawl on her property. She didn't know he had asked God to forgive him for his bitterness. That he was trying to be obedient to God's word, that he had a new joy and peace. And that he missed her and wanted to make things right with her.

He tipped his hat and smiled. Had she accepted his apology in his note to her? Perhaps now he might even be given a chance to beg her forgiveness in person.

"Good morning, Eliza." He started to climb down from the wagon. "I would like to—"

The scowl on her face made him stop halfway, one foot on the ground, the other still resting on the wagon board. Before he could move or say another word, she spun around, turning her back on him, and marched down the road, kicking up a cloud of dust behind her.

~

*E*liza hurried down the street, away from that despicable Caleb Morgan. What had he been doing at the jail? Trying to convince Benton to go into cahoots with him? Plotting how together they could get the Double E away from her?

She had seen enough. She certainly didn't need to stand and listen to him smooth-talk her into believing anything he said. Especially with that smile, the way it made him look so honest, so guileless, so...appealing. *Hmph.* She quickened her pace. If she didn't keep her distance from him, he probably would be able to hoodwink her again.

After finishing her errands in town, she needed to get back to where she had hitched Biscuit and the buggy. George, kind as always, had insisted on harnessing up Biscuit himself and giving Rosey a day off as well.

"Miss Wilkins—Miss Wilkins!" a man's frantic voice called out behind her.

As pounding steps gained on her, Eliza stepped aside before she got knocked over in the man's haste. But when he reached her, he stopped, his sides heaving from exertion.

"Excuse me, Miss Wilkins. I'm Harvey Garrett. I bought one of your horses in—"

Eliza looked at the stocky man in surprise. "I'm sorry. You must have me mixed up with someone else. I'm not Miss Wilkins."

The man stared her full in the face, then his eyes widened. "So you're not. I beg your pardon, ma'am." He peered at her again. "You look so much like her, though, you sure could be related. Your hair, your height... I'm sorry. Please forgive me."

Eliza smiled at the rattled man. "Of course."

"Are you?"

"I beg your pardon?"

"Related to Kitty Wilkins?"

"No, I'm not." Who was Kitty Wilkins?

"Surely, you realize why I mistook you for her, though."

"No, I'm afraid I don't. I've never even heard of her." Eliza smiled ruefully.

He looked at her incredulously. "Never heard of Kitty Wilkins? Why, she's the most talked-of woman in the state. Mighty tall like you, lots of hair your same color. That's why I mistook you for her. Why—" He scrutinized her again, shaking his head. "You even got her blue eyes and perty smile."

"I'm rather new here. Who is she?"

"She's the Horse Queen of Idaho. She breeds and sells horses all over the country. Just back in the spring, she came to Boise to prove up a homestead. The newspapers are declaring her the only woman in America earning her livelihood by horse trading alone. Being a spinster and all, I guess she had to figure out some way to fend for herself."

"An unmarried lady breeding and trading horses?"

"Yep. Mighty profitable too. As I said, she's the talk of the state."

Horses.

If this Miss Wilkins could run a profitable business with horses, then perhaps there was a way to save the Double E. While Eliza didn't know anything about cattle or roundups, she did know some about horses.

"Sir, I'd like to hear more about her, if you have a few minutes?"

He pulled out a pocket watch and checked it. "I have a train to catch, but yes, I have a few minutes. What would you like to know?"

"All you can tell me. How she got started and grew her reputation. Who she does business with, whether ranches or individuals. What breeds of horses she works with."

He chuckled. "Are you thinking of getting into the horse-breeding business as well?"

"Oh, no, sir. I wouldn't want to compete with Miss Wilkins, and I don't know anything as far as breeding and selling. But I was thinking maybe I could train them to be saddle horses."

He nodded. "You have spunk, just like Miss Wilkins, I must say. I'll tell you what I do know, and I'm sure if you ask anyone who's around horses much, they can add to it."

Eliza listened raptly to Miss Wilkins's history. Trained as a pianist but turned horsewoman. How, unlike Eliza, Miss Wilkins had been around the business of horses her entire life, learning from her parents. And how her success had grown.

Surely, Eliza could learn a new trade, especially if she found the right horse trainer to teach her.

"I hope this helped, young lady."

"Yes. Thank you, Mr. Garrett, for taking time to talk with me."

"It's been my pleasure. I wish you well in your ventures. Maybe one day I'll be hearing of you right along with Miss Wilkins." He tipped his hat. "Again, please forgive my mistake."

Oh, Mr. Garrett spotting her and mistaking her for Kitty Wilkins had not been a mistake at all—but providential.

"Good day." Eliza stared after him.

When Eliza returned to the Double E, Nellie was bustling around in the kitchen.

"Nellie, where's George?"

"Out in back of the barn, probably waiting to hear the dinner bell."

"Is it time to ring it? I need to talk to both of you."

"Is this about the ranch?"

"Yes, but this might be good news."

"Well then, go ahead and ring the bell." Nellie took a steaming pot of chicken stew off the burner. "By the time he gets himself washed up, I'll have these biscuits ready."

Once the three of them were seated around the table, they bowed their heads as George asked the blessing. Faithful

George. Even with the burden of running what was left of the ranch falling totally on him now, he insisted he wouldn't abandon her and Nellie. And if her idea worked, she could pay both him and Nellie soundly for their loyalty through the hard times.

And, Lord, Eliza added silently to George's prayer, *please help as I share my plan with George and Nellie. Only let them agree to it if this is from You.*

"Amen," they all chorused and began eating Nellie's savory stew.

After a few bites, Eliza set her spoon down. "Nellie, George, have you heard of Kitty Wilkins?"

"She's that horse-selling lady." George dipped a biscuit into his stew.

Nellie harrumphed. "Horse Queen of Idaho. If I were younger, I could do that myself. Not the breeding part, but anyone who knows a lick about horses could trade them and make a living at it."

"Do you really think so, Nellie?" Eliza leaned forward, hardly daring to consider her idea herself.

"Of course. Even you could, if you had a notion to."

"Well..." She took a deep breath and smiled. "A man in town today mistook me for Miss Wilkins. We got talking, and I had an idea, so I asked him questions about her and her business."

"What's your idea?" Nellie took another bite from her bowl.

"I was thinking, what if we could do something similar and save the Double E?"

Both Nellie and George stopped chewing their food and stared at her.

Nellie swallowed first. "Breed and sell horses?"

"No, neither one. But what if we could buy horses, saddle train them, and then sell them as riding horses?"

Silence.

Eliza tucked her head. She'd try to come up with another idea, one her trusted workers considered reasonable.

"Could we?" Nellie looked at George.

Slowly, he resumed chewing. At last, he swallowed. "Reckon we could."

Eliza wanted to jump up and shout hallelujah. But she needed to be practical, to make sure this could really work. "Did you ever train wild horses?"

He nodded. "Some. But I learned plenty from watching the best of them—Caleb Morgan and Gus."

"Gus was a horse tamer?"

"Yep. Every year at roundup, he'd close down his saddle shop and come out to help Mr. Roberts."

"His saddle shop? He was a saddlemaker too?"

"Yes. Tried at one time or another to teach all of us ranch hands that were here back then. Caleb was the only one who took to it much, though. That's why Gus sold his shop to Caleb when—well, when he was ready to put aside his tools."

Eliza could picture Caleb gentling a wild stallion, as patient and kind as he was with animals. But Gus? All the time she had spent talking with him, she had never known any of this about him. "If we decide to try this, would you and Gus—if he'll help us—train the horses? And figure out where to get them."

"That's easy." George finished off another biscuit in two bites and pushed his bowl away. "Buy an unbroken string from someone—or ride out to the Owyhees and see if we can find a few wild ones."

"Which would be the quickest?" Eliza's heart was beating faster as they talked about the possibilities.

"Finding a string would be easier than climbing the mountains—but paying for it might be near impossible."

"Maybe we can sell what cattle are left." Nellie looked at Eliza, then George. "Only keep what we'll need for milk and meat."

"Yes." Eliza looked at George also. "What do you think? Change over completely from a cattle ranch to a horse ranch?"

George grinned. "They're fatted up. Should sell quickly."

"Well, then." Eliza gave her schoolmarm clap. "When can you take the cattle to market and find us a few horses to start our business with?"

Nellie stood. "He can go tomorrow. I'll start cooking up some food for his journey."

George rose also and shrugged. "Guess I'd better tidy things up around the ranch if I'm going to be gone a few days."

"I'll go out and help in the barn." Eliza stood and trailed George out the door. "Tell me what you need, and I'll gather up supplies." Together they headed to the barn.

"Miss Eliza, could you get me all the ropes you can find?" George asked.

"Certainly." Eliza hurried to the tack area and retrieved every one hanging over the worktable, then looked around for more. As she scurried about, a piece of paper fluttered onto the barn floor. Where had it come from? Only her Morgan saddle was nearby. She reached for the note, not recognizing the handwriting.

Dear Miss Eliza,

I am most sorry for my bad behavior. I had wanted to protect you from Benton Calloway, but in so doing, I did not abide by your grandfather's order to never step foot again upon his land. If I had not compromised his wish, perhaps you would not have been attacked nor witnessed such disorderliness in myself. From henceforth, until my name has been cleared, I shall honor his request as well as your own. Rest assured that I shall not visit the Double E nor bring reproach to you again.

Sincerely,

Caleb Morgan

How long had this note been lying here? She turned the paper over, looking for any clue. The last time he was here was the day of the fight. Had he placed it here then, perhaps when he had returned the harness rigging after taking Benton to jail? If so, then how rude he must have thought her this morning when she'd stormed off without speaking to him.

She read the note again, a warmth filling her heart. *I had wanted to protect you...*

He was a strange one, all right. Ever since she had met him, he had been bitter. Yet today, there he was with a smile on his face. One that had certainly looked real. Well, she had another idea. Tomorrow she would ride out and ask Gus if he would help break horses for the ranch to sell. And while she was there, she had a saddlebag of questions for him. And this time, she wasn't leaving until he had answered every one of them.

CHAPTER 19

*T*he next morning, Eliza left as soon as breakfast was over to pay a visit to Gus, eager to lay out her plan for a horse ranch. At his cabin, she stepped onto the porch and raised her hand to knock just as he flung the door open.

"Good morning, Eliza. I spotted you coming. Get inside now, out of the cold."

Eliza welcomed the warmth wafting from Gus's small home. Shivering, she stepped inside.

"How about some coffee to warm you up a bit?"

"Yes, please." She took the seat he motioned to with his head. Within moments, he was sitting on the other chair and scooting a cup of steaming coffee across the table to her.

"Well, now, it's too early for pie." He winked. "And you look like you're all business today."

"That I am, Gus." She smiled in her excitement. "I'd like to ask your advice—and your help."

"Certainly. What can an old coot like me help a young lass with?"

She took a deep breath. "I understand you're the best horse tamer around."

"You been listening to old gossip down at Daniel's place?" But his eyes were bright with interest.

"No. George told me. I have a plan to salvage Grandfather's —my—ranch. I'd like to buy some untamed horses, gentle and saddle train them, and sell them."

"Ah, the horse-trading business. Another Kitty Wilkins, eh?"

Eliza laughed. "Not exactly, but something similar. I was wondering if you could help us out with breaking the horses to sell as riding horses."

Gus pursed his lips, then nodded. "Perhaps I can... Yes, I think I'll do just that."

"Thank you. But before I can take you on as an employee" —she directed a no-nonsense, schoolmarm look at him—"I have some questions that you need to answer." Eliza squelched a smile. If she wasn't mistaken, Gus had squirmed in his seat like one of her students caught passing notes in class.

He sighed loudly. "Well, Eliza, what is it you're hankering to know now?"

"Why Grandfather dismissed Caleb Morgan as his foreman."

"I should have known you wouldn't leave well enough alone." Gus lapsed into silence until Eliza gave him another pointed look. "Why are you so bent on knowing things?"

"I think perhaps an injustice has been done."

"And you're the one to right it?"

Eliza smiled. "Perhaps."

"Just like Elliott." He got a faraway look in his eyes, then laid his hand on top of Eliza's. "He loved his family...including you. He hated being separated from them and always felt bad that they didn't understand. He felt God called him here. But his love wasn't just for the land. It was for the people here."

Grandfather Roberts sounded exactly like the kind of man she yearned for, one who loved a plain-looking woman and had a passion for God. At one time, she had thought Caleb Morgan might become a man like that. But perhaps there would never be another man like Grandfather. And yet he had been misunderstood and judged by his own family.

Gus released her hand. "Well, since you're bound and determined to know things, I'll tell you. You'd be hearing it from someone eventually, anyway." He began slowly, as if some things were too hard to speak of.

"Caleb's had his share of troubles, all right. Now there was an honorable man, Elliott and I thought, if there ever was one. But we're all sinners, through and through." He leaned forward. "Caleb was the best foreman Elliott ever had. Hard working. Quick to learn. Picked up on saddle making right quick too."

"From you, isn't that right?"

He opened his mouth as if ready to evade the question, but then closed it with a sigh. "Yes, from me. And gentling horses. Why, even wild animals seemed to know they could trust him. Anyway, Caleb kept the books for the ranch. He was so good at it, Elliott never checked them over. Which turned out to be a mistake. If Caleb said the money was coming in, that was all that mattered. His word was good."

"Grandfather said in his letter he trusted Caleb."

"He had. Up to that point." A sadness crept into his eyes. "So when Benton brought concerns to his attention, Elliott checked the ledgers for himself. When he saw the entries, he had no choice but to believe the figures. It seems Caleb had been entering wrong numbers, stealing money from the Double E a little here, a little there, until the ranch was having trouble. When Elliott confronted him with the ledger page proving this, Caleb stormed out. And promptly got into an all-out fight with Benton Calloway. Left Caleb with a few broken ribs and a limp. Even if Elliott hadn't fired him, he wouldn't have been able to ride roundups anymore or do the lifting and hard work required of a foreman. Benton became the new foreman on the spot."

"How did Benton discover this 'evidence'?"

"Well, now, he'd become suspicious, and one day when the men were out in the field repairing fences and Elliott had gone into town, Caleb needed more wire from the barn, and Benton volunteered to go. Apparently, he took that opportunity to sneak into the house and look at the ledgers. Nellie came in, and he tore out a page before she chased him out. Later that night when Elliott returned, Benton showed it to him. Your grandfather, of course, didn't want to believe it and checked the ledger himself, especially the nearby pages. But he was convinced after seeing the entries."

Eliza wrapped her hands around the now-cold cup of coffee. "The day Benton was put in jail, when both he and Caleb came out to the ranch, Caleb told Benton the ledger page had been altered."

Gus shrugged. "That's been his story from the start. Never would admit guilt. Elliott wanted to believe him, but Elliott had the page to prove otherwise. Now, don't get me wrong. Up until then, Caleb had always been upright. But facts are facts."

"What made Benton suspicious in the first place? As he wasn't the one doing the books then."

"He— Well, I don't rightly know. I guess that part was between him and your grandfather. Elliott never told me."

Eliza sighed. "I see. So the whole town knows this?"

"Well, I wouldn't say the whole town. Caleb is closed-mouthed. Mostly, people like to speculate. And Caleb's saddle making has brought a lot of business into town, so many don't want to turn totally against him."

"Was Caleb always bitter?"

"Ah, that's another sad outcome of this story." Gus shook his head. "He used to be very pleasant. He was like a son—or grandson, I should say—to Elliott and Elizabeth. He was very godly."

A godly man.

Eliza wanted to weep for Caleb, for his hurts, his losses, for what he had let bitterness do to him. Yet the way he had smiled at her yesterday—there had been no hint of bitterness in his eyes, on his face. What had happened to change that? If anyone knew, Gus would. And today Gus was finally talking.

"Yesterday I saw him in Caldwell outside the jail. And he was smiling."

"Humph. No wonder there. He must be quite satisfied, getting revenge on Calloway, getting him locked up and all."

Surely, that wasn't it, was it? If so, what was she doing here, thinking she could right a wrong? "Perhaps." She stood. "Thank you for telling me these things, Gus. And for agreeing to help train the horses. Once George and I put our plan together, I'll be back to discuss your wages."

Gus waved her words aside and walked her to the door. "Don't worry about that yet. Just send word when you get your horses, and I'll be ready."

"I will."

So she finally had her answers from Gus. But she still wasn't satisfied. What if Caleb was telling the truth? Strangely, she wanted to believe in him again. If he was innocent, she had to help him prove it—though she had no idea how. Benton was capable of much deceit—that she knew. But Caleb?

With a heavy heart, she walked down the steps, mounted Rosey, and headed her back to the ranch. All the way down the dusty road, the memory of Caleb's earnest smile kept her company.

*C*aleb had been working since early morning on another saddle, one a man over in Boise had ordered. At least he had plenty of orders to keep him busy, keep his mind off...well, off things he most certainly wished to not dwell on in all the peace and quiet in the shop.

"Caleb, you back there?" Now what did Gus want? For avoiding him for months, Caleb sure had been crossing paths with him too often lately. Here it was only midmorning, and already he was in town. "Hello?"

"I'm here. I'll be right out." Caleb set down his tools and walked out to find Gus making his way around the big room, stopping at each saddle, and almost reverently running a hand over it. Did he miss his old shop, the feel of leather under his hands? The workmanship and satisfaction of creating something that endured rugged days of cattle roping and horse wrangling?

Even though this job wasn't Caleb's initial dream, he had found in Gus's training of how to work with horses and how to make saddles something fulfilling. Maybe something that now he did love, possibly even more than being foreman. Like a calling.

And strangely, maybe he had Benton Calloway to thank for that. Or God. Had God used circumstances to move him from the ranch right here to this shop? And even that Gus had sold it to him, considering how Gus felt about him?

"Nice work, Caleb." Gus didn't turn to look at Caleb, just kept making his way from saddle to saddle until he'd touched every one of them. "I hate to say it, but I couldn't do any better."

Oh.

"Thank you. You came to see me? Or"—he tried for a lighter tone—"are you looking for a new saddle?"

"If I didn't have one, I'd be proud to own any one of these. But I did come to see you. About some business."

Of course. "Yes?"

"I told her."

"You told who what?"

"That purty Miss Eliza. Elliott's granddaughter. I knew she wouldn't leave well enough alone, and she shore didn't."

"Gus, why don't you sit and explain yourself."

Gus pulled up a chair and plunked himself down. And Caleb sat, too, figuring this was not going to be good.

"Yessir, she come riding out early this morning and point-blank asked me why her grandfather fired you as foreman out at the Double E. She wasn't about to let me dodge any questions again, so what could I tell her but the truth?"

"Of course." The truth that he should have told her to begin with. "I should have been the one to tell her I'd even been the foreman. But I didn't. She learned it from Benton Calloway."

"That doesn't surprise me one iota. But I told her exactly what Elliott told me."

"That numbers don't lie? Mr. Roberts was adamant about that. And they don't. But people do." Caleb tamped down the anger—or maybe it wasn't even so much anger anymore but an emptiness. A sorrow that he could never fix now with Mr. Roberts gone.

"I told her the facts."

"Right. The 'facts' that Benton just happened to share."

"Now hold up, son."

Gus eyed him steadily, as if assessing him, looking for something, and Caleb refused to look away. He was innocent with nothing to hide—and no need to be belligerent. Especially not toward Gus. Gus, who almost appeared to be here as a...friend?

"Now let me finish." Gus settled back in his chair. "I told her the facts as related to me by Elliott. Now, have you ever asked me if I believed them?"

Caleb drew in a deep breath while he tempered his words. "I know you did."

"And you're right. I did. But I believe your Miss Eliza was there asking questions on your behalf. She thinks an injustice has been done."

"An injustice. She said that?"

"She did. Her very words."

Caleb crossed his arms. "Toward me?"

"Yep."

Now he was beyond confused. Why would Eliza ever say that? Considering how she'd scowled at him just yesterday. Turned her back on him and wouldn't even listen to a word he said. Even after apologizing in his note to her.

"And," Gus continued, "she's the one asking the right questions. The very ones all of us should have asked. Maybe Elliott did. I don't know. Even if he did, who knows what Calloway told him. But I admit, I did not." He looked Caleb straight in the eyes. "And I'm sorry for that."

Caleb nodded in acknowledgment. If Gus could admit that, Caleb could at least be gracious. "So what questions would those be?"

"How and what. How did Benton discover the evidence— the ledger page—he presented to Elliott?"

"You know as well as I do. He was snooping around and tore it out of the ledger. But he altered it before showing it to Mr. Roberts."

"Yes, so you've said. And her other question was what. What made Benton even go looking for numbers when he wasn't doing the entries himself?"

"I don't know. What's the answer to that?" Caleb was itching to be done with this conversation. He had work to do and—

Gus reached over and put a hand on Caleb's knee. "That, I don't know either. Elliott never shared it with me. And now I'm wondering if he ever asked. But that makes me wonder. It seems mighty convenient."

Caleb looked Gus in the eye. "Are you saying—"

"Yes. I believe you."

"You—" He cleared his throat from the sudden clog in it. "You believe that all along I've been innocent and telling the truth?"

"I do now. All thanks to your Eliza. Persistent, just like her grandmother, is all I can say."

Caleb blinked his eyes that were suddenly misty. Gus. Eliza. Both supporting him? *Thank You, God.*

"But hold up, son. I said *I* believe you. And I'm apologizing to you right now for believing otherwise. But we still need to somehow prove this. Do you understand?"

"I do. And thank you."

Gus lifted his hand from Caleb's knee and held it out, then retracted it. "Oh, forget a handshake." He stood and pulled Caleb up and into an embrace. One that felt like being in Mr. Roberts's presence again. Accepted. Loved. Like a grandson.

And just as suddenly, Gus released him. "All righty, now that we got all that out of the way... Eliza told me you were smiling when she last seen you yesterday by the jail. I told her you were just satisfied, what with you getting revenge on Calloway, getting him locked up and all. But now I'm seeing something in you. And again, I'm a-thinking I was wrong."

"I'm the one who was wrong." Caleb shook his head. He was still overcome by it. "But I forgave Benton. Asked him to forgive me too."

"Well, I'll be. Did he?"

"No. But I'm going to try to live God's way again. As Eliza says, glory to God and peace. And that's why I can smile."

"Glory be." Gus slapped him on the back. "And actually, I might be in the market for some saddles, after all."

"Is that right?" Caleb lifted one brow.

"Not me, but the Double E. In case you haven't heard, it looks like the ranch is going to get back on its feet. Eliza appears to be quite a businesswoman. She's going to buy or have George locate some untamed horses, and then him and me are going to train them as riding horses."

"Eliza came up with this idea?"

"Yep."

Caleb shouldn't be surprised, as spunky Eliza, of course, was very capable.

"And on top of that, we got to come up with a plan to prove your innocence to the whole town. And I'm here to help. And" —he winked—"I do believe our Eliza Roberts will be more than glad to help us out too." He tipped his hat and walked out of the saddlery.

"Glory be is right," Caleb whispered. He wasn't much of a talking man, but he sure could use someone to talk about this with right now. But the only face that came to mind was Eliza's.

And though from Gus's story she apparently now did believe him, as of yesterday, she still wasn't wanting to talk to him.

CHAPTER 20

*E*liza spent the next few days making plans for this new business of the Double E, hardly daring to believe it was possible. And that she'd already been blessed with having knowledgeable workers in Gus and George. But even in the busyness, at the most inopportune times—such as clearing away the supper dishes tonight—Caleb's smile would sneak into her thoughts again.

What had changed the gruff, bitter man into one with an open gaze and a smile? And he'd been coming out of the sheriff's office with that expression. The place where Benton Calloway was locked up. The more she thought about Gus's assessment, that it was one of satisfaction in getting revenge, she was sure that couldn't be the cause. It wasn't a sly, victorious look. But one of— If she didn't know better, she'd say peace. Crazy. And yet that's exactly what was radiating from Caleb's eyes.

More and more, she sensed an injustice had been done to Caleb. But how could she ever prove his innocence?

Kep jumped up from lying under the table, and Eliza all but

tripped over him with the last of the dishes in her hands. Wagging his tail and barking, he trotted to the kitchen window.

Eliza set the dishes down and followed Kep to see what his commotion was about. With one look out the window, Eliza ran to the door to let Kep out. "Nellie! Come quickly! The horses are here!"

She and Nellie grabbed their coats and ran outside just as George rode into the yard guiding three skittish horses roped together. Quickly, he loosed them in the paddock and dismounted his own horse.

"Gus should be here soon." He grinned. "He saw me passing by."

"They're beautiful!" Eliza stepped up onto the rail, watching the horses as they bolted from one corner to another now that they were free from the tether.

"They're rambunctious now, but they are a godsend. I found a man north of Boise who had bought them and already started training them. But he ended up needing to move and sell the horses. So we already have a head start for our first attempt at this."

Nellie grinned at Eliza and George. "Well, well. It looks like the Double E is back in business. George, you get yourself cleaned up and get on inside. There's leftover biscuits and chicken I'll warm up for you."

George nodded. "Will do."

Shortly after George had eaten and all three stepped outside again, Gus rode up. He studied the new horses a few moments, then nodded to Nellie. Some signal passed between them, and she hurried back to the house.

"Good-looking group. Eliza, you start with the bay. George and I'll get these other two separated from him."

"Me?" Eliza squeaked out. "I don't know anything about training a horse. That's your and George's job."

"We're not doing any training tonight. They need to rest after their trip. You're just going to get him to calm down."

"But how?" The bay was bigger than any of the Double E horses.

"Introduce yourself, make him feel welcome. That's all we'll do tonight."

"You can do it," George said. "Gus taught all of the ranch hands. And these horses are used to people already."

"But they're so—so—" She watched the horses paw the ground and toss their heads. "Lively."

"All the better," Gus said with a laugh. He and George moved quickly to separate the others from the bay. "All right, Eliza, get in the paddock with him."

"Wait." Nellie came trotting out of the house, holding a bunch of carrots with the stems still on top. "Here you go."

Gus took them from Nellie and handed them to Eliza. "Put these in your pocket."

Eliza did so, then climbed over the railing and stood clinging to it. "What do I do now?"

"Just stand there. Don't move."

Eliza pressed herself tighter against the boards while George and Gus seated themselves atop the rails. It was just her and the bay alone in the training area.

The horse eyed her and pawed the ground. Eliza stood rooted to her spot, not daring to move. The big bay took a step forward, shortening the distance between them.

"Gus—"

"Stay still," he whispered.

Eliza closed her eyes, breathing hard. *Stay...still. Breathe.* She opened her eyes and there was the horse, barely five feet away, looking her right in the eyes. He had stopped pawing the ground and shaking his head. He seemed...curious? Eliza gripped the fencepost at her back as she realized the horse was coming yet closer.

"The carrots—give him a carrot."

Eliza could barely hear Gus's soft command. With slow movements, she pulled out a large carrot from her pocket and thrust it like a sword toward the horse. The bay shied away, then stretched his head forward, sniffing. Fear paralyzed Eliza as the horse's huge head came closer and closer to her. With a quick fling of his head, he grabbed the carrot from her hand.

"Oh!"

With two swift chomps, he devoured his treat.

"Give him another one." George grinned from his spot on the rail.

This time, when Eliza held out a carrot, the bay walked right up to her and stood at her feet as he munched it.

"Why, you liked that, didn't you, boy?" Eliza murmured. Tentatively, she touched the horse's face. "I was just as scared as you were. But it's not so bad, is it?"

"You did it." Gus slid off the railing into the paddock and stood a few feet away from Eliza.

She moved her hand to rub the bay's neck. "We did, didn't we, boy?"

"Now walk across the paddock." Gus pointed as he spoke.

She took a few steps away from the safety of the rail. Her heart pounded again as the big animal turned and followed her. A few more steps, and he was right behind her, all the way across the enclosed area.

Eliza turned to the horse. "Why, you're a good boy, aren't you?"

In reply, the horse pushed her with his big head.

"Oh! You're a smart one, aren't you?" She laughed and dug into her pocket one more time. "You knew there was one more carrot for you, didn't you?" This time, she laid it on her open palm, amazed at the gentleness with which the horse ate it from her hand.

"Come on back." Gus grinned at her. "You're a natural. You

have that special gift, just like Caleb. Tomorrow we'll start work with them. And already the other two have calmed down too. Well done, Eliza."

She smiled at Gus's praise. And whether she had a special gift like Caleb had or not, it seemed that God's blessing was indeed upon this new endeavor.

~

*E*liza found she loved working with the horses, winning their confidence and trust. And she fast lost her fear of the huge animals. Once they were comfortable around her, Gus and George stepped in, working with bit and saddle. They discovered the horses were farther along than George had thought, and toward the end of the second week, he and Gus were confident that these three were ridable for experienced riders.

On Saturday, George and Eliza headed off to market in Caldwell with their first three riding horses in tow.

"Do you think anyone will buy them?" Eliza asked. What if she'd made a mistake? Or the horses needed more training?

"We won't know until we get there." George tipped his hat up as he rode. "But with asking a fair price for gentled horses, I expect they'll sell quickly." He turned around to look at the bay they had first started with. "I'm going to miss him."

"Me too. We'll be able to buy more horses with the money we get for him and the others. But once we're established as horse trainers and start making a good profit, I'm hoping we'll be able to increase the number of Double E horses as well."

When they arrived at the horse market, the area was already teeming with wagons and carriages and fine-looking horses. The Double E horses added to the noise with their own snorts and whinnies. While many of the horses looked to be wild mustangs from the mountains, hopefully, there would be homesteaders and businessmen here wanting to buy tamed riding horses.

George raised his voice over the screams of wild horses and shouts of cowboys. "Let's find a spot to wait and then one of us can go check in."

"Over there?" Eliza pointed to a less-congregated section under a tree, and George led the way over and dismounted as a man he seemed to know walked over.

"Heard you were entering the horse-training business now. This your stock?"

George patted the bay on the neck. "Yes. The Double E's first ones. Saddle-broke, good riding horses."

"Already trained?" The man cocked his head. "That's interesting. I'll be looking around. Good to see you, George. Ma'am." He nodded at Eliza and walked on to view another group of horses.

The three horses sold quickly, and more people gathered around Eliza and George afterward.

"Do you have any more to sell?"

"Didn't know the Double E was in the horse-training business now. You going to be bringing more horses?"

Questions were flung at them from all directions.

"Well, what do we have here?" An old gentleman looked from Eliza to George. "Looks like we've got our own Horse Queen of Idaho right here."

"Nah, that's Kitty Wilkins's title," a Caldwell resident said. "Eliza is the Horse Princess of Caldwell."

"She's more like an angel with her golden halo of hair," someone else put in.

"Yes, sir, that's it! She's an angel—our own Angel from the East!"

While the crowd loudly grabbed onto the name, all Eliza could do was force a smile. When she had arrived in Caldwell, that was exactly what she had wanted to be—a model of the angels at Jesus's birth, someone joyfully praising God. Someone proclaiming glory to God in the highest and on earth peace.

But now, after the hardships here—of nearly losing the ranch, being hoodwinked by Benton and let down by Caleb, and nearly trampled—her joy had been extinguished, replaced by fear. She was so undeserving of such a beautiful name. Yet the crowd was not listening.

"Shall we head back?" Eliza asked George.

"Yes, ma'am. I'd call our first market day a success."

She nodded. "The money from today is a good start to getting the ranch back on its feet." And once it was up and running again and with George and Gus in charge of the horses...well, she'd see what her next step would be. As she'd be free to leave.

So, tired and weary, she and George saddled their horses to head back to the Double E. But as they passed the penned area still holding horses, Eliza felt someone staring at her. She turned to search the faces of the folks lingering. And there on the edge stood Caleb Morgan, eyes on her. But the look he gave her was unsettling, for this time, there was no doubt about it. He was a man of peace.

But how could that be when her own heart was no longer so?

❧

*C*aleb stood in the shadows of the horse pen watching Eliza and George ride off. He hadn't expected Eliza to catch him staring at her. And yet, what else could he do? This was the first time he'd laid eyes on her since she turned her back on him after his visit with Benton at the jail. Even still, though she wanted nothing to do with him, he couldn't stop thinking of her. Had wanted just to feast his eyes on her for these moments.

He was so proud of how she was endeavoring to save the Double E. And the Angel from the East. What a befitting name for her.

Yet something was shadowed in her eyes, her features, in that brief glance. Of course, he expected that they would be around him, but something was missing. That spark she'd had.

The joy she had come to Caldwell with.

"Mister Caleb!" Virginia Billings came skipping up to him, ahead of her mother and two sisters.

"And what are you all doing out here at the horse market?" He ruffled the girl's hair.

"We came to see all these horses. Aren't they pretty? But I came to see you because Mama says you're a goodly man."

"No, Virginia." The elder sister, Lila, caught up to her. "Godly. Mister Caleb is a godly man."

By now, Mrs. Billings and Rosita approached as well. "Yes," Mrs. Billings said, "we heard the sheriff talking over at the mercantile about how you came to visit Mr. Calloway one day back with a canteen of water and a pot of savory stew."

"And you forgave him for being mean to you," Rosita added. "But he wouldn't forgive you even though you were being nice to him."

Mrs. Billings smiled at Rosita, then him. "I told my girls what a godly man you are. Just like the Bible says, heaping coals of fire on his head with kindness, asking for and offering forgiveness. Thank you for being an example of a godly man to my little ones. It means a lot to me to be able to point out to them how a man of God lives."

Never before had Caleb been held up as a good, much less godly, example for anyone to follow. "Thank you, ma'am." He knelt on one knee before the girls. "Your mama is right. Those words are from the Bible—if your enemy is hungry, feed him, if he's thirsty, give him a drink. I was just trying to do what God said to do. But that doesn't mean it's easy. It was a very hard thing to do. I prayed real hard for God to help me. And He did. So, girls, remember that it's always better to obey God."

Lila solemnly nodded. "We will, Mister Caleb."

"Me too," Rosita and Virginia chorused.

"We came to see Miss Eliza's horses," Virginia added. "She's so pretty too."

"That she is." Caleb looked in the direction Eliza had ridden off, catching one last glimpse of her golden hair among the crowds.

"Come along, girls." Mrs. Billings gathered her brood around her, and they all waved, then headed toward their home.

He turned to go back to the saddlery, and a couple men here and there nodded in greeting. And then there was Gus in front of him.

"Caleb. You come over to see the Double E flourishing again?"

Caleb shrugged. "Guess so. You all did an impressive job."

"Once word gets out about the caliber of these horses and the Angel from the East, I expect sales will be high. And the Double E will be known across the state. And that brings me to a proposal for you."

"Which is?" Caleb couldn't imagine what that would be. Certainly, he wasn't being invited back to the ranch.

"Buyers of a new horse will likely need another saddle. I was thinking, we could sell each horse *with* a saddle—a Morgan saddle. What do you think?"

That would bring in all the business he could handle. He could expand his shop, offer specialty saddles, work on new designs— "Did Eliza agree to this?"

"Uh, well now. Not exactly, seeing I haven't run it by her as of yet. But I don't 'spect there's going to be no objection."

"When she does agree, let me know." With that, he nodded to Gus and walked off.

As nice as the prospect of joining in with the Double E sounded, he wouldn't pin his hopes—or his business—on it. She hadn't responded to his letter. And with his new vow to honor, he couldn't approach her.

Unless...

CHAPTER 21

When Eliza reached the ranch after their trip into town, she greeted Nellie and told her about the sale of the horses. Then she went into the parlor to work on the mending. Maybe keeping her hands busy would also keep her mind occupied so she wasn't thinking about Caleb. But thoughts of his smile that day outside the jail still puzzled her. Even his look of peace today—as of a new man—had so taken her by surprise that she'd failed to respond in time with a pleasant greeting or wave. How she had believed Benton over him. How—

"Eliza?" Nellie stood in front of her wringing her hands.

She stopped stitching George's torn shirt. "What is it, Nellie?" Something surely was wrong.

"I feel so bad about what Benton did to you."

Eliza shivered, reliving the fright of Benton attacking her, his viciousness. "He's locked up tight. We're fine here."

Nellie shook her head. "He's a mean one, he is."

Eliza couldn't agree more, but she didn't want to worry Nellie any further. Still, Nellie didn't look relieved. "Is there something else bothering you?"

Nellie hung her head. When she lifted it, she didn't meet Eliza's eyes. "Yes." She took a deep breath. "This was my fault."

Eliza set the mending aside. "What do you mean? How could it be your fault?" She patted the chair next to her.

Nellie sat stiffly. Eliza got up and knelt down in front of Nellie, taking her hands in her own, rubbing them. "Why do you say that?"

The elderly woman sniffed a couple of times and wiped her eyes with her sleeve. "I always knew Caleb was innocent."

Eliza opened her mouth. How did she know? Why hadn't she said something? And proof—did she have proof? A kernel of joy wanted to burst in her heart that maybe Nellie did.

She closed her mouth. Pelting Nellie with questions would do no good. Better to listen.

"One evening several weeks after Caleb was dismissed as foreman, I announced at supper to Benton and George that as soon as the dishes were cleaned, I'd be taking a pot of stew over to sick Mrs. Barnes down the road. Folks all over were getting the fever. Mr. Roberts himself was already ill and quite weak, and I helped him into a chair in the parlor. George had some work to finish in the pasture, and Benton had chores in the barn, so I told Mr. Roberts I'd hurry right back so he wouldn't be alone for long. I packed up the meal, and on my way out I saw Benton coming from the bunkhouse. He offered to hitch up Rosey and the buggy for me so I could be off quicker. Such a gentleman, I thought." She shook her head.

"He stood on the porch, watching me go. But I'd forgotten the basket of rolls. I turned the buggy around and came back to get them. By then, he had disappeared. Back to the bunkhouse, I assumed. But when I stepped into the kitchen, I could hear Benton through the closed door to the parlor. 'Where is it?' He sounded so threatening. Mr. Roberts was very weak, so I wanted to be sure he was all right. I peeked through the keyhole, and Benton had his fist raised at Mr. Roberts! 'I don't know how you found it, but you'd better give it to me! Or you'll be sorry,' he said." Nellie's eyes were wide. "I didn't know whether to burst right in there and demand that he leave Mr. Roberts alone or what to do." She stopped.

"What *did* you do?" Eliza asked softly.

"I...didn't do anything." She hung her head. "That brute barged right into the kitchen door, about knocking me over. Then...then..." She began sobbing.

"Oh, Nellie." Eliza wrapped her arms around her friend. "What did he do when he knew you'd heard him?"

"He said I'd better not tell anyone what I heard and that I'd better find the ledger page myself. That if I told anyone, he'd..." She shuddered. "Then he left the house, and I locked the door. He's such an ill-tempered man, I knew he'd carry out his threats."

"He can't hurt you now that he's in jail. You're safe. And"— the thought comforted her even as she said the words—"Caleb promised he'd never let him bother us again."

Nellie wiped her eyes again. "When I went in to check on Mr. Roberts, he asked me to bring him a pen and two sheets of paper. After I did, he asked me to leave the room. He stayed up quite late. Then, when he called for me, he was so exhausted, I barely got him upstairs for the night. The next morning, he was feverish and mumbling things and so much worse that I summoned the doctor. But poor Mr. Roberts never recovered. Just like with the missus, within two days, he was gone."

Eliza fought back her own tears, imagining her grandfather during his last days.

"I found the letter he wrote to you. It was sitting on top of his Bible right there." Nellie pointed to the table next to the overstuffed chair. "I gave it to the lawyer, hoping he'd pass it on to you."

"He did," Eliza said. "It was attached to Mr. Taylor's letter and a copy of Grandfather's will. But it was only one page long. Did he write a second page or another letter?"

"The last thing he mumbled before falling asleep that night was, 'Please deliver the letters.' But I never found a second letter." Nellie frowned. "Not even the pen. I don't know where he could have put them. He was too weak to move from this chair without help. And once upstairs, he never left his bed."

"Did you tell Caleb about this?"

"Oh, no. I was afraid to even talk to Caleb because of Benton's threats. But I searched and searched for the ledger page. Even if I had found it, I would never have given it to Benton. I was going to give it to Caleb. But I have no idea where Mr. Roberts could have put it."

Eliza stood and helped Nellie to her feet. "Shall we look again? I'm thinking maybe if we find the second letter, we'll also find the missing ledger sheet." Again, the warm memory of Caleb's note cocooned itself around her heart. He hadn't been guilty of deceiving her grandfather—and he had come to protect her. He was honorable. And she desperately wanted to do the honorable thing, to help clear his name if she could.

Nellie shrugged. "Might as well. Maybe you'll find something. I've been over the area time and again."

Eliza walked over to the chair her grandfather had used. "Is this chair in the same place it was that night?"

"Yes. Everything is exactly the same. The Bible, the table, everything both down here and upstairs."

Eliza pulled open the table drawer. Empty. "Could Grandfather have given it to the physician?"

"No. He carried nothing upstairs with him. Even if he somehow had given it to the doctor, I'm sure the doctor would have told me."

"You said he was too weak in the morning, so he must have done the writing before he went to bed." Eliza sat in the chair and pulled the Bible onto her lap, flipping through the pages. "I don't understand why Benton would want the ledger page back. If he used it as proof against Caleb, how can we prove otherwise with it?"

"I certainly don't know."

"Well," Eliza mused, "if it's that important to Benton, we have to find it before he gets out of jail and comes back looking for it. Did Grandfather keep the books locked up when Caleb was doing the accounting?"

"Of course not. He trusted each and every one of his employees."

"Did Benton know about the letters?"

"No. Mr. Roberts wrote them after Benton left that night, and Benton didn't return to the house until breakfast the next morning. Even then, he ate in the kitchen and went straight back outside afterward."

"Do you think Benton snuck back into the house that night?"

"No, he couldn't have. I bolted the doors the moment he left. I never did deliver the stew to Mrs. Barnes, even."

"So if Grandfather did write another letter, it should be right here, within reach of his chair. Or at least we should find the pen and sheet of paper." She tapped the table.

Eliza got down on her knees and looked underneath the chair, running her hand along the underside, then doing the same for the table. Finding nothing, she lifted the edge of the rug, checking underneath. Again, nothing.

Nellie shook her head. "It's like even the pen just disappeared."

Suddenly, an image flashed through Eliza's memory. She must have been about six, back in New York, and her grandparents were still with them. Grandmother had been writing a letter, and her hand had curved and looped across the paper.

"Eliza, would you like to see this pen disappear?"

"Oh, yes!"

"Well, then, my little angel, close your eyes."

Eliza had obeyed, and when she opened them, the pen was gone.

"You put it in the drawer, Grandmother. That's no trick."

"Check and see."

When Eliza pulled the table drawer open, it was empty. "It disappeared! You did make it disappear!"

Grandmother had laughed. "Close your eyes again." When Eliza opened them, Grandmother held the pen in her hand.

"That's a great trick."

"No, dear, it was no trick. Your grandfather made this little table for me. Look." She had pushed on the side of the table. Silently, below the drawer, a shallow, hidden compartment had slid open. Inside was a stack of writing paper.

Now, Eliza stood. Could it possibly be? That her grandparents had brought that very table with them to Idaho? Other than that memory, she didn't recall seeing Grandmother's secret table again.

She touched her hand to the tabletop, then ran her fingers along the side. She applied a bit of pressure. And held her breath.

"Eliza!" Nellie shouted. "Look!"

The camouflaged drawer slid out. And there was the missing pen atop three neatly folded pieces of paper.

~

*C*aleb pulled at the strangling tie around his neck, shrugged his shoulders beneath the binding, coarse suit jacket, and stepped into the church building. Early. With a deep breath, he took a step past the rear pew where he had isolated himself for months. Then another step, and another, until he had walked almost the entire length of the aisle toward the front. The Roberts's pew seemed to invite him yet another row up, but he stopped at the row behind it and slid to the center, right behind where he hoped Eliza would sit.

He clasped his hands in his lap, wringing them the way Nellie used to in the kitchen. What if no one sat near him? What if people glared at him or told him he had no right to sit up so close? What if—

"Oh, Mama! May we sit with Mister Caleb?"

He looked up to see Virginia tugging on her mother's arm. Once Mrs. Billings nodded, three little girls vied over who would get to sit on either side of him.

"Good morning, Caleb." Daniel Jacobs patted him on the shoulder from behind.

"Glad to see you," Gus added.

Caleb smiled as he greeted the men and shook their hands. Now, if only Eliza would come in and sit right in front of him, where he could study her bitterbrush-blossom hair. It'd be soft and silky-looking, whether she wore it down or up in her usual bun. He'd be so close, he'd be able to hear the lilting sound of her voice as she sang the hymns. If she turned her head slightly, he might catch the sparkle in her blue eyes.

The church filled. Folks seemed genuinely pleased to see him sitting down front. A few asked him to be sure and stay for the church meal afterward. From the aisle, a couple of men told him they wanted to talk to him about ordering saddles soon. Even the sheriff greeted him and said he'd speak with him after the service. And still the pew in front of him remained empty. Where could Eliza and Nellie be? Had something happened to them? Should someone—he?—go check on them?

The preacher stood to greet the worshippers, and scurrying down the aisle came the two Double E ranch women. Silently, they slipped into their pew.

This close to her, Caleb could see her blushing cheeks. She'd probably never been late to church in her life. But now he could relax. Almost. He had hoped for a chance to talk with

Eliza before the service, but that could wait. What mattered now was that she was here, sitting right in front of him. He had begged the Lord to let her see the difference in him, and by His grace, after the service, she would understand that he was trying to be the man of God he should have been all along.

"Let us remain standing for the reading of the Word of God," Pastor Thompson said. "I will read First Peter chapter 3, verses 8 through 11. 'Finally, be ye all of one mind, having compassion one of another, love as brethren, be pitiful, be courteous: Not rendering evil for evil, or railing for railing: but contrariwise blessing; knowing that ye are thereunto called, that ye should inherit a blessing. For he that will love life, and see good days, let him refrain his tongue from evil, and his lips that they speak no guile: Let him eschew evil, and do good; let him seek peace, and ensue it.'"

Pastor Thompson looked up at the congregation. "And I will now read First Peter chapter 4, verse 8. 'And above all things have fervent charity among yourselves: for charity shall cover the multitude of sins.' May God add His blessing upon the reading of His Word. You may be seated."

Caleb sat as upright as he could with a heavy heart wanting to pull him down. Why had he picked today of all days to sit up front? Where the entire congregation, except the two ladies on the pew in front of him, could point and whisper behind him that he needed this message? Eliza and Nellie were too well mannered and refined to turn their heads or nod to each other over his sins. Indeed, this sermon was meant for him alone.

Each word of the sermon went straight to his heart. The price of bitterness was steep. But that was what he had chosen for months. What if he was too late in his repentance to win the affection of the most wonderful woman he had ever known? That brought a sorrow so deep, it seemed about to cut off his breath. But yet, God offered hope. Forgiveness. *For charity shall cover the multitude of sins.* He would cling to that verse.

As the sermon ended, Pastor Thompson prayed, giving a few moments for the congregation to silently bring their own petitions before the Lord.

Dear God, Caleb, *I just want to say again how sorry I am. And...even though Eliza may not ever see me as You do, please don't let that discourage me. Please help me to live for You alone each day...and to love fervently.*

As soon as the pastor's final amen was echoed throughout the worshippers, Caleb stood with a hand outreached to Eliza. Before he could get her attention, elderly women gathered around him, inviting him to stay for the noon meal being served at the reverend's house next door. Eliza and Nellie headed toward the door before he could extricate himself.

From behind, Gus slapped him on the back. "Follow us. We got to hustle to get over to that food line. Don't want to miss out on Mrs. Ramsey's chicken drumsticks."

Daniel added another clap. "Gus, don't run anyone over. You know she brings plenty to every dinner the church has."

"Caleb." The sheriff stopped in the aisle at the end of the pew. "Stop by my office tomorrow morning. I have some business to discuss with you."

"I'll be there."

"Good." The sheriff shook his hand and nodded to a few others as he departed.

Being summoned to the sheriff's office didn't bode well, but Caleb would deal with that tomorrow. He snuck a glance to the back of the church to see if Eliza and Miss Nellie were still inside, but they were gone.

He hurried outside and started across the yard. Biscuit and the Double E buggy were under a tree, so she must be inside the reverend's house. But he needed to find her. To ask her in person to forgive him. To tell her that he was a changed man. And if she was ready to hear it, to declare that he lo—

"Caleb Morgan!" And of course the screech from behind him reverberating in his ears was Callie.

He stopped and turned to her. "Now what?" Every moment with her was a delay in getting to Eliza. "I already told you—"

"Is that any way to greet me just coming out of church?" She put her hands on her hips.

He closed his mouth. Her words lodged in his heart as surely as God's. *For charity shall cover the multitude of sins.* "No, you're right. It is not. Did you wish to speak with me about something?"

She cocked her head, lowered her hands. "I do. Seeing that your holy Eliza was the cause of Benton not marrying me and *you* are the reason he's in jail and I can't marry him there, I expect you to get him out."

"What?" The word sounded like Callie's own screech. He cleared his throat and tried again. "What do you mean?"

"Just what I said. I want to marry Benton, and until you get him out of jail, we can't get married."

"Callie." It didn't matter why she still wanted to marry the man. Caleb needed some help, but the reverend wasn't anywhere to be seen. "Callie." He prayed with his eyes open for words or wisdom or something. "You've seen what kind of a man he is. He fights. He attacks people—ladies, even. Is that what you want in a husband?"

She lifted one side of her mouth in a smirk. "It seems to me that you're a fighting man as well."

"I— You're right, Callie. And I'm ashamed of that. But I'm trying to live as a God-honoring man now and—"

"Hmph. Not that it's your concern, but Benton's good to me. He made a mistake in trusting Eliza. Anyway, it's only your and that Eliza's word against his as to what happened."

"You've been to visit him?"

"Of course. Now, all you have to do is tell the sheriff you

made a mistake in what you saw and ask old Flint to release Benton so we can get married. He loves me, and I love him."

Caleb shook his head. "Callie, I'm afraid that even in that he's—"

"Lying? I should have expected as much from you now that you think you're so righteous." She spun on her heel and stomped off.

Benton was exactly where he belonged. Locked up so he couldn't hurt anyone else, especially Callie. As that's exactly what Benton Calloway would do to her.

Now he needed to get inside the parsonage and find Eliza. He took a dozen steps across the yard and—

"Mister Caleb!" Virginia came running out the front door. "I've been looking for you. We've already eaten, and now Mama says it's time to go home. But I saw you and wanted to tell you my story I made up. Can I? It's long and no one else wants to hear it."

How could he say no to that? But would Eliza slip away again before he got the chance to speak with her?

CHAPTER 22

*T*he aromas of fresh rolls and roasts and pumpkin and cinnamon that had welcomed the parishioners to the parsonage after the service were now lingering memories and still no Caleb. Eliza needed to ask his forgiveness, to find out what had happened, why he was so different. So sweetly different. But she had offered to help serve the meal. And he hadn't come inside yet.

By now most everybody had come through the line. Gus and George twice.

He could be somewhere reading Grandfather's papers she and Nellie had delivered early this morning to Sheriff Flint. That must be it. From the clear-eyed look on Caleb's face, his grin of happiness, the sheriff must have already shown Caleb the evidence of his innocence. Plus, she had seen them talking together after the service, shaking hands. But by the time they unloaded their food at the parsonage and helped with the setup, they slipped into the service just as it was starting. And her heart sank when Caleb wasn't in the back pew.

But when she discovered he was sitting right behind her seat, her heart had seemed to skip a beat. Though she hadn't had a chance to speak with him, during the songs she'd treasured the beautiful, strong tenor voice singing hymns of old practically right into her ear. The change in him was remarkable. And after the service, people were swarming around him while she needed to hurry to the parsonage to help set out the hot dishes.

From her position now of dishing up food behind the tables, she had a partial view of the window, and Ruby was still hitched in the church yard. So where was Caleb?

"Nellie," she whispered, "could you cover for me serving? I just want to peek through the window and see if Caleb is coming."

Nellie winked and took a serving spoon from Eliza's hands. "Go on now."

Eliza walked to the window and peered out.

And there he was, with the three Billings girls circling him, listening intently to something Virginia was telling him. When she stopped talking and smiled, Caleb bent and gathered the girls into his arms. Virginia wiggled free and reached into her dress pocket and pulled out her customary red-and-white candy. When she offered it to Caleb, he bowed and laughed. Truly laughed. Eliza gasped at how joy changed his appearance. His whole face lit up, making him even more handsome than ever. If only she could hear the sound of it. A low rumble? A musical lilt? Eliza rubbed sudden tears leaking from her eyes. No doubt about it, something had changed Caleb.

How could this sociable, laughing man be the same forlorn saddlemaker she had met upon her arrival in Caldwell?

If all of this wasn't enough to prove it, all she had to do was to look at the gentle expression in his eyes. What she saw there summed up what had happened to him.

Peace.

Somehow, he was filled with God's peace. That had been her message to the people here, God's peace. Yet her own heart was in turmoil. Which was why she was leaving. And today's sermon confirmed she'd made the right decision.

She had accomplished what she had set out to do here—visit the Double E and learn about her grandparents. And so much more had happened. Beholding the land as they must have. Helping to restore Caleb's good name. Setting the ranch on its way to being successful again. Most of all, meeting Caleb Morgan.

But she couldn't stay here. She wasn't the Angel from the East people were proclaiming her to be. After this morning's message, it had become clear. With her lack of discernment about so many things, she had failed God and the dear people of Caldwell. The only person she had whispered her decision to had been Mrs. Billings. She would tell Nellie and George when they got home.

So once the Double E sold—with the caveat that Nellie and George and Gus would stay on if they chose—she would be on her way. The California school had told her their invitation was open for whenever she wanted to come, as schools were popping up all over the Los Angeles area, and there was bound to be something for her somewhere.

She couldn't risk running into Caleb Morgan every Sunday or anytime she came into town. His gentle, shy smile told her he had forgiven her. But she had believed the worst about him, not trusting his word. There weren't enough miles between here and California to erase those memories. At least in California, she'd be far away from the saddlemaker who had captured her heart. But of whom she was not worthy.

"Eliza," Gus said with a grin as he passed by holding a plate with two slices of pie, "make sure you get some of Nellie's pie before it's gone."

"I'll try." Though she doubted she'd be able to eat a bite of it or anything else. She peeked out the window again. She had to get to Caleb. Never had she seen so many people around him at church. But as soon as the little girls left, she was heading out there to ask Caleb's forgiveness. Before she lost her nerve. As she couldn't leave Caldwell without having begged his forgiveness. And having one last positive memory of him.

Mrs. Billings walked up to them—surely, a signal that she was ready to take the girls home. And then Eliza would be out the door before anyone else could gain his attention. Apologize and welcome him back onto the Double E.

That was all she needed to do before anyone interrupted them.

⁓

"We'll all miss Eliza," Mrs. Billings said as the girls bent their heads together, laughing over something silly Rosita said.

"Miss her?" Caleb looked over their heads, not comprehending. "You're not—are you moving away?"

"Not us. Eliza is."

Not one word formed in his brain.

Mrs. Billings's gaze darted inside—perhaps looking for Eliza? "I'm so sorry. Apparently, I spoke out of turn, but she mentioned you—"

"No, no. This has just taken me by surprise. Where, may I ask, is she going? Surely, not to—"

"California." Mrs. Billings affirmed his fear.

California. Why would she be leaving? According to Gus, the Double E had a good start to getting back on its feet thanks to the success of the horse market yesterday and Eliza being dubbed the Angel from the East. She loved the ranch and wanted to stay to honor her grandfather's sacrifice which he had made when he had moved his wife to Idaho to make the ranch their home. So how could this possibly be true?

Oh, Lord, please don't let her leave.

"What will she do out there?" Not that it was any of his business, but he needed to know. To understand why. Or at least to be able to picture her there when his heart longed for her to be here.

"I believe she'll be taking a teaching position. That was the purpose of her trip originally before she stopped here to be with us in Caldwell."

Teaching. Of course. A teacher was what she was at heart, not a horse trainer.

"Do you know when she will be leaving?"

"Soon is my understanding. She's been such a blessing to me and my girls. To the whole town. She'll be sorely missed."

Oh, that she would be. He couldn't even imagine the emptiness of the town without her presence.

Soon. Did that mean a week or a month? And what would she do with the ranch?

"Mrs. Billings, excuse me. I best be heading back with Ruby." He tipped his hat to her. "Girls, good day to you also."

"Bye, Mister Caleb," they each chorused and waved.

He mounted Ruby and turned her out of town, away from everyone he knew. Alone, as usual. Except this time, he had no dream of any possible future with Eliza left.

But...if she was intent on heading to California, she wouldn't be stepping on that train without knowing how he felt about her.

CHAPTER 23

Caleb was there one moment, then gone the next. And by the time Eliza wove around people on their way out of the parsonage, he'd already leaped on Ruby and taken off. As if being chased.

"Caleb!" Eliza's cry fell flat as Ruby gained speed, taking Caleb farther away. Not even in the direction of his shop, where she could have walked over to talk to him.

And she hadn't told him anything. Not how sorry she was for the way she'd treated him. Not that he was welcome on the ranch. Not that he was the one she wanted to sell it to. And mostly not that he was a godly, honorable man.

And the fact that he had won her heart would always have to remain unspoken.

Eliza stood rooted to the ground as church people walked around her, many loading their wagons and buggies with their baskets and pans.

At her side, a hand fell on her arm. Hope leapt into her heart. Had Caleb returned?

"Eliza, dear." Nellie. Not Caleb.

Eliza blinked hard and fast, and thankfully, Nellie didn't ask about the tears she must surely see. "I'm sorry. I left you with serving while I..."

Nellie wrapped her arm around Eliza's waist. "I wanted to check on you, is all. Let me pack our basket and find George, and we'll head home."

Eliza shook her head. She waited until she was fairly certain she could get words out. "No. I'll help with the cleanup." This might be her last time at a church potluck. Her last time working side by side with these women. She took Nellie's arm and led her back inside.

Tomorrow. Tomorrow she'd fix this with a ride back to Caldwell. If Mr. Taylor was back, she'd arrange the legalities of selling the Double E with him. But most important, she would talk with Caleb. In the quiet and privacy of his saddle shop.

Tomorrow was her hope.

Eliza pitched in helping pack leftovers and thoroughly cleaning Reverend Thompson's kitchen and common areas with a renewed energy. Once the remaining men took out the extra tables and put the furniture back in order, George loaded the Double E buggy.

Nellie took Eliza's arm and followed him out. "I love the fellowship meals, but I'm also ready to get home. How about you, Eliza?"

"Yes, I'm ready as well." She had yet to form the words to tell George and Nellie about her decision.

She appreciated the quiet in the buggy as they started for home. While Biscuit clip-clopped through the town she'd grown to love, Eliza soaked in the buildings, the people they passed, everything she wanted to remember from her time in Idaho.

The town with alkali and sagebrush as far as she could see. The town with swaggering cowboys and too many saloons but not enough churches. The now snow-covered dust that had often covered her shoes, the dust she'd thought surrounded the town when she'd arrived those weeks ago. Weeks that had at first trudged along like years and then, all of a sudden, flown by.

Thankfully, their route didn't take them past the one place she couldn't bear to see today. C. Morgan Saddlery. The place of so many memories she'd never forget. Caleb bent over his saddles, crafting them with such skill and care. Discovering he was the man Grandfather wrote about. His offer to help her save the ranch. The hard muscles under his shirtsleeve as she'd placed her gloveless hand on his arm.

But he wasn't inside working this afternoon, as he'd been headed out of town. Maybe they'd pass him on the way? If they did, she'd ask George to wave him down, she'd jump out of the buggy and tell him...everything in her heart, even if she had an audience.

But they didn't pass him.

Upon arriving at the ranch, George took care of Biscuit and the buggy while Eliza and Nellie carried in the potluck dishes. Maybe over a cup of tea with George and Nellie, Eliza would find the words. But none came. Of course, she'd make sure they were cared for with the sale of the ranch, but how devastated they'd be.

Nellie finally pushed back her chair and stood. "Eliza, you look like you could use a rest. Why don't you go upstairs? I think we all should retire to our quarters."

Eliza went up to her room. Perhaps before the day was over, she would think of how to break the news to her friends. She laid Grandfather's letters out across Grandmother's bitterbrush quilt as today seemed to be a day of reliving memories.

She picked up the first one he'd sent and sat in her chair to read it. What surprise and joy when she'd received it at Aunt Belinda's home. He'd started their correspondence by telling her of his love for her and the beauty of the Double E. In each successive one, the story unfolded of the life he had here with

Grandmother and the people of Caldwell. He spoke so openly of God and His goodness.

Finally, she came to the last letter, written shortly before he died. This time, she would read it in light of Caleb's innocence, because Grandfather had known the truth about Benton and Caleb at that moment.

My Dear Eliza,

When you receive this, my farewell to you, it will mean that I have left this earth.

Now she could picture him sitting in his big chair downstairs, laboring to write these words, weak as he was.

Though grief will be in your heart, rejoice also that I will be with the good Lord above. As you know now from my will, I have given you the joy of my last years, the Double E. Its prosperities should keep you comfortable for years to come. It has been my refuge, my place of seeking and walking with the Lord. May you find His peace here also, whether riding beneath the stars or sitting on the porch steps.

Surely, Grandfather would be grieved to know she was leaving the Double E and selling his dream.

I hope that in heaven we are given the privilege of watching down upon the earth, as I long to see you finding joy each step of the way, my little angel.

May God bless you, dear one.

Love, Grandfather

She ran her hand over the letter, savoring each word of how Grandfather had trusted Caleb. Not only trusted him, but also wanted her to trust him, to lean on him. She chuckled, remembering how she had thought Mr. Morgan must be an elderly, frail gentleman. Quite the opposite—he was the strongest, yet gentlest, most honorable, godly man she had ever met.

Eliza, if you ever find yourself needing help in this land, seek Caleb Morgan. He is a good man and will assist you. I trust him with all I have.

She read it over again. Grandfather had known the truth as he wrote the letter that night. The truth about both Caleb and Benton. Yet there was something missing. He wrote not one word of condemnation against Benton. He only wrote of trusting Caleb. Could Grandfather possibly have forgiven Benton before he died? In all the letters Grandfather had written her, he had penned not one word against either man— not when he thought Caleb had betrayed him, nor when he knew that Benton had.

Lord, how can this be? Did Grandfather forgive them both freely? I don't want to forgive Benton. But if Grandfather did—and You did... Oh, Lord, please help me to forgive. I need so much forgiveness myself. So...with Your power—only with Your help—I—I—

The ugly sneer on Benton's face rose up before her. The gun raised and pointed at Caleb...the cruel words that had come from his heart...pinning her against the door...his flailing fists...

Oh, Lord—

Weeping, Eliza sank onto her knees in front of the bedroom chair. How could she possibly forgive Benton for all of that? How could God expect her to?

> Let all bitterness, and wrath, and anger, and
>   clamor, and evil speaking, be put away from
>   you, with all malice. And be ye kind one to
>   another, tenderhearted, forgiving one

another, even as God for Christ's sake hath
forgiven you.

New pictures formed in her mind. Her unfairness to Caleb.
Her vindictiveness toward Benton, barely being able to wait to
testify against him. Her believing that her dear, loving grandparents had abandoned their family, without knowing the facts.
Yet she had been forgiven.

Eliza wiped her eyes. Amazingly, God had forgiven her. For
Christ's sake. Christ, who had died an ugly death to pay for her
sins...for Benton's sins.

Lord... Eliza placed her arms on the chair seat, then her forehead atop her arms. *Lord, as You have forgiven me...
I...forgive...Benton.*

In the quietness of the room, another verse, God's answer,
settled in her heart.

And the peace of God, which passeth all understanding, shall keep your hearts and minds
through Christ Jesus.

Peace, amazing peace. That's what she had. God's peace.
Was this perhaps the same peace the angels had sung of? *Glory
to God in the highest, and on earth peace.*

Eliza stood and walked over to the window. When she
looked out this time at her favorite view, there was so much
more than the beauty of the vast land. She heard Caleb's laughter. Saw his eyes filled with peace. Felt again the warmth of his
lingering hand upon hers as he helped her mount Rosey.

She closed her eyes, holding fast to the memories. And a
tear slipped out. For even though Grandfather had trusted him,
Caleb Morgan had stolen something.

Not from Grandfather or the Double E, but from her. He
had stolen her heart.

So maybe there was something more she needed to say to Caleb tomorrow.

~

*E*liza set three cups of breakfast coffee on the table and joined Nellie and George as they also sat. She had let the whole day go by yesterday without saying a word to them about selling the ranch and heading on out to California. But she must do it today. And then she'd ride into town and make the rounds she had planned.

She opened her mouth. And nothing came out.

"Eliza?" Nellie studied her a moment. "Is something on your mind?"

"I hope it's not about the ranch." George now looked at Eliza too. "I spoke with some sellers on Saturday and have some good leads for our next group of horses. I'm hoping to go look at them this week and—"

Barking from the porch interrupted him.

George jumped up. "What's gotten into that dog?" He swung the door open, and Kep immediately quieted and sat on his haunches, tongue hanging out, panting. "What have you got on you, fella?" He bent over the dog, then straightened.

"Eliza. Come here. He has something for you."

"For me?" She walked outside with Nellie behind her.

"Nellie"—George nodded inside, amusement in his voice—"let's go eat breakfast."

Nellie looked at Kep, then Eliza, and grinned. "Yes. Of course." And the two scurried inside, leaving Eliza on the porch with Kep and an envelope hanging from a red ribbon around his neck. There was no mistaking that it was for her since her name was written neatly in block letters.

Eliza looked around. Where was the person who had tied this to Kep? And who was it? But she didn't see or hear anyone.

She untied the ribbon and Kep licked her face. "Good boy, Kep. You did a good job delivering this message."

But from who?

She opened the envelope and withdrew a sheet of paper. Looked at the end to see who had signed it, and her heart skipped a beat.

Caleb.

She looked around again but knew she wouldn't see him. Not if he was still keeping his vow to not intrude on the property until his honor had been restored. Did he not know yet?

"Oh, sweet Caleb." Had he been at the entrance gate and slipped this around Kep's neck, then sent him back to the house?

She wanted to laugh at the wonderful thought—but what if the message was not good news? Though if he'd gone to the trouble to find a red ribbon and ride all the way out here and trust Kep—

She'd better read it right now. Though the morning air was nippy and she was outside without a coat, she sank into Grandmother's rocker and soaked in the words penned to her.

Dear Eliza,

If it is true what Mrs. Billings inadvertently told me, that you are leaving Caldwell to head on west to California, please know that you will be missed beyond words. You have done what you declared was your intent—you have brought the message of God's peace to the people of Caldwell. And to me. For that, I am most grateful.

If you can find it in your heart to stop by the saddlery before you leave, I have something I would like more than anything to show you. To tell you what is in my heart, if you will hear me out.

But if not, know that you were used by God to restore this poor soul to Him. And that is a treasure beyond words.

I wish you the best in your travels and journey through life.

Though truthfully, I am saddened to see you leave, as the ranch, the town, and, most of all, my life will be empty without you.

May God's peace rest upon you as you have shared it with me.

Sincerely,

Caleb

Eliza sat in the rocker, tears streaming down her face.

The door squeaked open, and Nellie burst through with a coat in her hands. "Dear child, whatever is wrong?"

Eliza laughed. Cried. Stood and hugged Nellie. "Caleb—I have to go to town and see him." Or could he still be at the ranch entrance?

Nellie looked at the ribbon and envelope and letter still in Eliza's hand. "Well, goodness, child, put this on and go. No, wait. Come inside and eat fast and George can saddle up Rosey."

Eliza couldn't eat a thing, but maybe Nellie was right. A few bites would do. She shrugged into the coat while Nellie gave George his orders, then passed George in the doorway on his way out.

"Rosey will be ready in a jiffy," he called as he ran down the steps.

And by the time Eliza got ready and ate a few bites of eggs, George was standing outside with Rosey saddled. George gave her a boost up, and Eliza was on her way, hoping that Caleb might even still be waiting at the entrance to the ranch.

When she reached the Double E sign, Caleb wasn't there. But she knew exactly where to find him. And that he'd be waiting for her.

She urged Rosey toward Caldwell, but C. Morgan Saddlery wouldn't be her first stop when she got there.

There was one person she needed to visit before Caleb.

CHAPTER 24

aleb set down his saddlery tools and wiped his brow. Between yesterday afternoon into the night and early this morning before his ride as far as the entrance to the Double E, he was almost finished.

Now he only prayed Eliza would come.

The door to the shop opened. Closed. Was she here already? Which meant not only had Kep done his job but that Eliza's heart was open. Or at least curious.

Caleb hurried out front to greet her, but it wasn't her.

"Howdy, Caleb." What was the sheriff doing here so early? His eyes were haggard looking, the same as his own must be.

"I know I told you to stop by my office this morning, but I had to go to Boise after church yesterday and am just now getting back. I figured you'd want to see this, now that I've had a chance to look it all over." He handed Caleb a slim stack of papers. "Go ahead and read them. They're from Elliott Roberts."

Mr. Roberts? Where had these come from? With trepidation, Caleb looked at the top sheet, a letter.

Caleb,

I ask your forgiveness. I know now Benton betrayed both you and me. You are a man of honor, and I should have believed you without one question. I trust you with all I have. I am dying.

Could you please watch over my granddaughter, Eliza, when she arrives to run the ranch? I entrust her to you, as she is most precious to me.

I pray you will find it in your heart to for

Had Mr. Roberts been too weak to continue writing? Caleb's own hand was shaking now. Of course, he forgave Mr. Roberts.

He reread the short note. What mattered most was knowing Mr. Roberts had believed him. So now he would be able to return to the Double E with honor. He could go there and talk to Eliza face-to-face. And to think that Mr. Roberts had placed her in his care.

"Aren't you going to look at the other pages?" the sheriff asked.

Caleb blinked. "Yes." He set the letter aside and then he was looking at a sheet torn from the ledger. The old anger started burning in his chest as he held it.

Lord, please forgive me again. Thank You that Mr. Roberts trusted me.

So with that assurance, he looked at the figures. Nothing had been changed on the page. He looked closer. The writing was his. There were no erasures or any appearance of tampering with it. It didn't make sense. These were the correct figures. So why would Mr. Roberts ever have doubted him? What had Benton's plan been? Much less, how had he carried it out?

The sheriff sighed loudly. "Caleb—there's another page. Keep going."

Caleb turned to the next page. Another ledger sheet. Ragged edges showed that this also had been torn from the book. Except...though the written item entries matched up between the two pages, the numbers did not. And upon close inspection, though very similar so even he had to look carefully to be sure, the writing was not his. He blocked his letters carefully like these were, but he never put a little squiggle on his *a*'s. So this must have been the page Benton had shown Mr. Roberts. No wonder he had been tricked. And yet Benton had never destroyed the original copy. Somehow, Mr. Roberts must have found it and compared the two.

Benton, why did you do this?

"Well?" The sheriff crossed his arms. "What do you think about that? Your name has been cleared."

"This is... I don't even know what to say. Overwhelming. It's completely overwhelming. Thank you."

"Don't thank me. Thank Miss Eliza Roberts."

"Eliza? What did she have to do with this?"

"She's the one who found these papers and brought them to me before church yesterday to clear your name. But then as I said, I got called away. So as soon as I got back, I brought them over to you."

Eliza did that for him? "I will thank her. Thank you again also."

The sheriff clapped him on the back. "You're an honorable man, Caleb. And I'll be the first one to spread the word throughout town. I best be getting back to the office now." And before Caleb could mumble much of anything after him, the sheriff walked out the door.

If only he could leap and kick up his heels right in the middle of his shop. He settled for tossing his hat in the air. He'd been given back the thing that meant the most to him, the thing he thought was impossible with Mr. Roberts gone—his good name. And just maybe, he had a chance to win Eliza's heart as well.

~

*E*liza opened the door to the jail.

"Eliza." Sheriff Flint looked up from his desk. "What brings you by today?"

"I wanted to ask if I might have a visit with Benton Calloway."

The sheriff pushed back from his desk. "Why? Seeing he attacked you, I don't think it's a good idea."

"I'm not here to cause trouble. There was just something I needed to ask of him. I'll be brief. If I may?"

He studied her a long moment. "I still don't think any good will come of it or you'll get any answers, but all right." He stood. "Follow me. I'll take you to him. You just give a holler if you need anything."

Eliza trailed him to the back of the building until they stopped in front of a cell. Benton lay on a thin cot, his back to them. Sleeping? Or at least ignoring them.

Sheriff Flint rattled the cell door. "Calloway. You have a visitor."

"I don't want no visitor," he mumbled.

"Sit up. You have one whether you want one or not."

Benton very slowly, methodically, sat up. His black hair was longer and shaggier than ever, his face whiskered. When his eyes landed on Eliza, the smoldering hate in them seemed to ignite before he looked away. "Especially not her."

"Pipe down, Calloway." The sheriff rattled the bars again. "You be respectful now and listen to what she has to say. You hear?"

"Hmph." He glared at both of them.

"Thank you, Sheriff Flint." Eliza stepped up to the cell door once the lawman left. "Benton, I came to say I know how you cheated Grandfather."

"You don't know nothing—"

Eliza held up a hand. "I found the original ledger sheet and the altered one where Grandfather hid them. But I didn't come to talk about that. I came to say that I forgive you—"

With one leap, Benton was at the bars and grabbed them with both hands. Eliza jumped back. "I don't want your forgiveness, just like I told Morgan I don't want his—"

"Wait—what do you mean?"

"Just what I said. He came waltzing in here a couple weeks ago with a pot of stew and a canteen of water. Spouting babble about if his enemy hungers and thirsts and being overcome with good. Thinking he was obeying God or something. Saying he forgave me. But I told him I didn't want any of it. Not his stew, not his water. And not his forgiveness"—he spat the words —"and not yours."

Stew and water? Forgiveness and obedience? Caleb had truly done this, forgiven Benton Calloway? But if she was standing here offering him forgiveness, of course, God could have spoken to Caleb too.

"Then you have two—no, three—great offers, Benton. What could be more wonderful than the blessing of being forgiven by others? Except knowing the forgiveness of God and His peace."

He looked her in the eyes, a burning fury in his. "I want nothing from you or Morgan. Do you hear? And you both had better be on the watch. This isn't over. One day, I'll make you both pay. Now get out. Sheriff!"

Sheriff Flint appeared at the cell. "What's going on here? Miss Roberts, are you all right?"

"I want her out of here. Now." Benton growled the words, and Eliza backed up.

"I'm finished. Thank you, Sheriff." And with that, she left

the jail. Shaken but with a peace that she had extended forgiveness to her enemy. Amazingly, just as Caleb had.

And now she was on her way to see him, to ask his forgiveness. To tell him, even if it was considered forward, what was in her heart. Wholly. Plainly. So he knew precisely what he meant to her.

No matter how he responded, whatever he wanted to show her, she was now going with a heart once more filled with peace.

And this visit with Caleb would determine whether she even needed her third stop of the day.

CHAPTER 25

*C*aleb brought the saddle he'd just finished out to the front of the shop. Set it in a prominent place and ran a hand over the polished leather that he'd worked so meticulously on. Though he'd just finished it, he'd started it weeks ago, tweaking the design in his head until he knew exactly how he wanted to build it. And this morning, he'd known the perfect etching to add to his maker's mark.

The door opened.

Caleb looked up.

And there was Eliza.

Still outwardly resembling her grandmother—tall and stately like a pine tree with hair almost as yellow as the late-spring blossoms of Miz Elizabeth's bitterbrush. But now he also knew her heart, how she loved and cared for others just as Miz Elizabeth had. And how he loved her.

"Eliza. You came." He took a step toward her.

"Of course." She chuckled. "As soon as I got Kep's note. With one stop on the way."

"Eliza—"

She held up a hand. "Please. I came here to say what I

wanted to say yesterday and didn't get a chance to. And I don't want another day to go by that you don't know. So many things have happened that I hardly know where to start. But I'll start with this—I'm so sorry for not believing you. I know you're a man of honor."

She stopped to take a breath, and Caleb took the opportunity to speak. "Sheriff Flint came by this morning and showed me the papers you found."

"This morning?"

"Pretty early. He left after services yesterday to go to Boise, and he was on his way back."

"Then you didn't know yesterday you'd been exonerated?"

"No. That's why I couldn't step on the ranch—"

"So you sent Kep."

He nodded.

"He was a good messenger. But I also came to ask your forgiveness, just as I stopped by the jail first to ask the same of Benton."

"You did?"

"I did, and he told me that you did too."

Caleb shook his head. "He said he didn't want it."

"That's what he told me also. But will you forgive me for the things I said? Things that were untrue and wrong. For not trusting you." She looked deep into his eyes, hers so blue, so clear, reflecting what he felt in his heart. Peace.

"I do." He took another step to her and held out his hands, which she took, and the connection was as strong as a cord unbroken. "I do," he repeated, wanting to never let go. "And will you forgive me as well? You've shown me such light, Eliza. You're beautiful and so precious." Never had he spoken words of that nature to anyone, and yet with Eliza, they poured out of his mouth, his heart.

"Of course, I do. You're the most honorable man I know. Loving and kind. And godly."

In a wild moment, he almost pulled her to him. For a hug? A kiss? He wanted both. "Now may I show you what I wanted to?"

She nodded, her eyes bright, trusting.

He released one hand, keeping her other one tight in his as he led her over to his newest saddle. Finished just in time. The polished leather gleamed in the sun's rays coming through the window. "I wanted to show you this."

Her brows puckered as she reached out and ran her hands over the seat, the cantle, one of the fenders. "It's beautiful. But this is different. It's wider here."

Caleb nodded. "I've made the swell wider. I've been working on this style for some time, trying to make it just right for—to make it for a more secure ride on a rough horse."

"It's lovely. I'm sure it will make a good working saddle for someone." And as she continued to examine the saddle, her quick intake of a breath revealed the moment she discovered his special engraving on the skirt. "A bitterbrush bloom?"

"Yes." As Eliza took her hands off the saddle, Caleb placed his on the horn, gripping it tightly to still the shaking. "I placed it there for all it symbolizes."

"And that is?"

"A reminder of God's goodness and faithfulness. But this saddle isn't for just someone. I made it for you. For training your horses."

"Me? But if I go to California, I'm not going to be training horses anymore. And I won't need a saddle at all if I live in the city of Los Angeles."

"Yes. But I...want..."

"What is it, Caleb?" She looked him straight in the eye, maybe the way she'd look at a student not speaking an answer forthrightly. But she seemed to be asking him something beyond her words. Maybe hoping for the truth in his heart?

If he were talking to Ruby, he wouldn't have any trouble

with words. He'd say exactly what was on his mind. So... *Lord, give me boldness.*

Before he could think why he shouldn't do it or change his mind, he grasped both of Eliza's hands in his again, ignoring the shock on her face. But also registering that she hadn't pulled away. "Eliza, I love you. I wish you would reconsider leaving. If you would stay here, I would ask you what's in my heart. If I could court you. With the intention of marrying you."

Her jaw dropped.

He couldn't blame her. He also was shocked, but he'd asked for boldness. Had he said too much too soon—offended her, even? For tears sprang to her eyes. "I'm sorry, Eliza, if I was too forthright. But I can't let you leave Caldwell without knowing exactly how I feel. And the truth is, I do love you. I love your spirit, your love for others, your determination. Your sweetness. I love you now and I want that love to grow."

"You love me?"

"I do," he said firmly. Definitively.

"And you—you want to marry me?"

"That is my heart's desire. I know I'm not yet the man I need to be, but with God's grace, I promise you, I'll always try to follow Him. And to always love and care for you. To treasure you as a precious gift from God."

Eliza withdrew one hand from his—but seemingly only to wipe tears from her eyes. Nothing indicated she was angry with him. Could they be tears of happiness? With that hope, he forged ahead with what he wanted her to know.

"I made a promise once that I would make a special saddle for my wife. That's why I made this one for you, Eliza. I offer it to you, you alone, with that in mind. If you'll accept it."

Now the tears that had pooled in her eyes ran down her cheeks.

"Oh, Caleb." She rubbed her fingers across her eyes, her face. "But I didn't stand by you when you needed me to."

"Shh. Remember, I said I forgave you." Just as he had been forgiven. "But you're also the one who cleared my name, so I am indebted to you."

Eliza loosed her other hand from his, stepped up close, and wrapped her arms around his neck. "I love you, too, and yes, I'll court you—because I'd love to marry you and be your wife."

"So does this mean you won't be moving to California?"

She laughed. "That's exactly what it means. And it means I do still need a saddle and that now I don't need to talk with Mr. Taylor about selling the ranch. Though I also came here today to offer it to you first."

"Me?" His heart swelled with love for her in that show of trust.

"Yes. You love the ranch and its legacy and people. And now you can be a part of it again. I expect you to be a frequent visitor until we're married."

And proper or not should any customer come in, he drew her close, his arms sheltering her back, and lowered his lips to hers, kissing her to seal his promise that he would love her all their days.

When they pulled apart, he grinned at her. "Should I telegraph your parents to ask their permission to court their daughter?"

She smiled. "They'll be most surprised that someone wants to marry their spinster daughter."

"No. Their beautiful, spunky, loving daughter." He placed his work-worn hands on her soft cheeks and gazed into the face of his beloved. "Glory to God in the highest!" He looked around, embarrassed by his uninhibited outburst, and Eliza giggled. "I can't help it. God brought you to Caldwell for a purpose. How faithful He is for sending me my very own Angel from the East."

EPILOGUE

MAY 1898

*E*lizabeth Rose Roberts Morgan walked out onto the wide porch of the Double E after supper to watch her husband. He had wanted just a little longer in the daylight to work with the white stallion. And of course, this horse would be staying on the ranch, because Caleb had given him a name. Paxton—*one of peace.*

"Mrs. Morgan—"

Eliza turned and grinned at Nellie, who teasingly had been calling her that ever since the wedding of just four weeks ago.

"Shall I bring coffee out here for you and your new mister? Maybe another piece of pie too?"

"That'd be lovely. Thank you. And you and George are welcome to join us."

George came out onto the porch as well, and he and Nellie exchanged a look—and a grin. "No thank you," George said. "I already had my second helping. So, 'night." With a tip of his hat, he clomped down the steps.

"Nellie, how about you, then?"

"There's only two rockers here."

Eliza blushed but smiled. "Thank you for our gift of time alone tonight. But you and George are part of the family and are always welcome to join us."

Nellie eyed her for a moment, then nodded. "Just like your grandmother. Just like her." Humming to herself, she slipped back into the kitchen.

Thinking of all the plans they had for the growing Double E, Eliza looked back to Caleb working with Paxton. Ruby would become her riding horse, and sweet Rosey could spend her aging years resting, except when the Double R's were both needed to pull the wagon. Now that C. Morgan Saddlery had moved out to the ranch, there were bound to be more frequent trips in to Caldwell.

Paxton searched Caleb's pocket for a treat, and Eliza smiled. Caleb's lips moved, though she was too far away to hear his words. But she imagined his usual murmurs of soft words and affirmations to the horse. It had taken a while for Caleb to win Paxton's trust, but now the huge, wild horse stood momentarily as still as the two mares.

Once Caleb was done, he would come straight to the porch and sit beside her in Grandfather's old rocker, her in Grandmother's. But she didn't have to wait until then to enjoy a fiery sunset. There was one going on right now in her heart. Every day since their wedding, her love for Caleb exploded with such breathtaking color that even an Idaho sunset had a hard time competing with it.

Still holding onto their stubbornness, no one from her family had made the trip from New York to Caldwell for the occasion. They had missed something special. A town event with three little girls wiggling on the second pew at church. And, if Eliza wasn't mistaken, the new man in town hadn't just been sitting in the same pew as Mrs. Billings and the girls but with them. Or maybe Eliza just saw romance everywhere through eyes of love.

And news had come from home that Aunt Belinda had a beau. So maybe there would be another Roberts wedding coming up shortly.

Caleb looked over at her and winked, his grin full of peace and promise. Her heart swelled with love as she waved back.

Was this how her grandmother had ended each day? From all she had learned of Elizabeth and Elliott Roberts, she and Caleb were headed down the same path of lasting love. She truly hoped they would have many years sitting out here in the rockers watching the sunset together. Caleb was the kindest man she could imagine, one who tried to follow God with all his heart. Exactly the kind of man she had prayed for.

She watched Caleb a moment longer, then hurried around to the field behind the house. There, on the edge, Grandmother's bitterbrush had bloomed overnight. No wonder her grandmother had insisted on keeping that bush for all generations of occupants on this land to see. For what had looked just like the rest of the sagebrush when Eliza had first arrived now was bursting with rose-like blooms of yellow.

And that's exactly what God had done in her life. He had taken the worries and unforgiveness of her bitterbrush life, and through a season of growing, made her burst with love and joy, the colors of a God-fearing woman. This bitterbrush was part of the legacy of the ranch. The maker mark Caleb put on every saddle he created now.

So, just like Grandmother, she would pass on the directive that it must always remain. It was like God's smile upon their land, their lives. A beautiful reminder of His goodness and faithfulness.

She picked a few sweet-smelling blossoms and held them close to her heart as she hurried back to the house. After arranging them in a jar filled with water, she placed the vase with the vibrant flowers on the porch railing just as Caleb walked up.

"Darling." With a smile, he reached for her hand and bent to smell the petals. Then pulled her into a heart-bursting kiss. Too soon, he pulled back but still held her hand while looking deep into her eyes. "How's my sweet Angel from the East?"

Eliza leaned her head against his shoulder, content. No longer did she need to prove herself as a teacher or a rancher. Or even as the Angel from the East.

"You know, I have a new calling, one I love more than anything else."

Caleb kissed the top of her hair. "And what is that, sweetheart?"

"That," she whispered against him, "is simply to be your godly wife in the West."

Did you enjoy this book? We hope so!
Would you take a quick minute to leave a review where you purchased the book?
It doesn't have to be long. Just a sentence or two telling what you liked about the story!

Receive a FREE ebook and get updates when new Wild Heart books release: https://wildheartbooks.org/newsletter

Don't miss the next book in the Blooms of the Bitterbrush series!

AUTHOR'S NOTE

Dear Reader:

Thank you for taking this first leg of the generational journey in the Blooms of the Bitterbrush Series. I hope that you enjoyed meeting Eliza and Caleb and watching them fall in love and grow in their faith.

I invite you to join in their continued story in *As Far as the West*, where their daughter meets Benton Calloway's son. And Benton is back, too, making good on his threat to the Morgan family. But Elizabeth Roberts's legacy of the bitterbrush plant still stands as a reminder of God's goodness and faithfulness.

May you, too, cling to His faithfulness.

Barbara

ACKNOWLEDGMENTS

There are so many parts involved in a book—from writing the first word to the final publishing—and so many people working mostly unseen on the various steps. To each person, I would like to say thank you. As well as an extra expression of gratitude to:

Misty Beller for giving *Angel from the East* and the Blooms of the Bitterbrush Series a home at Wild Heart Books.

Denise Weimer for her overhaul where needed and her expert editing.

Leah Berecz for setting up my author page and website and for her photography.

Alex Curtis for my hand-drawn cover years ago when I started this story as a novella, printed it off, and had it spiral-bound. I still treasure it and your encouragement to write.

For each one who had a part in the book along the way—the many who offered encouragement, prayers, research help, and marketing aid.

From my heart—thank you!

Barbara

If you love historical romance, check out the other Wild Heart books!

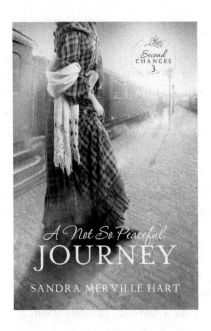

A Not So Peaceful Journey by Sandra Merville Hart

Dreams of adventure send him across the country. She prefers to keep her feet firmly planted in Ohio.

Rennie Hill has no illusions about the hardships in life, which is why it's so important her beau, John Welch, keeps his secure job with the newspaper. Though he hopes to write fiction, the unsteady pay would mean an end to their plans, wouldn't it?

John Welch dreams of adventure worthy of storybooks, like Mark Twain, and when two of his short stories are published, he sees it as a sign of future success. But while he's dreaming big with his head in the clouds, his girl has her feet firmly planted, and he can't help wondering if she really believes in him.

When Rennie must escort a little girl to her parents' home in San Francisco, John is forced to alter his plans to travel across the country with them. But the journey proves far more adventurous than either of them expect.

~

Ranger to the Rescue by Renae Brumbaugh Green

Amelia Cooper has sworn off lawmen for good.

Now any man who wants to claim the hand of the intrepid reporter had better have a safe job. Like attorney Evan Covington. Amelia is thrilled when the handsome lawyer comes courting. But when the town enlists him as a Texas Ranger, Amelia isn't sure she can handle losing another man to the perils of keeping the peace.

Evan never expected his temporary appointment to sink his relationship with Amelia. Or to instantly plunge them headlong into danger. But when Amelia and his sister are both kidnapped, the newly minted lawman must rescue them—if he's to have any chance at love

~

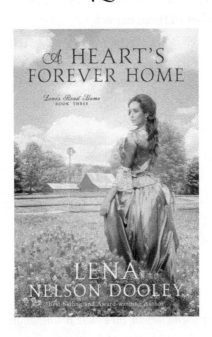

A Heart's Forever Home by Lena Nelson Dooley

A single lawyer whose clients think he needs a wife.
*   A woman who needs a forever home...or a forever family...or a forever love.*

Although Traesa Killdare is a grown woman now, the discovery that her adoption wasn't finalized sends her reeling. Especially when her beloved grandmother dies and the only siblings she's ever known exile her from the family property without a penny to her name.

Wilson Pollard works hard for the best interest of his law clients, even those who think a marriage would make him more "suitable" in his career. And when the beloved granddaughter of a recently deceased client comes to him for help, he knows he must do whatever necessary to make her situation better.

As each of their circumstances worsen, a marriage of convenience seems the only answer for both. Traesa can't help but fall for her new husband—the man who's given her both his home and his name. But what will it take for Wilson to realize he loves her? Will a not-so-natural disaster open his eyes and heart?

www.ingramcontent.com/pod-product-compliance
Lightning Source LLC
LaVergne TN
LVHW011941100525
810893LV00008B/131